Grave Reckoning

A McCall / Malone Mystery

Glenn Harris

Grave Reckoning is a work of fiction. Names, characters, places and incidents either are the product of the author's imagination or are used fictitiously. Any resemblance to actual persons, living or dead, or events is entirely coincidental. Portland, Oregon, actually exists of course. Major landmarks like Pioneer Courthouse Square and the Justice Center are where they belong, as are the streets and neighborhoods, but I have moved a few buildings around, put restaurants where none exist, erased houses that do exist, and wreaked other minor havoc with Portland's reality for the purposes of my story.

Grave Reckoning

CHAPTER ONE

He sat behind his desk, listening to the creaks and groans of the rotting floors as his followers moved about the building. He tried to ignore the stale odors of mold and ancient dirt that the newly painted walls of his space could not entirely keep out. He wanted no reminders that outside this room the building was anything but the palace he deserved.

It would not be forever. No, far better things were in store despite the sickness deep within him. He tried to ignore the sickness as well.

He focused instead on his God and the Great Plan that God had for him. The sickness would be defeated. That he knew. The ungodly would fall before his wrath. That he knew. America would be purified by his hand and his hand alone. That he knew. Then he would be well. Then they all, and all things, would be well. It was God's will.

Through the open door in front of where he sat at the old desk, he could see the top of the stairs at the end of a long corridor. There was a window in the stairwell on his level with bright sun shining through. Two people appeared at the top of the stairs, coming from the first floor. At that distance he could only see their outlines against the harsh sunlight. Then the larger of the two urged the smaller onward and their features clarified.

He had known already who they were. It was the newest of The Chosen and her escort. He couldn't remember offhand which woman had birthed her but it made no difference. That person was no longer her mother. The Chosen had no one but God and God's representative here on earth. They needed nothing and no one else.

The two figures continued walking toward him along the bare wooden floor of the corridor and he could see as they came closer, as they came into the light of his own window, just behind where

1

he sat, that the larger of the two was holding onto The Chosen's arm, continuing to encourage her forward. There was no need for that and he'd have to chastise his follower at the right time. This was not the right time.

This was the first meeting of The Chosen with her destiny, always a bright moment in both their lives.

At last they arrived and, after a respectful nod of his head, the larger of the two left The Chosen behind, disappearing back into the glare toward the far stairway.

The child stood in the doorway of his space, her face pale and her eyes darting around the brightly lit area, looking everywhere and finally directly at him. He smiled and gestured that she should come forward. He had no idea how frightening that smile was and felt a slight irritation when she hesitated.

Did she not know what glory awaited her? Did she not know that she was of The Chosen and that there was no higher calling? Well, she would know soon enough. Soon enough all fear and doubt would be behind her.

There was nothing to be frightened of. That he knew.

Nothing at all.

CHAPTER TWO

Robert Moseley was the first person I killed.

It was almost six years ago, when I was still apprenticing with Johnny Crew and Hap Harbaugh. I was in pursuit of a very dangerous man who, it turned out, had gone in another direction. Then Moseley stepped out from behind a dumpster in a deeply shadowed alley with a gun in his hand.

I imagine he was there just to pick up a few bucks from an easy mark. He couldn't have guessed I was a private cop with a gun of my own already drawn and ready to fire.

Johnny and Hap got the bad guy. I killed a young man who probably didn't need killing.

There was no question I had reacted properly. When someone suddenly accosts you with a gun in an alley, even if you aren't already looking for a vicious killer, you can't take the time to inquire politely about their intentions.

There was an investigation, of course, a hearing, and I was cleared of all blame. In due course I got my private investigator's license and set up my own agency. I tried not to think too much about Robert Moseley because I wanted to survive the next confrontation with an armed man in a dark alley, if and when it came. Hesitation could be just as deadly for me as instant response had been for Moseley.

I had never mentioned him to Devon Malone, the woman who was now my partner in the agency and for the last three months my lover, but it looked like I was going to have to tell her now.

As is so often the case, she apparently had already sensed that something was wrong.

"What's with the pretty postcard?" she asked from her side of our partners desk where she'd been going through her own Monday morning mail.

I turned it over and looked at the picture of a pre-eruption Mt. St. Helens. It was pretty. I turned it over again and looked at the message scrawled in red ink:

"HOKE IS OUT. Yours, Melissa."

Just a few simple words that brought back that night in vivid detail.

"We need to talk," I said. I flipped the postcard across the double-size desktop to Malone, who picked it up and frowned down at the red ink.

Devon is a beautiful woman, at least as far as I'm concerned, even when she frowns—which she does rather often. She's slender but wiry and physically very tough, a little over five feet tall, currently wearing her tousled brunette hair down to her shoulders, hair that sometimes smelled of cinnamon. This morning she had on her standard outfit of tank top, form-fitting jeans, and boots.

She looked up at me. "Okay. So, who are Melissa and Hoke?"

"Melissa and Hoke Moseley. The mother and brother, respectively, of Robert Moseley, shot to death by an apprentice private investigator in an alley quite near here."

She looked down at the card again. "Ah ha."

I took a long, slow breath and dived in. "It was one of my last cases when I was still with Johnny and Hap's old agency. You know I apprenticed with them. You have to do that to get a license if you haven't previously been in law enforcement."

"I know that."

She also knew I was stalling.

"It was a domestic abuse case that turned into a murder investigation," I went on, "a really nasty one. The cops couldn't find the husband and the wife hired us because she believed her son's accidental death wasn't accidental—and she was right. We were on the killer's heels late one night here in downtown and split up in pursuit. I headed down one alley while Johnny and Hap went on to the

4

next one. We knew the guy was armed and desperate, so we all had our weapons out and were ready to use them if necessary."

I paused for just a moment. "Robert Moseley, 19 years old, high school dropout, petty thief and mugger, was waiting in my alley for his next victim. He had a .32 revolver that he'd apparently inherited from his father and he led with it when he jumped out in front of me.

"He was dead before I had a chance to see he wasn't my quarry, that he was a young punk in the wrong place at the wrong time."

She took it all in. "Why haven't you told me this before?"

I shrugged a little. "I don't like to think about it. It's done. It's past. And it's not like you don't have plenty of things you don't talk to me about."

I immediately recognized my partner's do-not-fuck-with me look.

"Oh, we don't want to go there," she growled. "You don't share with me until I share more with you? What, are you in the third grade?"

I held up my hands. "You're right. It was a stupid thing to say. I don't know why I haven't told you. It's just not something I talk about, with anybody."

Malone held eye contact for another moment and then looked back down at the postcard. "So. I gather that brother Hoke has been in prison. Was he in the alley, too?"

"No, he was already serving ten to fifteen for armed robbery. Their dad died in prison. Clearly it runs in the family."

"Why does mom want you to know he's out?"

Another little shrug. "Probably because he said he'd kill me when he got out. And she's cheering him on."

"Oh. Well, the 'yours' is a nice touch. You can almost see the 'up' in front of it."

CHAPTER THREE

The McCall-Malone Detective Agency is located on the second floor of an old two-story commercial building on the northwest edge of downtown, above Previously Owned Books. The floor also houses the agency's attorney, insurance broker, and accountant, which is convenient to say the least. The remaining tenant is a small firm that does telephone surveys, a service we have yet to need.

It's a good location not only because we have support people right there, but also because some clients are sensitive about friends and neighbors knowing that they need a private detective. Portland may be the state's largest city, but it can be a surprisingly small town when it comes to keeping your business to yourself. If someone is spotted heading up in our direction they can always pretend they have legal, insurance, accountancy, or survey issues to be resolved.

Our office itself looks almost like something out of an old Humphrey Bogart movie with the ancient (but well-polished) partners desk in front of a pair of slightly dirty windows, the two barely padded visitor chairs that looked like refugees from a cop shop, the old file cabinets, the wooden hall tree, and the sparsely decorated walls. The most modern touches—besides our computers and phone system, of course—were on the table in one corner: a small modern fridge and good-quality coffeemaker.

Except for the big old desk, which we acquired when Devon Malone joined the agency, it looked about like it had when I was here by myself. My partner was not into personalizing her space, at least not this space. Oddly, I had yet to see the interior of the apartment where she still lived most of the time. For all I knew, it was sparse and undecorated as well.

After a little more thinking time, she flipped the postcard back to me. "You going to be proactive or wait for him to come after you?" she asked.

"I think the first thing I'm going to do," I said as I picked up the phone, "is make sure I'm interpreting the message correctly." I dialed the Records Division of the Portland Police Bureau.

It was picked up immediately. "Records."

I recognized the all-too-familiar voice of Joy Castle, civilian manager of the division; I'd rather have gotten one of her clerks.

"Hello, Joy," I said as brightly as I could. "How are you?"

"Clint."

That was it. The silence began to thicken and I figured I'd better cut through it before she hung up on me.

"I got a postcard from Melissa Moseley today," I said, "kind of cryptic. It seems to say that Hoke is back on the street. Could you check if he has a release date?"

I held my breath. She knew all about the Moseleys and Hoke's threat. It went back to when she and I were lovers.

"Give me a minute," she replied tersely.

Okay. We were up to six words now. Over the hump. All she had to do was a quick check of one of her databases.

"He got out yesterday."

"Thanks."

"Good luck," she said, her voice fading out as the handset headed for the receiver. It was possible that on some level she even meant it.

I hung up. "He's been out for a day," I told Malone.

"Clever. So Ma Moseley timed the postcard for maximum effect. You would know Hoke had already had twenty-four hours to take you out while you were ignorant and vulnerable."

She looked at our closed office door. "And even now he might be on the other side of that door."

I gave our closed door the finger. "I hate to disappoint Melissa, but I am *not* going to sweat it."

Which doesn't mean I didn't jump when someone knocked on the frosted glass of the door right then.

CHAPTER FOUR

My current weapon of choice was a Smith and Wesson Bodyguard Airweight. It's a five-shot revolver chambered for the .38 Special cartridge with two-inch barrel and a shrouded hammer to eliminate the possibility of snags on clothing. I keep it in the top right-hand drawer of my desk. I gently pulled the drawer open and rested my hand on the butt and trigger guard. Not sweating is one thing; being careless is another.

Meanwhile, Malone was still chuckling. Nothing like a supportive partner.

"Come in!" I called as affably as I could. Don't want to be rude to a friend or discourage a possible client even if you are prepared to shoot them.

The door hesitantly swung open to reveal a person who was definitely not Hoke Moseley. My immediate impression was of frailty. She was tall, rail-thin with long hair so fine and blond that it was almost white. For a moment I thought she was very old, but as she stepped fully into the office I could see that the lines on her face were more from hard living than age. Probably around forty, I was guessing as she finally spoke.

She focused on me, then looked at Malone, then back to me. "Mr. McCall?" Her voice matched the hair, wispy and pale.

I closed my drawer, noticed that Malone was also pushing hers back in, and stood up. "Yes," I said to our visitor, "I'm Clint McCall. And this is my partner, Devon Malone. Come in. Have a seat."

Her eyes took in the office as she slowly closed the door behind her and then she examined the two of us again as she crossed the room to sit down. She exchanged a nod with Malone and seemed slightly flummoxed.

"You aren't quite what I expected," she said as she settled into the chair nearer me.

"Oh?" I wondered what she had expected. What she'd found on my side of the desk was a medium-height, stocky, 53-year-old male with thinning hair wearing brown chinos and white polo shirt. And on the other side a somewhat shorter, wiry, mid-thirties female with shoulder-length brunette hair wearing black jeans with matching black boots and white tank top. Our usual appearance, though sometimes Malone pulled her hair back into a ponytail. I thought we looked as much like private detectives as anybody else.

Our visitor frowned slightly. "I mean...I don't mean anything by that. Nothing bad. I just mean...." She glanced over at Malone. "I didn't expect a man and a woman."

"Dogs and cats...." muttered my partner from her side of the desk and I made a little gesture to shush her.

No point in pursuing the gender diversity of the office. "What can we do for you?" I inquired. I wasn't optimistic about the answer. Everything about this woman's face and general demeanor said poor and downtrodden. On the other hand, her light blue summer suit was clearly both new and expensive, so there was some hope.

"My name is Diane Austin. I'm looking for my daughter."

Ah, a runaway kid, probably a teenager. We could do that. Out of the corner of my eye I caught my partner sitting up straighter. Before getting her P.I. license, Malone had spent the latter part of her law enforcement career working missing persons out of the Portland Police Bureau. This could be a slam dunk for her.

I grabbed a pen and notepad. "Okay, Mrs. Austin. What's her name and how long has she been gone?"

She looked a little dismayed. "It's Miss Austin. My daughter's name is Noelle and she's been gone eleven years."

I was more than a little surprised at the answer. "Eleven years? How old was she when she left?"

Again she looked uncomfortable. "Six months."

Malone and I locked eyes for a moment across the desk. So much for runaway teenagers. A child born out of wedlock—I was assuming—eleven years ago who's been missing almost all that time? Definitely not a slam dunk.

"Let's start over," I said. "You tell us the story and then we'll talk about how we can help you."

"I'm from Ketchikan, Alaska," she began. "I flew in from Juneau last night because I think Noelle was brought here by her father. I hope so."

"You mean, eleven years ago?" Malone asked.

"Yes. I know it must look funny, that I show up now looking for my daughter after all these years. But I just wasn't in any shape...and I only have the money to do it now, from a friend of mine in Ketchikan. When I hooked up with Noelle's father I was eighteen, stupid, on drugs and in every kind of trouble you can imagine. Paul Gregory was his name." She paused until I wrote it down. Malone was also taking notes.

I mentally corrected one of my assumptions. If Diane Austin was eighteen when she had a daughter who's now eleven, then I'd been off by more than a decade on her age. Of course, the kind of life she was describing could do that.

"Paul hung around until Noelle was born but left just a few weeks later. I named her Noelle because it was Christmas time. It was tough. The worst time of the year and me with a new baby, no money, no father, no nothing."

"So he left the baby with you." Malone again, and I was happy to let her take the lead as it was her area of expertise.

"Yeah. He didn't take her then. It was six months later. I'm sure it was him."

"Go on." Again we exchanged a glance. This wasn't sounding very promising.

"We made it through the winter somehow," Austin continued, "but then one day in June, just about eleven years ago today, she...disappeared."

"Disappeared how?" asked my partner.

"I was...working...out of my home one night. Things were really tough and I had to do what I had to do. Noelle was asleep in the other room, but when my...client...left and I went to check on her, she was gone. Just gone! I was crazy, running all over the neighborhood screaming for her, but she was nowhere. Just gone. I'm sure Paul took her—or had somebody take her."

I decided to jump in here. "Do you have any real reason to believe that? Couldn't it have been your client or someone else?"

"No, no, I know it was Paul. The guy I was with was well known in town and for sure didn't want my baby, I'll tell you that.

"I didn't get all my schooling, but I know people. Paul thought it over and decided he wanted Noelle. He'd already told me he didn't think I'd make a good mother. He didn't even like the name I gave her. He couldn't take her right after she was born, a tiny baby like that, not and run away somewhere. He waited, that son of a bitch. I know it. I have clues."

"Clues?" Malone again.

"I hired a detective this past year, when I first got some money, and he found clues. The police, back when it happened, couldn't find out a thing. They didn't really care. The bastard baby of a whore and one of her boyfriends. What did they care? But this guy, my first detective, all these years later he found out some things—but then he quit, the fucking...well, you know."

This was getting interesting. I leaned a little toward her. "No, Miss Austin, we don't know. You're going to have to explain it."

CHAPTER FIVE

"He told me to talk to you, Mr. McCall." Her tone was plaintive, as if I were supposed to know all this already. She turned toward Malone. "I'm sorry. He didn't mention you."

"It's okay. I'm new here."

A little frown. "Oh."

"Who told you to talk to me?" I asked.

"My detective. He called around down here and came up with your name. He wouldn't follow the trail anymore and he told me not to, either, but said that if I wouldn't let it go I should talk to you. He heard you were supposed to be a good fighter. What's that mean? You're a boxer or something?"

This was rapidly going from not promising to terminally confusing. "I'm a fourth degree black belt in taekwondo. Maybe he heard something about that. Do you know who he talked to?"

"No. You're a black belt?" She was looking at me the way people usually do when they hear about my training, wondering why I don't look like some hunk they've seen in a martial arts movie. "You, too?" she asked Malone.

My partner gave a little snort at that. "Nope. I don't do martial arts. I just kick ass."

"Okay," Miss Austin assented a little hesitantly. I wanted to tell her she wasn't alone in not knowing quite how to take Devon Malone, but instead I got her back on track with her story.

It took another half-hour, but eventually we had it all, everything that she had. It wasn't much.

The detective Diane Austin hired in Alaska determined that a man using the name Tommy Cling had registered in the motel nearest her trailer park the day before the kidnapping, giving a home address in Portland. She thought this was significant be-

17

cause, she said, Paul Gregory had talked often about having friends in Portland and what a great place it would be to live. It was the whitest city in the country, he told her.

That made sense to me. Portland has the well-deserved reputation in mainstream America as a liberal and friendly city, but out on the dark periphery of society it's got a whole different appeal. Portland is Mecca for some racist, right-wing extremists because it's so white. From what she was telling me about her old boyfriend, he sounded like he would fit right in with that circle.

The Alaska PI, however, hadn't been able to find any further traces of Tommy Cling or Paul Gregory. Not any guys with those names who'd likely been fathering or stealing children in Ketchikan, Alaska, anyway. Then, according to Diane Austin, he abruptly announced he couldn't work for her anymore, telling her it was useless to pursue the case. Apparently he even got in touch with her "friend," who I gathered to be a quite elderly but highly enthusiastic sugar daddy, and told him to stop wasting his money.

Instead, sugar daddy got the detective to make a few more phone calls and come up with my name, then bankrolled the lady's flight, hotel room, wardrobe, etc., all of which brought her to this point.

She gave us a full description of the Paul Gregory she'd known and a vague one of the Tommy Cling who'd been in the nearby motel. Apparently the front desk clerk had been employed there for life; at least he was still at the desk when the Alaska detective showed up to inquire. And he claimed to actually remember Cling from eleven years before—a memorably nasty person, according to the report the detective submitted. I doubted there was any validity to the description, but I made a note.

So that was it, not much besides her friend's money and a desperate hope that somebody *maybe* named Tommy Cling had kidnapped her baby for somebody *maybe* named Paul Gregory, then *maybe* brought the kid back to Portland, Oregon, and *maybe* eleven years later they were all still around here using the same names. Yeah, right.

We both told her as plainly as we could just how dismal those odds were, but she begged us to at least give it a try. I didn't know about Malone, but in my years as a private investigator no client had ever begged for my services before. Not to mention that this was a mother pleading with us to help find her child. It didn't take me long to learn that I am a total sucker for such an appeal and, of course, my partner is always ready to test her own expertise at finding missing people.

We agreed to give it at least a few days, assuming Austin had no objection to our normal per diem rate plus expenses. She didn't even blink at the figure, just whipped out a signed check and filled in an amount big enough to cover a week. She had a very good friend indeed back home, apparently.

Our new client said she couldn't stay in town because her friend needed her, as a caregiver I suspected, and she left her contact information so we could get in touch if we learned anything.

I didn't even have her sign a contract, though I assured her she'd have a refund if we didn't work a full seven days. I was privately certain she'd get about five days back. There was going to be nowhere to go with this.

CHAPTER SIX

Devon Malone kicked back in her ratty old recliner, glass of wine in hand, and stared at her small TV. The wine was cabernet sauvignon from a box and the TV wasn't on. In fact, it didn't work.

Her apartment was sparsely furnished and minimally decorated, which was the way she liked it. There was nothing new, nothing fancy, nothing that didn't have a necessary function.

It occurred to her that her life was defined much more by what she didn't have than by what she did. Which was not an atypical thought for an evening alone with her wine and her TV.

Even though she seemed to be spending more and more evenings—and nights—at Clint McCall's house, she still needed the occasional evening to herself and her minimal surroundings.

Nothing minimal about Clint's house, with the two cats demanding attention and the man himself wanting always to be more intimate. And that was the question, wasn't it? The really Big One: how far could this thing between them go?

McCall made a great partner in their work. He was fun to talk to. The sex was good. She'd had better but she wasn't about to tell him that.

Which came right back to the Big Question, again. How much would she tell him? How much *could* she tell him? This morning he'd shared—finally—something from his past that he preferred not to talk about. Didn't she owe him the same? They were lovers. He said he loved her. She'd said she loved him—not many times, though she thought she sort of meant it.

She finished the current glass of wine in one good slug and sighed. It had been quite a day. First McCall's past comes around to possibly bite them both in the ass and then they get a genuine missing person's case, right up her alley but so cold that she practically got frostbite just trying to contact someone, anyone, who'd been involved in the original investigation in Alaska.

And, speaking of alleys, Clint had spent a good part of his day calling local informants to see if he could get a bead on where Hoke Moseley might be staying and then making still more calls to see if he could track down anything about a Paul Gregory or a Tommy Cling. Too bad little Miss Accountant/Hacker Eleanor Ivory had been tied up with client meetings all day. In any event, apparently Clint had had no success on either front.

Meanwhile they had other ongoing cases that either needed follow-up or reports written.

By late afternoon she and McCall both were tired, frustrated, and grumpy. She had learned nothing useful. He had learned nothing useful. They readily agreed that it would be a good evening to just rest up and take some space.

So here she sat. She looked around the plain and simple room. *Clint has never been here. Another item on a very long to-do list.* So: no lover, no cats, no working TV, and no wine in her glass. At least that latter problem was easily remedied.

She'd gotten up and was halfway to her small and, yes, sparsely equipped kitchen when the phone rang. Almost certainly a salesman, a wrong number, or McCall, she thought, since there were very few other people who might be calling. Maybe he'd come up with something new. Or was horny after all. She picked up the phone.

"This is Devon Malone," she said as always. There were a few seconds of silence and she was about to hang up, thinking the wrong number guess was the correct one, when she heard a familiar, whispery, and unwelcome voice, one she hadn't heard in years.

"Devon? Is that you?"

Oh, fuck. "Sherry?"

"Yes, yes, thank God. It is you. I'm in trouble, sweetheart. I need your help."

Malone almost dropped the empty wine glass but managed to set it on the table next to the phone. Meanwhile she had a hard time getting her own voice to work. "What...? How...? Where are you and what kind of trouble?"

"I'm here. In Portland. At a Motel 6 on...Sandy Street, I think. You've got to come help me."

Oh, double and triple fuck. She couldn't believe it, didn't want to believe it. "You're in Portland?"

"Yes, and I know everything will be all right now that I'm back with my sweet little girl. Come quickly." She rattled off the address and room number, apparently reading from something because she got the Sandy Boulevard right this time, and hung up. Just like that.

And now I've got my goddamned mother to deal with, Malone thought as she set the phone back in its cradle, her hand shaking slightly.

CHAPTER SEVEN

I was in the office ahead of Malone the next morning. The late-June sun was shining and the Tuesday morning traffic had been good to me between the Hawthorne District and downtown, plus I was eager to see if I could actually get something accomplished today. Yesterday had been pretty much a bust on all fronts.

The first thing I did after Diane Austin left was look in the Portland phone book for Paul Gregory, Thomas Cling or Noelle Austin. Never hurts to try the obvious. There was a Paul Gregory listed, it being a fairly common name, but when I called he claimed to be an eighty-three-year-old retired railroad engineer with a bad heart and a worse wife. Sounded to me like he was telling the truth.

The second thing I did yesterday was check to see if our accountant and Internet expert, Eleanor Ivory, was available to do some research. Alas, she was not. So I made a bunch of other calls, looking for any kind of lead on the Austin case or the Moseley threat. No luck.

Meanwhile Malone had been pursuing her own, more sophisticated, avenues of investigation, checking with the Ketchikan PD for instance, but apparently with no more success than I was having.

I started this morning off with a call to Johnny Crew. Even though he and his old partner Hap Harbaugh had been retired for some time, they still backed us up upon occasion and had a few informants who were still alive.

Johnny is a vigorous seventy-two years old, a short and burly but very well-groomed fellow with a full head of luxurious gray hair. At the Bureau he'd been known as "Dapper John."

Hap is sixty-nine and has at least eighteen inches of height and a hundred pounds of weight on his partner. While Johnny always looks immaculate, Hap is a total schlump who thinks nothing of wearing the same clothes a week at a time. A completely bald mountain of a man, he complains constantly about his back, bunions, knees, neck, and all the other parts of his body he can no longer reach. His nickname on the force had been "Hap the Hulk."

Johnny never complains about anything. On the other hand, he has an incredibly foul mouth in private among friends while Harbaugh never says anything more potent than "dang."

Johnny's wife Geraldine answered the phone, sounding cheery as usual. She asked after my daughter Colleen and my partner Devon, then handed the phone over to her husband.

"Hey, Clint," Johnny boomed in greeting. His voice, like his partner, is about twice his size. "You ever heard of a fuckin' dog nanny?"

I laughed. The man is always on about something. "I've heard of fucking, nannies, and dogs, but never a fucking dog nanny."

"I was just reading in the paper about this fiftyish gal getting remarried and it said the bridesmaid was her dog nanny. Can you fucking believe that? How rich do you think this woman could be? Christ, a dog nanny."

"At least the pooch should live happily ever after. Johnny, I need to ask you something. This may sound odd, but did a detective from Alaska recently talk to you or Hap about me?"

"Well, yeah, as a matter of fact I did get a call from some snowbound shithead looking to pass off a case to a PI down here. I guess he hadn't heard that me and Hap are retired. He said it had to be somebody who could handle a lot of trouble, so I gave him your name. Why? Something come of it already?"

26

"Looks like. This guy didn't happen to mention what *kind* of trouble he was talking about, did he?"

"It didn't sound like emotional difficulties, if that's what you mean. Sounded like ass-kicking to me. I told him you teach people how to handle that kind of trouble. I guess it was what he had in mind if you've heard from him."

"I didn't hear from him, but his client came to visit us yesterday morning. The thing is, the case she hired us for, the same case the Alaska guy was working on, doesn't seem to have any trouble associated with it—not that kind, anyway. The only trouble I can see is that we probably can't do anything to help the lady."

"I don't know. That's what he said to me. Hey Clint, seriously, speaking of ass-kicking, I heard Hoke Moseley is back on the street."

"Yeah, I got a nice card from his mother sharing the good news. Sort of a murder invitation."

"Really? You mean, like a threat? I got some time right now if you want backup for a few days. I'll see if Hap's available, too."

I couldn't help smiling to myself. Other than backing up me and Malone occasionally, the two old detectives had nothing but time—as their wives would be happy to tell you.

"No, that's okay, Johnny." I had never actually seen Hoke Moseley but I imagined him as an older and harder version of his younger brother—blond and lean and very mean. There was no way I wanted Crew and Harbaugh trying to take him on.

I hung up with more questions than I had started with. Why would the Alaska PI be worried about handling violence of some sort if he hadn't made any progress on the case? And if he had, did he not tell his client? Or did she not tell us?

I was just beginning to speculate about how I might answer those questions when Devon Malone finally arrived. She was significantly later than usual and looked significantly more wrung out than usual. She looked downright devastated, in fact.

CHAPTER EIGHT

She more or less threw her summer-weight leather jacket at the hall tree and I was on my feet before she made it to her side of the partners desk. "What's happened?"

"What makes you think something's happened?" she asked irritably and plopped down in her swivel chair, immediately swinging it toward the window that looks out on Stark Street.

I knew better than to touch, much less hug the woman at such a moment but I came around and stood close, leaning over her just a bit. "Well, let's see," I said. "Could it be because you look like you haven't slept and are incredibly upset about something?"

After a long pause, she actually reached back over her shoulder for me. Then I knew something was *really* wrong. I took her hand.

"What is it, Devon? Tell me."

She just sat there squeezing my hand and staring out the window for what seemed like five minutes but was probably thirty seconds.

"My mother's in town," she said at last.

That was not among any of the things I might have imagined. "Your mother?"

"I don't want to talk about this."

"Devon...."

She abruptly let go of my hand and swiveled the chair to the desk. "I didn't say I wasn't going to talk about it. I said I didn't want to talk about it." She pointed at my chair. "Sit."

I stepped back a little. "Ookay," I said, and obeyed the command.

Once I was seated, she made a point of making and maintaining eye contact as she talked. "I did not have what you would call a happy childhood," she began. "My father was a drunken asshole who started raping me when I was eight years old."

I wanted to say something, do something, but her eyes said, *Let me tell this my way.*

"I killed him when I was twelve." No special emphasis, just another step in the narrative. I was beyond doing or saying anything at this point.

"My mother, who knew all along what he was doing and did nothing to stop him, confessed to the killing." A tiny twitch of the shoulders but no break in eye contact. "I guess she finally found *something* she could do to protect me. So she went to prison and I went into foster care."

Now, finally, her eyes said she was waiting for a response. There might even have been a little fear in them.

"Devon, I am so sorry. I had no idea...."

"Of course you had no idea. I haven't shared any of this with anyone since I escaped the final foster home—and, no, I didn't literally escape; I aged out of it, as required." She jabbed a finger in my direction. "But don't be sorry. I don't want sorry. If you want to be angry, that's fine. It's what I've always been."

She paused for another couple of seconds. "So, now that you know I'm a murderer...."

I leaned toward her pointing finger. God, I wanted to hold her, comfort her, something. "You're a survivor. You did what you had to do and you've survived. And I love you even more for it."

A little nod. Her hand dropped back down to the desk. "Okay. That's good."

"Your mother...."

"Is out. Just like your Hoke Moseley, except she's been out for almost ten years."

"And now?"

"And now I've finally heard from her, because she thinks someone is trying to kill her and she wants *my* protection."

"Good grief." What else could I say? Talk about having a lot to process.

"Yeah. Lots of grief. Not so good."

"Who's trying to kill her? And why?"

She finally looked away, out the window again for a moment. "You know, those are interesting questions. I just spent half the night talking to the woman and I can't answer either one, yet."

"She wants your protection but won't tell you what's going on?"

A shrug. "You'd have to meet my mother. In fact, fuck it all, you *will* have to meet my mother. Apparently she isn't going to do the big reveal until she's met you, which I can actually understand because I know the woman. A man is much easier to manipulate in her universe. So. If you're willing to help me out with this, whatever 'this' turns out to be...."

"Of course I'm willing to help. And, you know, meeting the parents is kind of traditional anyway."

She gave me a wide-eyed look at that and snorted. "Are you trying to make me laugh in the middle of all this shit?"

"A feeble effort, I admit, but yes."

"Well, kudos for the effort."

"So now what?"

She gestured to take in the whole office. "We've still got an agency to run. Cases pending. A new client. You weren't going to neglect those because of Hoke Moseley, were you?"

"Well, no...."

"Then we're not going to neglect them because of Sherry Malone."

CHAPTER NINE

I needed to know more. A lot more. My partner was a patricide, for God's sake, and her mother had gone to prison for the crime. I didn't blame her for letting her mother protect her that way. She'd been twelve years old and incredibly traumatized. But now is Devon's first contact with the woman in the ten years she's been free? That was hard. I couldn't even imagine how estranged they must have been, how hurtful it must have been that her mother didn't protect her until after she'd acted on her own.

Devon Malone's body was badly scarred by a madman who tortured her at length last year and the scars have never bothered me at all. I didn't have to get used to them. They are part of who she is and I love who she is. But now it appeared that she is just as scarred on the inside. That was going to be harder, because she clearly didn't want to let anyone in there. And I was determined to understand that, too.

I knew better than to press the issue and obsessing wasn't going to do any good. She was right. We had pending cases and a new client. Not that I could think of much more to do for Diane Austin. Well, maybe one thing.

I reached for the phone. "Having exhausted my own Internet skills because Eleanor was in meetings yesterday," I announced, "I'm going to check to see if she has some time today. I hope so."

Eleanor Ivory has been the agency's accountant since I started it and has her office right down the hall from us. I'd originally met her when I was still apprenticing with Johnny and Hap and she was a new Taekwondo student of mine. She was the reason I'd looked at this office space, in fact; then, once I was here, it was a no-brainer to use attorney Sam Bitterly and insurance broker Ray Witkowsky.

Recently turned forty, Eleanor is five-nine with long blond hair and the body of a fitness magazine model—not least because she's still doing martial arts, now a brown belt in the small private dojang that she and I and five other black belts co-own. She and Malone did not hit it off right away, to say the least, and my partner was still not entirely comfortable with using Eleanor for her computer expertise.

"She's probably still too busy helping clients cheat the government," Malone muttered.

"Maybe so," I said equably.

"Eleanor Ivory Accountancy," said a slightly throaty voice in my ear.

"It's Clint. You have a few minutes today to do some research?"

"Yes, the rush seems to be over for the moment. I'm just running some quarterly reports for corporate clients. Come on down."

"On my way."

I hung up and looked over at Malone. "You?"

She offered me a little grimace back. "I've got a report and an invoice to prepare for a woman who will be happy to learn that her husband is not having an affair."

"Good for her," I allowed as I stood up.

"She may be a little less happy to learn that he has an apparent addiction to strip joints."

"Ah. Well, one has to take the bad with the good. I'll be just a couple of minutes."

"I'll probably be here." She focused on her keyboard and I headed down the corridor.

I knocked once and opened Eleanor's door. Her office is a single room like mine and Malone's, though smaller. It's a little girly, with a doll collection on some shelves to one side and a small mobile of papier-mâché birds hanging from the ceiling.

As for Eleanor herself, there's steel under the femininity. I could name some guys who'd made overly aggressive moves on her and paid the price.

Today she was dressed sedately in earth tones, a brown sheath skirt that hit just above the knees and a beige wrap-over top. She turned away from an open file cabinet drawer and gave me a smile. "Come on in," she said. "I could use some excitement."

"Really?" I inquired as we took seats on opposite sides of her desk. "Aren't you currently dating some Latino playboy who claims to be related to Spain's royal family, drives a silver Ferrari, and lives in a Lake Oswego mansion? What's his name? Miguel?"

She grinned and waved that away. "He's just par for my course," she said. "Nothing like assisting my favorite private detective in his investigations. I assume that's what you need. You don't have a tax problem, do you?"

"No, we are looking for your help on a case, all right." I put a little emphasis on the "we," just for the fun of it. Eleanor was no more a fan of Malone than vice versa. Then I went on to tell her about Diane Austin, the long-lost baby, and the mysterious possible abductors.

"That poor woman!" she said when I'd wrapped it up. "It must be terrible for her to lose her child like that—and then to have to snuggle up to some old codger for the money to go looking...."

"Well now, she didn't *say* that's what she's doing. It's just our speculation."

"That's what she's doing. Believe me."

"Okay."

"And you want me to do a search for these guys, Gregory and Cling, right?"

"Plus the kid, not that any of it is likely to do much good after so many years."

"I'll give it my best shot and let you know."

I ambled back down to the office and the rest of the morning was relatively quiet. Malone and I fielded a few telephone inquiries, drank lots of coffee, and caught up on paperwork. Several times I thought about returning to the subject of her mother, but each time I thought better of it. The quiet office with the woman I care so much about right there in front of me, the two of us working in tandem.... That was enough for the moment.

CHAPTER TEN

Around eleven thirty Malone tapped one final key on her keyboard and swiveled square with the desk, placing both hands face down on the surface. "Time for lunch," she announced. No matter how distressed either of us might be, I could always count on her to remind me to eat.

We hit the sidewalk and turned right toward 2nd. I abruptly stopped with my hand on Malone's arm to bring her up short as well.

Standing on the corner was a tall, thin young man looking straight at me. He looked younger than I'd thought he would, no more than early twenties, and his head was shaved rather than displaying the blond hair I'd been expecting, but I had no doubt it was Hoke Moseley. He stood balanced a little forward on the balls of his feet as if anticipating an attack, shoulders curved slightly inward as if he'd already suffered defeat at the hands of whatever might come. His posture labeled him an inmate just as clearly as if he'd still been wearing his prison outfit.

I took a slow, deep breath. Well then, let the party begin.

His current attire was a gray tee shirt and blue jeans with canvas high top sneakers. The long white shoelaces were untied and trailed on the sidewalk as he took a step forward. The shirt and pants were too tight to conceal a gun. It might be nestled in the small of his back but as long as I could see his hands hanging at his sides, that wasn't a problem.

"Is that...?" Malone muttered.

"Yep, that is," I replied in a normal voice.

He took a step toward us and I shifted my hand a little nearer the holster hooked to my belt under my sport coat, in case he charged or one of his hands disappeared. I saw now that his complexion was light and freckled; maybe the missing hair was red. He had a prominent scar over his left eye and his nose had obviously been broken at least once.

"Moseley," I said.

He stopped and looked hard at me, then Malone. "So," he said slowly and distinctly, "you gonna shoot *me* now?"

"Not unless you try to shoot me first." I said.

Another two steps, shoelaces dragging. "My brother didn't try to shoot you first."

"I was in the alley looking for a guy I knew was a shooter. It was dark. I saw your brother's gun and I reacted. I didn't have a choice, given what I could see. I'm sorry. I know that's not enough, but it's all I can do. It's something I have to live with."

"Maybe not."

I didn't know yet what Hoke Moseley wanted. His body was tense but not poised for offense. Not yet. The stance said he expected me to attack. So maybe my out was to reassure him—and how strange was that?

I held up my hands, fingers spread wide. "I sincerely wish I hadn't hurt your brother and I don't want to hurt you. That's the truth. You've been on the street—what, twenty-four hours? Why don't you just walk away rather than put yourself back in a cell so soon?"

"You think it's that easy?"

Hands down again. "For today, this minute, this street corner, it can be."

38

He stood quietly, posture and expression unchanged, for what seemed like a full minute. Finally his mouth twisted as if with a sudden bitter taste. "Fuck you." He turned and walked away. The only thing in the small of his back was a sweat stain.

I couldn't see it, but I was pretty sure I had one of my own.

CHAPTER ELEVEN

"Did that strike you as weird?" asked Malone as we waited for the delivery of our burgers and fries in the Home Run Sports Bar across the street from our office.

The Home Run's ambience is casual with a color scheme that is warm golden yellow rather than fast-food orange. There are booths along three walls and a bar along the fourth, with tables spread across the open floor space and flat-screen high-def TVs visible from every seat. All of the TVs are tuned to one sports channel or another. The menu is heavy on burgers with sporty nicknames; the fries are fat but light on grease.

I set down my coffee cup. "It wasn't exactly what I was expecting," I admitted.

"It was almost like he didn't want to be there, like he expected you to attack him rather than the other way around, did you get that?"

"Yeah, I don't know what's going on with Moseley." I took another sip of coffee and observed a waitress headed our way with a loaded tray of goodies. "But I guess we'll find out eventually."

"I guess we will," Malone agreed as the waitress started unloading calories onto our table. My partner dug in immediately, as was her wont.

I enjoyed her enthusiasm for a moment before picking up my own super-sized Home Run Burger. It seemed that nothing could keep this woman from enjoying her food. "You didn't say a word out there," I noted before I took a bite.

She swallowed what must have been her fifth fry already and shrugged. "So?"

"You always mouth off when somebody confronts us."

Another little shrug. "He wasn't confronting us. Just you. I didn't think he posed a danger and I didn't see a reason to provoke him. I thought you handled it pretty well." Followed by another big bite of burger.

"Well, gee, thank you."

After about ten minutes of companionable consumption, Malone popped her last French fry into her mouth and gave me a look. "I guess we should make a plan for you to meet my mother," she said.

I'd been wondering how long it would take. "I thought we were going to do what we can for Diane Austin first."

"We are, but that might not be much and your past has already shown up. We might as well at least plan for you to see mine."

I really didn't know whether to be glad she was taking another step toward helping her mother or worried about where it would take us. "Okay."

"This evening? If we don't have anything else going on?"

Probably gladness and worry were both appropriate. "Sounds good to me."

She grimaced and pushed away from the table. "That's only because you don't know my mother yet."

CHAPTER TWELVE

Eleanor Ivory was coming down the hall toward our office as we topped the stairs, returning from our lunch. She stopped and waited for us at our office door.

"You found something?" I asked her as I unlocked and let us all in.

"Not really," she answered. We all crossed the room to the desk and took seats, her in the visitor's chair closest to me.

"I can't find Noelle Austin, Paul Gregory, or Thomas Cling in any local database," she went on. "As far as a general web search, I came up with zero hits on the girl, one that didn't pan out for a Tommy Cling, and sixteen hundred and sixty for Paul Gregory--mostly first and middle names rather than first and last, mostly genealogical listings. Not much help, I'm afraid."

"What was the one on Tommy Cling?"

"A website for something called the True Christian Brotherhood. I checked because it was the only one for him, but his name wasn't actually there. It could have been associated with the site in the recent past, but more likely it was a bogus hit."

"Well, write down the Internet address. I might look at it later. Was it local?"

"Northwest, I think, but I didn't pay any attention to the specific location. Ugly stuff. One of those hate-thy-neighbor Christian cults, looked like to me."

"There's plenty of that out there. Try one more thing for me, Eleanor. This first and second name business gives me an idea. Go back and see if there are any local hits with first name Paul and middle name Gregory. Try it the other way around, too: first name Gregory and middle name Paul. Most people aren't very creative about coming up with an alias."

"No problem. You're lucky this isn't tax season. I'd have to charge you a premium for the time."

We both ignored the tiny grunt that came from Malone's side of the desk. She'd been listening but saying nothing during my exchange with Eleanor, as was usually the case.

As soon as Eleanor had closed our door behind her, Malone sighed. "We're not going to be able to do anything for that woman."

"Don't give up yet," I said as I went for another cup of coffee, the last in the pot left over from this morning. I held up the empty pot as an inquiry whether my partner wanted more and she shook her head no.

I returned to the desk, took a swig of stale coffee, and looked at the note with the Internet address that Eleanor had left on my desk. "Let me check this website," I said.

Malone made a little disparaging noise. "The one that doesn't have Tommy Cling's name?"

This time I sighed. "Yeah, that one," I agreed as I typed in the address and hit enter. A stark website appeared, all black and white, with densely packed text that seemed to be mostly vitriol and condemnation directed at everyone who wasn't a true believer in whatever these morons believed.

"Yuck," I said, and started looking for an "About Us" button. It was probably hopeless, but I was here anyway. Way down at the bottom, in a much smaller font, I did find a "Contact Us" button. Good enough. I clicked it and ran my eyes down the short list of contact information. "Ah ha!" I said.

"Well," Malone responded, "we've gone from 'yuck' to 'ah ha.' That's some kind of progress."

I'm sure I was looking rather smug at this point. "Guess who is listed here as the leader of the True Christian Brotherhood?" I asked.

"Tommy Cling? And Eleanor missed it?"

44

"Good guess, but no. A guy named Gregory Paul Zoller."

"Ah ha."

I looked at my watch. "According to the website, they have an office in Salem. I guess it's too late to head down there today, but I suggest we go looking for Mr. Zoller first thing in the morning."

"That sounds like a plan, but you may have to go by yourself."

"Really? Why?"

Malone grimaced and then firmed up. "Because, one way or the other, we're going to find out this evening what the hell is going on with my mother." A little wave of the hand. "And I might have to do something about it."

CHAPTER THIRTEEN

There are a number of Motel 6 locations in the Portland area. Sherry Malone's was on a stretch of Sandy Boulevard mostly given over to fast food restaurants and fast sex streetwalkers. It looked just like every other Motel 6—big sign, utilitarian building with slightly grungy siding, narrow parking lot running from the office on one end past identical rooms to the maid's supply storage on the other.

I pulled into the lot and parked in front of Room 7 just before 6 p.m., as instructed by Devon Malone who was sitting in my passenger seat. I had insisted that we were going to spend the night together after our visit with her mother, so we were in my Outback with her Jeep still in the parking lot across from the agency.

My insistence was based on a strong feeling, or call it a fear, that if we weren't together after this meeting we might not get together again. The fact that my partner was so tense she was practically vibrating lent some support to my concerns. This was not going to be fun. Whatever "this" turned out to be.

Taking a deep breath, Malone bailed out of the car. I followed her to the door of the room and stood back a little as she knocked firmly on the laminated wood. I took a measured breath of my own.

My first thought when the door opened was, *Is this what Devon Malone is going to look like when she gets older?* My second, immediate thought was, *No fucking way.*

The woman who stood there looking wide-eyed at us was a heavily made-up bottle blonde wearing a low-cut top and Capri pants. She was taller than Malone and a good deal more voluptuous. It was hard to guess her age. If I hadn't known she was Devon's mother I'd have put it anywhere between a well-worn mid-forties and sixty trying to look mid-forties. Imagine if Marilyn Monroe had failed both at suicide and at aging well. I think my jaw dropped a little.

"Devon, sweetheart," she said with a somewhat brittle smile. The throaty voice, at least, was similar to my partner's.

"Sherry," muttered Malone as she swept past the woman into the small motel room.

Experienced detective that I am, I could discern that there was no genuine affection in either greeting.

I was still on the threshold, wondering if I should just follow Devon past her mother. Then Sherry Malone offered me her hand with a sort of half-smile. "You must be Clint McCall," she said. "It's good to meet you. Come in."

Her hand was soft and a little damp, not entirely pleasant. I let it go as I stepped past her into a typical small motel room dominated by the bed and accessorized with one armchair, a tiny round table with a single straight-backed chair, a dresser and somewhat dirty mirror. There was one other door that no doubt led to the bathroom. The air smelled of disinfectant and cheap air freshener.

Malone sat on the bed and I took the chair by the table, leaving the armchair for our hostess.

Sherry Malone settled there, crossed one leg over the other, rested her clasped hands on her knee, and looked from Devon to me. "As soon as my daughter told me she had a partner now," she said to me, "I knew I wanted you here when I told my story. I'm hoping you might be more understanding."

"You're hoping that he'll be on your side because he's a man," interrupted Malone. "It won't work."

After a moment of Sherry and I both absorbing what I, at least, took to be a testimonial of sorts, she went on as if her daughter had not spoken.

"Devon and I have not...been close...for a long time, as you may know."

"He knows it all, Sherry," Malone told her.

That stopped her for a little longer. "All?"

"All."

Sherry looked to me as if for confirmation, so I confirmed. "Devon killed her father who had been abusing her for years with your knowledge and you finally stepped up by taking the fall. You've been out of prison for a decade during which there's been no contact between you. And now you're here because you're in some kind of trouble. Does that about cover it?"

Her heavily painted eyebrows went up and her heavily lipsticked mouth turned down. "I guess it does, yes."

Malone shifted forward to the very edge of the bed. "So what's the damned story, Sherry? Why are you here?"

Her mother took a breath. "I've been in Fresno, California, most of the last ten years with a man named Marty Salazar. He's not a very nice man."

"That's who you're afraid of?" Malone asked, sounding like she was on the edge of losing it.

"Yes."

"Why? Come on, Sherry. Just put it out there. Why does the not-very-nice man want to kill you?"

"Because I ran away from him. The son of a bitch was an abuser, just like your father, and I escaped."

"That's it?" I asked, thinking that I should take some part in this conversation. "He wants to kill you because you got away from him?" I exchanged a look with Malone. Just a few months before we'd dealt with someone like that and I didn't welcome the prospect of another nutcase.

"Well," Sherry Malone responded slowly, "I might have taken some money and...other things...with me when I left."

That made a little more sense and I noted that Malone had an I-thought-so expression on her face. "How much money? What other things?" I asked.

"He had a safe in his office and he didn't think I knew the combination. I emptied it. Around thirty thousand dollars and the notebooks he used to keep track of his business."

"Jesus!" exploded my partner.

"How long ago was this?" I asked right on top of her.

"About six months. I've been on the run ever since."

Malone gestured at our shabby surroundings. "This is what thirty thousand buys you?"

Her mother grimaced and slumped a little. "It's gone."

My partner goggled at her. "What's gone?"

"The money. The money's gone. I spent it trying to stay ahead of Marty." Sherry Malone mirrored her daughter's wave at the room. "I could barely afford this." She reached over and patted a leather satchel that was lying on the bed near the foot. "I still have the notebooks, though."

Malone was on her feet by this time, clearly losing the struggle to rein in her emotions. "What the fuck do you expect me to do about it, Sherry?" she practically shouted at her mother.

The woman was not fazed by the outburst. She offered Malone a copy of that initial brittle smile. "I expect you to get Marty Salazar off my back. You don't want your mother to die, do you?"

Malone abruptly headed for the door. "I've got to get out of here, get some space for a minute," she said to no one in particular before she jerked the door open and plunged outside, slamming it closed behind her.

CHAPTER FOURTEEN

"Well," Sherry said as she moved from the armchair to the bed, sitting approximately where her daughter had been, "I guess she needs to think about my question."

I couldn't help noticing that the move had been totally unnecessary and that it brought her much closer to me. I had no reason (yet)to be particularly uncomfortable about that, but my gut turned over slightly anyway. What had I gotten myself into?

She leaned a little toward me, exposing a bit more cleavage, and practically purred, "I know you'll help me even if my daughter won't."

Okay. So. The second Devon was gone, Mom went straight to seduction. I resisted the strong urge to get up and move further away. Instead I held up a hand, palm toward Sherry Malone, and said firmly, "Devon will help you. We wouldn't be here if she hadn't already decided that."

She stared at my hand, which I was not lowering, and then sat back. "I hope you're right," she said, and this time it sounded genuine.

"This is very difficult for her," I offered and then waited for a response, maybe hoping to learn some more about the dynamic between them. That was obviously going to be important.

"You think I don't know that? I spent half of last night trying to make things right with Devon. Everything has always been difficult for her."

Which was not a big revelation. "But," I said, "I guess that didn't include telling her why you were here." She offered a little shoulder twitch. Time to focus in. "My understanding is that Devon was twelve when...her father died...and she's mid-thirties now...."

51

"Thirty-six," interrupted Sherry. "She's thirty-six."

Already I was learning new things. "Okay, and you've been out of prison for ten years?"

"Yes. I got out because they knew I didn't do it in the first place."

That was unexpected. "I don't understand. Devon said you confessed...."

"I did."

"Okay. Let's start over. Devon killed her father, your husband, right?"

She took a deep breath and sat back, her eyes a little unfocused as if she were picturing it again. "Yes. He was...a very bad man, my husband. Not as bad as Marty Salazar, but bad, and I was afraid of him. Too afraid to protect my daughter." She paused as if she wanted to go on justifying herself, but then shook her head.

"It happened in the kitchen. It might not have happened at all if it hadn't been in the kitchen, if that damned heavy mortar hadn't been right there on the counter...."

I had to interrupt. "Mortar?" I was imagining some kind of military ordinance sitting around their kitchen.

Sherry frowned at me. "Mortar and pestle, you know, to grind stuff up? I grind my own herbs.... Never mind about that. I had an old ceramic mortar and pestle that had belonged to my grandmother. Big. And heavy. The mortar weighed a couple of pounds probably."

"Okay. I gotcha."

"Devon had just had enough, I guess. Twelve years old or not, she'd just had enough. He was trying to...do something...and she picked up that heavy sucker and brained him with it. I don't know if she even realized what she was doing, though she likes to think she did."

"But you confessed to killing him."

52

She nodded. "I did. I found them in the kitchen, him already dead on the floor and her standing off in the corner. She was in shock or something. I knew right away what had happened and what I had to do. I picked up the mortar to get my fingerprints on it and dropped it back on the floor beside him. Then I called 9-1-1 and confessed. I didn't even use the excuse that he was hurting my daughter; I didn't want to embarrass her."

"And what happened then? You say they didn't believe you?"

"Oh, they did at first. They had fingerprints and a confession.... Why not? But I'm sure that after all the interviews and all the investigation, they knew, or thought they knew, what really happened. You can tell by the looks they give you and each other. But they let it be. I guess they figured he deserved to die and Devon deserved to live free."

"What about you?"

Her face fell and she looked even older for a moment. "I deserved what I got and worse. I let my baby down for a lot of years. She's not going to forgive me and I guess she shouldn't." She tried to perk up a bit. "That's why I was glad to hear she has a partner now, somebody she cares about. I figured maybe you would help me."

The logic didn't quite track, but probably Devon had been correct that her mother was used to depending on a man. Simple and sad as that.

"We'll both do what we can," I said. "Why do you think you're in any particular danger now? Does Salazar know you're in Portland?"

"Marty's got connections everywhere. No matter where I go he's on my heels and I'm tired. I can't keep running. I got no money left and no energy either. That's why I finally came here to see my daughter. I know she didn't want to see me. She wants nothing to do with me or the memories, but I didn't have any choices left." She leaned a little toward me again, wide-eyed and pale. "If Marty isn't here already, he will be soon. You've got to help me."

CHAPTER FIFTEEN

There was nothing else that Sherry Malone could or would tell me, so I reassured her one more time and excused myself. I found Malone pacing up and down the motel parking lot. Oddly enough there appeared to be a half-smile on her face.

"You seem to be feeling better," I said as she finally pulled up next to the car where I was waiting for her.

"There was a guy."

"A guy?"

"A pudgy middle-aged guy wearing a fucking Hawaiian shirt and a wedding ring who thought I was a whore. Offered me money." She snorted. "A lousy hundred dollars."

I glanced around. "Do we need to call the medical examiner?"

Now she grinned outright. "No, but I wouldn't be surprised if he stops by the emergency room on the way home to the little woman."

Then, just that quick, she shrugged off the grin and looked back at the motel room door I'd just exited. "You get anything else we can use?"

"So you are going to help her."

"I'm going to get her off my back so she can fucking move on."

"She didn't give me much that *we* can use, no." I had a strong hunch that my partner would not want to stand around a parking lot and deal with my learning more about her past, so I just let the emphasis on "we" serve as a hint that I probably knew more details of what had happened in that kitchen and the aftermath.

"She says this Marty Salazar guy has been close behind all along and could be in town now," I went on. "That's about it."

Malone looked away, seeming to watch the still-heavy evening traffic on Sandy, and then nodded. "Okay. I'll go back to the office and see what I can find out about Salazar and then tomorrow I'll go talk to our local crime boss to see if he has heard anything."

"You don't have your Jeep," I reminded her. "You were going to be at my house tonight. I still think you should."

She reached out and squeezed my arm. "I can't. I just can't deal with.... Drop me back at the office and go work out—or have a nice quiet evening at home. Or both. Tomorrow night. We'll be okay." Reading my mind again. "I'll be there tomorrow night."

Okay, she didn't want to risk having to talk about what had happened in that kitchen, nor probably about what was happening now with her mother. Not yet, anyway. I'd look forward to tomorrow night.

"Let's go," I said, and she leaned in to give me a quick kiss.

It's good to be an understanding partner.

CHAPTER SIXTEEN

I dropped off Malone as requested and then spent some time working out at the dojang. Carmen Gonzales and Daisy Mansfield, both third degree black belts, were kind enough to put in an hour or so of two-on-one and beat the crap out of me.

Around nine the following morning I made the forty-minute drive down Interstate 5 to Salem. It was the first of July, the sun was shining, and the ramshackle fireworks stands on Lancaster Boulevard in our state capital were doing a booming business. I didn't know if the True Christian Brotherhood would be a house, a storefront, a church...but I didn't expect it to be located in a strip mall.

There were plenty of spaces available and I picked one, then sat for a minute to absorb my surroundings. I noticed that four out of the other six cars were Subaru Outbacks—which is why it makes the perfect surveillance vehicle. Everybody in the Pacific Northwest is accustomed to an Outback driving behind them or parked nearby.

I hoped that this trip had not been a waste of time. I'd taken another good look at the website before leaving the office yesterday and it was not promising. Only self-professed Aryans and so-called Christians need apply to the True Christian Brotherhood. Must be heterosexual of course. Properly submissive if female. Poorly educated and dumb as a rock wouldn't hurt, either, I was guessing.

Groups like that were unfortunately a dime a dozen on the Internet. They could find a lot more followers in cyberspace than in the real world because a person could spew venom and hatred in their chat rooms and on their e-mail servers with impunity. There was no one to recognize them in their white robes and pointy hoods.

None of which provided any hint that the Brotherhood had anything to do with Diane or Noelle Austin. I was here mostly just out of nostalgia. My long-ago and infrequently remembered Pulitzer nomination had been for a series on Northwest cults and I was curious to see how they'd evolved, if that was the right word, since my youth as a reporter for *The Oregonian*.

The True Christian Brotherhood was just one among a half-dozen storefronts facing the small parking lot: dry cleaner, tobacco emporium, photography studio, trading card dealer, sewing machine repair shop, and cult headquarters.

The lower half of the Brotherhood's display window was covered by a dark brown curtain that set off the white lettering of the name on the glass and also provided some privacy for the office space inside. I exited the car and headed for the glass door (also curtained) that I hoped was unlocked.

It was. Inside I found a creepy-looking fellow behind a plain gray-metal desk. Nothing on the desk, no papers, not even a phone. Matching four-drawer file cabinet off to the side, two chairs, a couple of posters, and that was it. A door in the far right corner was slightly ajar; maybe there were secretaries back there who did the actual office work.

He gave me a quick once-over and remained seated. Dressed as I was in sneakers, khaki pants, and polo shirt with the tail out, I guess I wasn't impressive enough for him to stand up. "Can I help you?"

"I'm looking for Gregory Paul Zoller."

At that he rose and tentatively held out a hand. "I'm Gregory Zoller." I shook his hand, which was thin, heavily veined, and felt a little like moist paper.

Already I was feeling my time had probably been wasted. This man looked nothing like the Paul Gregory described by Diane Austin. About the same height, around six feet, but she'd described a man who was very fit, close-cropped blond hair, a bushy beard, generally uncouth with a nervous, jumpy disposition. Gregory Zoller was gaunt and sallow, with thick black hair almost greasy enough to bring the word "pomade" back into everyday English. He was clean-shaven and dressed in a neat if inexpensive suit and tie. Didn't look like he had a jumpy muscle in his body, nor even any muscles that had moved much lately.

His eyes were something else again. They managed to look mean and dead at the same time. Was the zombie apocalypse already here? I might be lucky to escape with my brains.

I introduced myself and showed him my ID.

"A private investigator. What can I do for you, Mr. McCall?" He gestured to one of the two wooden folding chairs in front of the desk and sat down again in the elderly swivel chair behind the desk.

The seat he'd indicated was decrepit enough to make me uneasy about keeping my balance—not to mention getting a splinter. "Your name came up in a case I'm working on."

"Concerning?"

"A missing person."

He sat back, hands spread in innocence, smile revealing teeth seriously in need of both an orthodontist and a hygienist. "We aren't one of those cults that brainwash people, Mr. McCall. We're simply a group of like-minded believers in Christ."

"Of course. I could tell that just by looking at the posters behind you there on the wall."

One was all white with the words "Christ is coming" in red letters dripping blood. The other featured a classic Old Testament God image pointing in the style of Uncle Sam with the words "God wants you!" at the bottom.

Mr. Zoller did not seem to appreciate my wry observation. He frowned intensely. I think he was trying to look fierce.

"How did my name come up?"

59

"I'm afraid I can't tell you that."

More exercising of the face muscles. "I don't see how my name could have come up in such an investigation."

"It happens all the time that the names of innocent people come up. They still have to be checked out. I'll only take a few minutes of your time." I had finally found a good balance point for my chair and poised myself for a quick interview. "Tell me something about the True Christian Brotherhood."

"We are a dedicated and growing group of Christians supporting God's plan for a proper government, a government of moral and righteous citizens, that will one day be restored to its rightful place of authority in America."

I almost looked back to see if there were another poster behind me that he was reading from. If that's how he was going to handle it, there was no point in asking many more questions. I knew from the website and my own experience that the "government" he hoped for would be anti-Semitic, anti-Catholic, anti-liberal, homophobic, racist, anti-immigration...the whole sick spectrum of hostilities and phobias. So much for nostalgia.

I sat forward carefully. "Let me cut to the chase. Do the names Diane Austin or Tommy Cling mean anything to you?"

Zoller in turn leaned back and contemplated the ceiling with his fingertips together as if in deep thought or prayer—just enough to keep me from reading his eyes. Very good move, actually.

"I'm afraid not," he told the ceiling.

I said nothing and finally he lowered his eyes again to meet mine.

"You are not a man of God, are you, Mr. McCall?" His face now was absolutely still and his pupils were contracting as he spoke.

"My beliefs are my business."

"Not if they go against the will of God. Then they are the business of all righteous people and must be set right."

Time to go. I stood up. "Not by you, my friend."

Zoller remained seated, though leaning a little more forward all the time. I couldn't imagine that the guy was looking for a fight, but he was definitely getting into this. "You don't respect our beliefs, Mr. McCall? You should. Isn't that the way of the liberals and godless, to say that all beliefs are equally worthy?"

I took a step backward toward the door. All my previous experience and disgust with characters like him boiled in my gut. If I didn't get the hell out of this office in a hurry, I was going to say some things I didn't need to say.

Zoller's mouth twisted with disdain and his pupils were down to pinpoints now. His voice suddenly boomed in the small office, as if he meant to attack me with sheer volume. "You are still mired in fearful obedience to men rather than to our Lord!"

That was it. Too late. I stopped. "I don't have to respect beliefs that are expressions of ignorance and hatred."

"Then you're the one who is ignorant and prejudiced."

"You know, Zoller, there is at least one thing it's okay to be prejudiced against."

"Christianity?"

"No. Prejudice."

His eyes flicked toward the door that was ajar. "Jerry," was all he said. He was speaking quietly again. It didn't sound like a command, but I suspected that it was.

CHAPTER SEVENTEEN

The door opened to reveal a very large man who could only be described as a bruiser. Six three or four, stocky even at that, bald, probably in his early forties, gray dress shirt hanging loosely over matching gray slacks, almost a uniform and probably concealing a weapon—as my shirt would have been if I hadn't left the damned gun in the car. I didn't like the eagerness with which he gave me a beady-eyed once-over as he came into the room.

"This blasphemer does not belong here, Jerry. Please remove him."

What the hell was this? I was about to be strong-armed in the front office of a lousy little Christian cult? I couldn't help noticing that Gregory Zoller looked significantly more animated than he'd been up to now. He was actually bouncing slightly on his chair and his hands, scrawny fingers splayed wide, were moving in the air as if he were conducting some invisible, evil orchestra. Maybe he wasn't a tough guy himself but he obviously enjoyed the hell out of having tough guys at his beck and call.

The muscle named Jerry, meanwhile, stepped over and gripped my right bicep with a meaty left paw, taking up a stance that fully exposed the front of his body to me. Big and ugly and strong, maybe, but with no idea what he was doing. It was more of a pose than a stance.

Still, it is not a good idea to let someone who's big, ugly, strong, *and* hostile get a good grip on you. I tightened the muscle under his fingers, ready to step back and pull free if necessary. "That's not a good idea," I said softly, glancing down at where he had hold of me.

His eyes widened momentarily with the apparent challenge and then narrowed in suspicion as he registered the fact that I was standing quietly and calmly, giving no sign of wanting one of the pissing contests he was probably used to. I guess he couldn't quite process what was really going on, however, because his grip tightened as he suddenly cocked his right arm back with a fist that looked only slightly smaller than a basketball. He was going to win the macho contest whether there was one or not. I could see him anticipating that punching little old me into the next county would definitely do the trick.

I feel guilty when it's as easy as this. If you're relaxed and your attacker isn't, you have all the advantage. He doesn't know when you're going to move and the move, when it comes, is much more explosive. My new friend was still savoring the moment when I shot a quick straight punch across my body, planting my knuckles right into his clavicle.

He let go of my arm with a tremendous "Oof!" and grabbed at his chest as he staggered back against the far wall. He rested there, probably trying to recall how to inhale. He'd be okay in a few minutes, after I was long gone.

Zoller was half out of his chair, eyes wild now, breathing hard and obviously trying to collect himself as if he'd just taken the punch. He looked over at Jerry, then back at me. "You surprised him," he said accusingly.

True enough.

"He's lucky he only lost his wind," I responded. "Just trying to let him know there are consequences."

"Get out."

"No problem."

I made my exit as gracefully as I could while kicking myself for letting Zoller provoke me into spouting off, which in turn led to the violence. It did no one any good except possibly teaching Jerry a new technique. Sometimes the Zen equanimity just fails me.

My cell phone went off while I was settling into the Subaru and clipping the Smith and Wesson back on my belt. I pulled the phone out of my pocket. It was the Pen and Pastry's number.

"This is Clint."

"Clint, it's Veronica. Are you anywhere near by?"

"Near the café? Not even close. I'm in Salem."

"Damn. Should I call Johnny?"

Veronica Fortune not only owns The Pen and Pastry but is the best-selling author of a book about her former life as a prostitute. Nevertheless, at times she is a less than logical communicator. "I don't know who you should call," I said. "It depends on what the problem is."

"Colleen is here and there's a young man sitting with her. I think it's Hoke Moseley."

Holy shit, he's after my daughter. "Call Malone. Johnny and Hap if you can't reach her right away. Mike Whitehall if you have to. I'll be there as soon as I can."

I tossed the phone onto the passenger seat and peeled out from the curb, headed for the nearest freeway exit, hoping that the highway patrol was on vacation today.

CHAPTER EIGHTEEN

Devon Malone unfolded her home-delivered *Oregonian* newspaper as she sipped her third cup of coffee, wanting to kill a little more time before setting out on the day.

"BOMBING ON MLK," shouted the front page headline, over the lead about an explosion on Martin Luther King Boulevard late yesterday evening. A homeless man had been injured when a bus stop enclosure blew up, according to the story.

A bus stop enclosure was an odd choice for a target, she thought idly to herself. Unless that homeless guy had some really impressive enemies. Maybe it was kids practicing for the Fourth? No, this blast was much too big to be fireworks gone wrong. A couple of nearby buildings were badly damaged. Maybe somebody had a serious grudge against Tri-Met.

Malone finally, and somewhat reluctantly, left her apartment a little after ten and headed downtown to see if Carl Gunther was in his office. She almost hoped he wouldn't be, but she'd learned nothing of interest through Internet searches and this situation with Sherry had to be resolved.

There was a protocol among modern big-money crime syndicates. If Marty Salazar came to town, he probably would make a courtesy call on the local crime boss, namely Carl. Maybe he'd even mention where he was staying. That could be all the lead she needed to get this shit done.

The offices of Gunther Global Import/Export were on the twenty-second floor of one of the newer downtown Portland office buildings, just off Pioneer Square, a building that was all pink-tinted glass and glimmer and a very snazzy business address indeed.

Malone picked one of six elevators in the lobby. The car she entered was trimmed in leather, sported a light floral scent, and included a comfortable bench in case you needed rest on the way to your floor. The ride was smooth and quiet. The doors opened without a sound to reveal a spotlessly clean carpeted hallway that extended some distance in both directions.

There was a small metal directory on the wall in front of her, the arrow for Gunther Global pointing to the right, but she already knew the way.

Framed works of modern art were hung along the glowing off-white walls of the wide corridor. She made no more noise walking on the thick carpet than the elevator had made getting her here. A fresh, slightly more masculine scent came faintly to her nose.

She entered a simple but tastefully decorated reception area. The plush carpet from the hallway continued inside, as did the fresh-smelling air. What appeared to be reproductions of old maps were hung, one on each of the walls. There was one other door, which she knew led into Gunther's office. A medium-size leather couch sat against the wall to her left and directly before her was a highly polished wooden desk with an older woman behind it who—despite her standard office attire —looked like Central Casting's idea of everybody's favorite grandmother. White hair. A round, cheery face with pink cheeks. Half-glasses over which she gazed at Malone inquiringly. A little free-standing nameplate sitting toward the front edge of her desk said she was Mrs. Agnes Pinkerton.

Malone knew from previous experience that there was a very big handgun in one of the upper desk drawers and that the rotund little woman was a hell of a lot more dangerous than she looked. She wondered if the woman would ask to see the Glock she had holstered in the small of her back under her summer-weight jacket.

68

"Hello, dearie," said Mrs. Pinkerton. "Do you have an appointment?"

"No, I just stopped by hoping to talk to him for a minute. I've got a question."

"And the question is...?"

"For Carl."

For a long moment the elderly receptionist, no longer cheery, just looked at Malone. "It's going to be like that today, is it?"

"Look, Mrs. Pinkerton, I know it's your job to protect Carl from intruders and you're very good at your job, but I'm not here to arrest the man or even interrogate him. I need his help." A sudden inspiration, too good to pass up even though the words tasted sour in her mouth. "Actually my mother needs his help. I'll only take a couple of minutes, okay?"

And it worked. Mrs. Pinkerton perked up immediately. "Your mother, dearie? Well, why didn't you say so?" She picked up her handset and punched a button on the base unit. "Mr. Gunther. Devon Malone is here to see you. She says her mother is in trouble and you can help." She listened for a moment, nodding. "Yes, sir. Right away."

Oh, shit on a biscuit, Malone thought to herself as the older woman hung up her phone and gestured toward the inner door. *Now Gunther's going to want to know about my mother. Fuck that.*

Gritting her teeth, Malone nodded her thanks to Mrs. Pinkerton and walked into the lair of Portland's most powerful gangster.

CHAPTER NINETEEN

Carl Gunther, Sr., looked every bit the part: a big man, expensively dressed in a gray pinstripe suit with a dark maroon tie, sitting behind a huge, highly polished desk. He was early to mid-fifties, Malone estimated, with a full head of dark hair and craggy features. He didn't get up when she entered, as of course he wouldn't, but she knew he was over six feet tall with thick legs to go along with the broad chest that loomed above the desk top.

He looked like a man who was used to getting his way, a man capable of hurting people who didn't cooperate. And Malone knew that to be true.

At the moment he was sporting a wide smile and gesturing to one of the plush visitor chairs in front of the desk. "Always good to see Portland's toughest chick," he rumbled as she settled in the indicated seat. "What can I do for you—or your mother?" The smile was about to split his face in half, Malone thought. He was loving this.

She took a moment to calm herself, absorbing the high-class atmosphere of Gunther's office. Leather couch along one wall, Victorian-looking coffee table, two matching leather arm chairs to complete the sitting area, framed reproductions—she assumed they were reproductions—of Monet and Chagall on the walls, all capped off by the floor-to-ceiling windows behind the desk looking out over the city.

"I just have one question, Carl, and then I'll leave you to your criminal enterprises."

His eyes were sparkling with amusement. "All my businesses are completely legit. Now, about your mother...."

"And here's the question. Are you aware of a guy named Marty Salazar being in Portland?"

Gunther's eyebrows took a little hop before he got them under control. "Hmm," he said thoughtfully. "Marty Salazar. I'm not sure that name rings a bell. What would your mother...?"

"Have you caught on yet to the fact that I'm not going to say anything about my mother? Marty Salazar. He's a crime boss—just like you—from Fresno, California, and I have reason to believe he's in town. Have you heard from him? Simple as that. If you can't answer the fucking question, I'm out of here."

Gunther sat back and laughed out loud. "God, I love your style. I don't know what you see in that shrimpy old guy you partner with." He leaned forward with an inviting grin. "You'd do a lot better working with me."

"Not a chance," Malone announced as she started to get up.

Gunther held up a big, meaty hand to stay her departure. "Hang on, hang on. Yes, Marty Salazar is in town. He stopped by for a few minutes yesterday to let me know he is here on personal business. Which I guess must involve you or your mother somehow."

"Shit," responded Malone. "Did he happen to mention where he was staying?"

"The Suites."

The Suites was a luxury hotel right here on the Square. Very convenient. This time she did stand up. "Thanks," she said. "That's all I needed."

The big hand went up again. "Watch your back," Gunther told her. "I never heard of Salazar before he showed up here so I did some checking. He's got a rep for being one very nasty son of a bitch."

Malone grunted. "Unlike you."

Gunther shrugged. "Everybody loves me. You know that. I guarantee that not everybody in Fresno loves Marty Salazar."

"I'll keep it in mind."

"Keep me in mind, too," Gunther said to Malone's back as she strode to the office door, jerked it open, and swept into the reception area. Ignoring his last comment, she closed his door behind her and nodded to Mrs. Pinkerton on her way out.

In the elevator she found herself wondering briefly how McCall was doing in Salem. Would he learn anything useful from the so-called True Christian Brotherhood? Probably not. And it was lucky for the true Christians that she hadn't gone along.

She stepped out of the elevator car into the lobby area already focused on what she hoped would be a confrontation with Marty Salazar, but then remembered that she'd felt her phone vibrating—several times—while she was talking to Carl Gunther. She stopped to check for messages.

There were three, all from Veronica Fortune and increasingly urgent. Hoke Moseley was at the café. He might be threatening Clint's daughter, Colleen. *Crap.* Salazar would have to wait. So much for convenience.

Devon Malone stuffed the phone back in her pocket and ran for her Jeep.

CHAPTER TWENTY

I didn't see any open parking spaces on Hawthorne so I stashed the Outback in my own driveway and trotted around the corner to Veronica's café.

My little house is just a half-block above Hawthorne, and the Pen and Pastry is one of the most popular gathering spots in the Hawthorne District. It's basically a coffee shop that specializes in pastry dishes for both breakfast and lunch. It seats probably eighty patrons when packed and it was getting there as the lunch hour approached and I burst in the front door.

I scanned the room. Owner Veronica Fortune was standing in the doorway to the kitchen area. She was wearing a bright green caftan with her long red hair pulled back into a kind of chignon, evoking the fabulous fifties as usual. All I had to do was follow her gaze to Devon Malone in the far corner.

It took only a few moments to work my way through the crowded space to where my partner was standing, arms akimbo, over a table at which my daughter and Hoke Moseley were seated. They were both staring up at her, a little wide-eyed, Moseley looking bemused and Colleen definitely pissed.

They made an interesting-looking couple, a thought that turned my stomach. Colleen was wearing her usual granny glasses with well worn sweatshirt and faded jeans. She had, thank goodness, finally given up on her punk cut and regrown her shiny blonde hair to a decent length. She managed somehow to look significantly older than Moseley. It could have been a young guy and his tutor sitting there. But it wasn't. It was my daughter and a man who might be a killer.

"What's going on?" I asked as I pulled up beside Malone.

"Don't know yet," she said out of the side of her mouth toward me. "I just got here. I was about to ask that question myself."

So I asked my own question: "What the hell are you doing here with my daughter, Moseley?"

He flinched a little and opened his mouth, but Colleen jumped in—and practically up—before he could speak. "I invited him," she said.

I am not often speechless, but for about ten seconds I had nothing. *She invited Hoke Moseley to meet her at The Pen and Pastry? What the fuck? How did she even know who he was?*

"Do.... Do you know who this is?" I finally asked.

She shrugged as if it were no big deal. "He's the younger brother of that guy you killed in the alley when you were first starting out with Johnny and Hap. He just got out of prison and everybody thinks he wants to kill you."

What the hell was I supposed to say to that? "Okay. Yes. That sums it up pretty well, however you found out. And...you invited him here?"

"I found out from Hap," she said. "I ran into him and Wilma downtown and he started telling me about this Moseley guy and the possible threat to you. So I thought I'd check it out."

"You thought you'd check it out." I repeated, almost mechanically. Malone was making some kind of muted sound beside me, possibly a suppressed chuckle, possibly an expression of disbelief to match my own.

It was at this moment that my brain apparently caught up with what I was hearing and anger nearly blinded me. I leaned down into Colleen's face. "What the fuck were you thinking?" I asked and then, without pause, turned my head to Moseley. "If you aren't out of here by the time I count three," I said to him, "you'll be leaving for the emergency room. One...."

76

The poor bastard still hadn't said a word since I arrived. He jumped up and looked down at Colleen. "Uh, thanks for the coffee," he said, and that was it. He headed for the front door.

Now Malone was definitely chuckling, but I found none of it even slightly amusing.

I glared at my daughter. "Colleen?"

She crossed her arms, sat up straight, and glared right back. "It isn't easy being your daughter, you know, with people trying to kill you all the time. I wanted to talk to him, to maybe talk him out of it if it was true. Hap said he was about my age and that he was staying with his mother. He didn't sound all *that* dangerous, so I called up and invited him to meet me here." She gestured around the café. "It's a public place. Veronica was keeping watch. I wasn't in any danger." She paused. "And I'm tired of people trying to kill you."

"You're...."

Malone broke in at that point. "What did you think of him?" she asked Colleen. "Do you think he wants to kill your dad?"

"No," my daughter answered without hesitation.

"Did he say that?" asked Malone.

"No. We didn't get that far before Dad barged in and chased him off. But he didn't seem like the killer type. He seemed confused, maybe even scared. I don't know...."

I jumped back in. "That's exactly right. You don't know. But here's what I know: You are not *ever* going to pull a stunt like this again. I can deal with my own death threats, thank you, and I don't need my daughter trying to fix them for me. Do you understand?"

She made a big show of reluctance but nodded. "Okay, okay. It's still not easy, I'll stay out of it. It was just this once. He's staying with his mother, for Christ's sake."

I know I gritted my teeth. "Colleen?"

77

She threw up her hands. "I agreed! I agreed already! You have my word, okay?"

I held her gaze for another moment and then nodded. I didn't know what else to say.

Malone gently backfisted my arm. "Now that that's settled, I have to go see a gangster about my mother. You want to come along?"

CHAPTER TWENTY-ONE

The Suites is located in a totally remodeled landmark department store building next to Pioneer Square in downtown Portland. Lots of color, open spaces, art, and elegance. Not where you'd expect to find a gangster from Fresno, not unless he was a very successful gangster.

The Square is an easy walk from the office and it was a beautiful sunny day anyway, so we left our vehicles in the usual spots and headed west on Stark Street. The day had turned hot and many of the pedestrians were in shorts. I didn't see any suits and ties, which was fairly typical for our business district.

Malone hadn't said much since we left the café and I was still stewing in silence myself. We'd gone about half-a-block when finally she said, "Your daughter is really something."

"Yeah, an idiot," I grumbled back.

"Hey, I resent that."

I frowned over at her. "*You* resent it. Why?"

"Because it's the sort of thing I might have done at her age. If I'd had a parent who was threatened instead of threatening, anyway. It's gotta feel good that your kid loves you that much."

I took a long moment as we continued walking. I wanted to be fair in my response. "The love feels good. Inviting a potential killer to have coffee, not so much."

"I think she's right."

"To have invited a killer to coffee?"

"That he's not a killer. I don't know what's going on with Hoke Moseley, but I don't think he's out to get you."

"Maybe he's not, but something *is* going on and whatever it is could still be dangerous."

"We'll figure it out."

We rounded the corner onto 6th about then and said nothing more until we entered the lobby of the hotel. It looked and smelled and sounded like money.

I let Devon have the lead as we approached the desk. It was her mother and her gangster. The nearest desk clerk, a young guy with immaculately combed hair and glistening white teeth, looked up and beamed at her.

"How can I help you today?" he inquired brightly.

Malone smiled back, going into her rarely seen ultra-feminine routine. "You have a gentlemen by the name of Anthony Salazar staying here. Could you please call and tell him that Sherry Malone is here in the lobby? He's expecting me."

Oh ho, I thought to myself. *That might work.*

And it did. The clerk returned to the desk and said, "He'll be right down."

"Thank you so much. I'll wait for him outside. Just let him know that's where I am."

The youngster seemed to find the request a little strange, but agreed.

CHAPTER TWENTY-TWO

We stood on the sunny sidewalk watching the glass entrance doors from a distance of about twenty feet. It was only about three minutes before a large, swarthy gentleman exited, scanning the sidewalk where we were standing but not really focusing on us because, of course, he was looking for Sherry. He was casually but well-dressed and had a lot of silver hair. Almost a pompadour. If they were casting for a *Sopranos* remake, this guy would definitely be in the running.

"I'm guessing that that's Marty Salazar," I said to Malone.

"Yeah," she said as the man registered that we were standing there staring at him. He headed our way, looking very angry indeed.

Malone immediately stepped up to meet him and got in his face—as best she could, given that she was a full eight inches shorter. It was a face that only a mother could love, by the way, what I believe they used to call a "mug." Leathery skin, nose broken probably multiple times, several scars almost lost in the proliferation of wrinkles.

"Marty Salazar?" Malone inquired.

"Who the fuck are you?" he responded, looking up and down the sidewalk. "Where the fuck is Sherry?"

"She's somewhere safe right now. We're here to talk about keeping her that way."

Salazar finally focused over Malone's shoulder on me. "We?"

"This is Clint McCall and I'm Devon Malone. We're private investigators."

It took him a moment. "Malone? You related to Sherry?"

"In a manner of speaking. Why don't we find someplace to sit down and have a little chat?" She indicated the food court across the street in Pioneer Square.

He looked over at the array of small tables and food carts, then looked at me rather than Malone. "Is she fucking kidding? I'm supposed to sit at one of those piss-ant little tables in the sun and...what? Have a fucking hot dog with you two? Maybe some fucking Fritos?"

Oh crap. Another one who wanted to diss my partner and deal with the male instead. That never, ever ended well.

She stepped in even closer, literally toe to toe with the big Hispanic, and poked him in the chest with her finger. "If you don't want to talk about Sherry Malone, we could talk about the notebooks that she stole from you." Another poke. "California law enforcement would probably love to talk about those if you don't want to." And another. I was edging my hand back to my Smith and Wesson in case this went *really* bad. "What do you say we go have that chat, Marty? You don't have to eat a single fucking Frito."

He pulled his eyes away from me and glared down at her, turning a good deal darker than he'd been when we first saw him. They held their positions for what seemed like a full minute but was probably ten seconds, and then, without a word, he turned and headed across the street toward the food court. And I mean right through what had been moving traffic, all of which came to a screeching halt as he stomped to the other sidewalk without a glance to either side. Horn blasts and curses also failed to faze him. Tough guy established. Even if he was doing what a woman told him to.

Without discussing it, and just to be ornery, Malone and I strolled over to the proper crosswalk and crossed with the light.

By that time Salazar was standing among the small round tables that populated the fast food area of the square, next to one of the few that was still available. It was the noon hour on a summer workday in downtown Portland and the Square was crowded. His arms were crossed and his expression was grim as we approached.

Malone gestured at the empty table, which conveniently enough had three chairs. "Have a seat, Marty," she said.

I was happy with her continuing to take the lead, not least because it really pissed off Salazar.

He jerked one of the chairs back from the table and sat down. We joined him and as we sat down I noticed that he did a quick scan of our surroundings, so I did the same. There were four large Hispanic males in sight, coincidentally enough, all casually dressed but none looking like they really belonged among the Pioneer Square lunch crowd. There was one at each point of the compass around us.

"You called for back-up before you came down," I said.

"You bet your ass," he agreed. "And it will be your ass, right here in the middle of the fucking square, if you make any kind of move."

Malone took a moment to scope out the same four that I'd recognized, then looked at Salazar. "We aren't planning any moves, Marty, not here and now anyway. We're here to get you off Sherry Malone. What will that take?"

He looked at me and I gave him nothing. Finally he had to deal with Malone. Which he did with a sneer. "You could kill her for me and retrieve my books. That would do it."

She didn't even blink. "Not gonna happen. How about a compromise? You get the notebooks and Sherry doesn't get killed? How about that?"

He held the sneer. "Why the fuck should I *compromise* with you? I'm here already. I got people here. We can find the bitch and get the books ourselves. She's given me a lot of trouble, she stole from me, and I like to give trouble back."

"You might find Sherry but you're not going to get your money back and you won't find the books, Marty, and that's more important to your long-range prospects. Sherry might not have known what to do with them, but we do. Like I already said, I'm sure the California AG's office would love to see all that information about your business. And they will, if you harm Sherry."

His mouth firmed up into a grim line. He said nothing for almost a full minute. Finally: "I'll think about it."

Malone reached in her pocket and pulled out one of our cards. "Here," she said. "Give us a call when you've decided. And, no, your notebooks are not in our office."

He took the card between two fingertips as it were a dead bug and stood up. "You'll be hearing from me," he said, and headed for the corner, apparently intending to actually use the crosswalk this time. The four goons formed up behind him as he went. A regular testosterone parade.

"I'm not sure he meant that he'd call," I said to my partner.

CHAPTER TWENTY-THREE

Salazar parted company with his crew at the entrance to The Suites and they headed south on 6th, probably staying at a nearby motel.

We were crossing the street ourselves when an early '70s model pink Cadillac pulled into a vacant space just past the corner ahead of us. Only one person in Portland drives such a car—Reuben Keys, long-time local drug dealer, fence, and pimp. He was coming around the front of the vehicle to intercept us as we approached, drawing the stares of everyone on the street. Reuben's wheels are not his only extravagance. He's quite possibly the last living pimp to dress like the old '70s stereotype, often—as now—in solid, brilliant turquoise head to toe. This colorful persona contrasts sharply with the coal black of his skin, the pepper-gray hair, and a face scarred by cuts, burns, and God knows what other misadventures. All the bright, cheery accouterments end up making him look even more scary and, believe me, he knows it.

We know each other because of Veronica Fortune. Keys was featured prominently in her bestseller as her last pimp, the one who got her off drugs and gave her a chance to escape the life. Yes, that's right: *off* drugs. It's Reuben Keys' most prominent eccentricity, that he's a major drug dealer who insists his whores have to be clean of drugs.

We get along. He's backed us up at times, but I can't say I like him a lot and Malone certainly doesn't; he's ruined a thousand lives for every one he's helped. He claims to like me and even my partner, but knows one of us could be the one to take him down someday. Call it an armed truce.

"McCall. Malone." His voice is rough, almost guttural. Some of those scars are on his throat.

"Reuben," I responded. "What can we do for you?" He shook hands with me but didn't even attempt it with my partner. Despite the gesture of civility, passersby were giving us a wide berth.

"It's what I can do for you, my man. I hear you lookin' for some crazy people."

"Really. Where'd you hear that?"

"I got it from Eleanor. She say you might be interested in those Jesus fuckers with the office in Salem and the country place out southwest of there."

Much to my accountant's dismay, Reuben had a serious and ongoing crush that led to him occasionally dropping by her apartment to see how she was doing. She would say anything to get rid of him. Apparently this time, luckily enough, she'd picked the website she'd just found as the distraction.

I exchanged a glance with Malone. "Ah. We didn't know about a country place."

"I figured that. Combination RV camping and war games, from what I hear."

"Interesting. The True Christian Brotherhood."

"Yeah, right. And I bet not a damned one is a brother."

"Or a Christian, either," offered Malone.

Reuben grinned at her. "You got that."

I watched a Portland patrol car slowing down to give us a close look, then moving on. There were no pedestrians anywhere near us now.

"What else do you know about them?" I asked.

"I know they're mean fuckers. One of my girls ended up in the hospital after seeing one of them pricks. Did her and then got all righteous about her being a whore. I guess he was a conflicted motherfucker."

"You're sure he was part of this group?"

"Yeah, he told her all about it while he was beating the shit out of her. He's like second in line to make Heaven after they take out all the bad folks. Name was Tommy something."

"Jesus! Cling?"

Reuben took a half-step back and looked at me hard. "What? You not goin' weird on me now, are you?"

"Sorry. I mean, was his last name Cling? Tommy Cling?"

"I got no idea. He didn't leave her no phone number, neither."

The vague description that Reuben had of "Tommy," however, matched the vague description we had from Diane Austin of her child's possible abductor, he of the motel clerk's remarkable memory: short, built like a tank, black hair, ugly, nasty disposition. Not conclusive, but intriguing.

Reuben was able to give us fairly detailed directions to the True Christian Brotherhood's rural location; apparently they had bought an old abandoned farm between Salem and a little unincorporated community called Pratum. His information was that about a dozen people, mostly men but a few women and children, lived in the camp and a dozen more showed up on weekends. He hadn't heard one way or the other about weapons, except for the rumors concerning war games. Maybe they shot paint balls at each other. Thinking back on those posters in Zoller's office, not to mention my new friend Jerry, I doubted it.

CHAPTER TWENTY-FOUR

I awoke the next morning with a warm female body spooned against my back and a warm feline body snoozing beside my head. There is, in my opinion, no better way to start the day.

After our encounter with Reuben yesterday, we'd stopped by the office thinking that we'd go check out the True Christian Brotherhood's rural camp if nothing else was cooking. But something else was.

We had a message from a Mr. Albert Zualaga who said he owned the Corner Mart chain of seven stores in the Portland area and wanted to meet with us right away.

One of the things about living off a private investigation agency is that, even if your mother is in trouble and you have a lead in another case, you still have to put food on your table and clothes on your back. So we stayed put and I called Mr. Zualaga to say we were available to meet. He said he'd come to the office, probably wanting to see what it looked like.

He was an abrupt little man with thinning hair and sharp features, mid-sixties, over-dressed for the season and the city in full suit and tie. He told us that all seven of his stores had been robbed at least once in the past six months and he wanted someone to look them over and make recommendations about added security measures. After talking for an hour or so, he concluded that we would do.

I told him we couldn't start until next week because of our current caseload, which he grudgingly said was fine. We signed a contract, he gave us an advance payment, and we were left a little more flush but without enough time to go looking for the purported rural encampment.

Our intention was to get going right after breakfast this morning. Meanwhile, I was very much enjoying the warmth fore and aft. Likewise the ambient sound. Maxine was purring and Malone was humming softly, which was normal for Maxine but something of a surprise from Devon.

"Are you awake?" I inquired without turning over.

The humming paused. "No."

"Then you're humming in your sleep. Or maybe it's your version of purring. I've got Maxine over here doing her version."

At which point Maxine's sister, Stella, bounced onto the bed, our voices having alerted her that we were awake and breakfast was in the offing. So now we were four. I turned over to look at the other human. "Are you ready to get up?"

"No."

"Then would you be interested...."

"No."

I sighed and rolled onto my back to stare at the ceiling. "Oh God. We're like an old married couple already."

That sat Malone up abruptly. Stella was startled and jumped off the bed with a yip. Maxine just kept purring—or maybe it was snoring. "You didn't seem to feel that way last night," my partner said as she punched me in the arm.

I then used the arm to pull her down and kiss her. "Remind me again what that was like," I whispered, but she pushed herself up on one elbow and looked down at me.

"Old married couple, my ass," she said. "Up. We've got shit to do."

And so we all got up.

Half-an-hour later Malone and I were at the kitchen table eating bacon and scrambled eggs while Maxine and Stella—on the floor nearby—plowed through salmon and beef in gravy.

My partner popped one last sliver of bacon into her mouth, drained her coffee cup, and pushed back from the table. "We haven't heard anything from Salazar," she said before she stood up.

I was already done, so I stood as well. "No, we haven't. You think he's going to make a move?"

She shook her head. "I don't know, but we'd better stop by Sherry's when we get back from this summer camp or whatever the fuck it is. I told Salazar we have his notebooks. So we should have his notebooks."

"Sounds like a plan," I agreed. "You ready to go?"

"Sure."

We strapped on our weapons, mine covered by my shirttail left out and hers by a light linen jacket, and headed outside. My Subaru was parked behind her Jeep in the driveway, so that's the one we would take.

I locked my front door and hadn't even taken the first step off the little front landing when Malone reached back from the walkway to stop me. "What?" I asked, adrenaline kicking in. She pointed across the street.

Hoke Moseley was standing there staring at us. His shirttail was out also.

CHAPTER TWENTY-FIVE

Without even thinking, I reached for my gun and he whipped both hands up high in the air.

"You're dead set on capping me like you did my brother, ain't you, McCall?" he yelled across the street.

I left the gun in its holster. "Just being careful, Hoke. You know how it is. What are you doing over there?"

"Watching."

"Why?"

He shrugged a little, hands still held high. "Can't seem to stay away, I guess...but you should be glad."

"Oh? Why's that?"

"Can I put my hands down?"

"Why don't you come on over here, slowly, and let Malone pat you down. Then you can lower your hands."

"Sure. That sounds like fun."

As instructed, he crossed the street at a very sedate pace. Fortunately there was no traffic. Even more fortunately, it was still early enough that probably few if any neighbors were witnessing this little drama. Malone met him halfway up my walkway and quickly patted him down while he smirked at me.

She stepped back and nodded to me. "He's clean," she said.

I left the landing to join her facing him. "Okay, hands down. Now, why are we supposed to be glad you were watching the house?"

He glanced over at the Outback. "Because I saw a guy plant something under your car there. A tracker, maybe, or a bomb? He was under there for a while."

I glanced over myself and then focused on Moseley, a chill playing across my shoulders. "You're kidding."

"Nope." His smirk was, if anything, even bigger.

Malone poked me. "Give me your key. I'll go back in and get a flashlight. And a hand mirror." I handed her the key without taking my eyes from our unwelcome visitor.

"When was this?" I asked him. "What did the guy look like?" I didn't want to believe what Moseley was telling us but couldn't figure his angle. Why would he lie about it? On the other hand, why would he tell the truth about it?

"Half-an-hour ago maybe, pretty soon after I got here myself. He didn't see me because I was hiding then, behind those bushes over there. I didn't get a good look; there wasn't a lot of light yet. A short, beefy guy with dark hair. Kind of funny looking, about as wide as he was tall. Nobody I know."

"Shit."

"Sounds like you might, though."

"Could be." It matched the description that the Alaska detective had gotten from the old desk clerk who claimed to remember Tommy Cling. And the description Reuben had given us of the assaultive True Christian Brotherhood member.

Meanwhile, Malone had reappeared with flashlight and mirror in hand.

"I appreciate the information, anyway, if it's true," I said to Moseley, "and I'd appreciate it even more if you left now in case it isn't."

He actually chuckled a little. "You mean you don't want me to hold the light while you stick your head under the vehicle?"

"Maybe next time," I said. "Malone can do it this time. See you around, Hoke."

He gave me a last long look. "See you around."

We watched him out of sight down the street, then walked over to the Subaru. Malone handed me the mirror and we both crouched at the side of the vehicle. She lit up the under-carriage while I slowed panned the mirror.

And there it was.

It was an explosive, all right, but no need for the bomb squad. No tangle of multi-colored wires, no flashing red numbers. Just a small battery, a dab of plastique, and a simple circuit set up to trigger when the driver's side door was opened. All neatly held in place with electrical tape.

Malone leaned over and took a look in the mirror. "What the fuck is that?" she asked no one in particular. "That wouldn't do much more damage than a cherry bomb." She glanced around as if looking for the bomber to complain about the quality of his work. "It would have scared the shit out of you, but that's about it."

"Me? What about you?"

"I don't scare that easy."

"Right. It would have been a very big bang, at least. You'd have shit in your panties."

"Says you. Anyway, that's obviously the point, to scare us. This sure wasn't going to kill us."

We took another couple of minutes to look it over, made sure we weren't missing anything, and then I pulled one of the wires loose from the battery. No problem. I removed the tape and gathered up the pieces to add to our increasingly bizarre collection of evidence.

"Did you hear Moseley's description of the guy who planted this?" I asked as we stood up.

"Yeah. It could be coincidence that it sounded like the descriptions we have of Tommy Cling. There are a lot of short, chunky guys with dark hair on the planet."

"It could even be someone working for Marty Salazar."

She grunted. "Maybe, but you know what we think of coincidence. I'm betting on Cling—and, if we can find the guy, no question we need to have a very serious talk."

"So," I said, "let's go looking."

CHAPTER TWENTY-SIX

We didn't talk much during the drive to Salem. Some idle speculation that came to nothing. Malone related a news story about a bus stop shelter being blown up and we decided it probably wasn't related to the "bomb" under my car.

I swung by the True Christian Brotherhood storefront but it appeared to be closed. So we went looking for the encampment Reuben had described.

Just beyond the Salem Hills area we hit mostly open farmland. There were patches of the remaining Northwest timberland scattered among the green peas, onions, snap beans, and sweet corn. According to Keys, the True Christian Brotherhood camp was located in one of those wooded areas. I found an unmarked gravel road about where Keys had said it should be, going off to our right up into some trees, and I made the turn.

The road twisted in among the heavy foliage, quickly leaving civilization behind. Within a few hundred feet we could have been in the middle of a wilderness area—an impression that changed again in less than a half-mile when we encountered a heavy steel gate blocking the road which then curved out of sight twenty yards or so beyond the obstacle.

There was a man, about the same size and demeanor as my buddy Jerry from the Salem storefront but with the sallow skin tone of Zoller himself, leaning casually against the gate. He was slipping a cell phone into his right pants pocket as we pulled up. No doubt he'd heard us coming and alerted the camp. He was dressed in hunting clothes, all brand new, and carried a shiny new hunting rifle in the crook of his left arm like in the magazines. He straightened and ambled toward our vehicle, grinning real big, just a guy who was out hunting and happened to be standing there taking a break when we arrived. The only way he could have been more obvious was if he'd been carrying a sign that said, I AM NOT WHAT I SEEM.

Before he got to the car I eased my Smith and Wesson out of the holster and tucked it under my right leg with my hand resting lightly on the butt. I saw in my peripheral vision that Malone was making a similar move.

"You must be lost, friends," the man said when he got to the driver's side window. He leaned over a bit to give Malone the eye. "This road doesn't go anywhere."

"Really? What's the gate for then?" I asked politely.

He looked back as if seeing it for the first time. "Hell, I don't know. I guess it's to keep cars out of the hunting preserve."

"That's what you're doing, hunting in the hunting preserve?"

He hefted the rifle. "You bet."

"Bagged anything?"

"Nah. Not yet."

"Well, I wouldn't hold my breath," I said. "Not much wildlife in a small uncleared patch of farmland like this. You might get a woodchuck if you're lucky. More likely, you'd knock off a member of the True Christian Brotherhood. Seen any of those around here?"

He stepped back, dropping the grin from his face and the rifle from the crook of his arm into both hands. He didn't raise it, though, so we left our own weapons in place.

"Who are you?" he demanded.

"Just a couple of curious folks," I answered. "We heard the Brotherhood had a camp out here. Thought we'd pay a visit."

He went squinty-eyed, probably trying to process the idea that somebody just happened to hear about the location of their secret camp.

"No visitors allowed here, brother...and sister. You have to apply at our office in Salem." He let go of the rifle with one hand and reached into his pants pocket, the one without a cell phone. He handed me a business card with the storefront address.

"We were just there," I said. "I don't want to apply. I need to talk to Gregory Zoller. Is he here?"

His face went expressionless. "Father is always here."

A chill plunged down my spine, in sharp contrast to the heat and humidity seemingly trapped by the trees that surrounded us. The capital "F" in what he'd said was clear, as was the mindless rote. I'd heard that ritualistic tone before and too often it meant followers who would do anything. Kill themselves. Kill you. Anything. I could feel Malone tensing up. She'd heard it, too.

My grip on the Smith and Wesson tightened, my finger curling snugly around the trigger. I eased the gun out from its cozy spot under my leg.

"If he's here, we'd like to talk to him," I said, maintaining a nice, neutral timbre. No tension in the voice. It was all in my right forefinger.

He opened his mouth to reply but just then the sound of an approaching vehicle drew his attention—and ours—to the gravel road beyond the gate. A few seconds later an old Jeep appeared around the curve, moving fast and kicking up gravel as it came toward us. Another Jerry clone was driving, accompanied by an even bigger and uglier fellow in the front passenger seat. Neither one matched Tommy Cling's description. Between them I could see Gregory Zoller hunched in the back seat, eyes looking as big as the headlights on his vehicle.

The Jeep slid to a halt just short of the gate. The two in front bailed out, bringing with them a couple of small but nasty-looking automatic weapons, old Ingram "room brooms" or something very similar. Right then I was more interested in the orientation of the weapons than their manufacturer. They were pointing at us through the front windshield, as was the hunting rifle through the side window. So much for our own little popguns.

"Shit on a fucking stick," muttered Malone. We slowly raised our hands.

CHAPTER TWENTY-SEVEN

"We just want to talk!" I called through the open driver's side window. It was becoming more difficult to maintain an unstressed voice as my heart threatened to pound through the rib cage.

On one hand, I knew it would not be very smart for these guys to shoot two cops, even private cops, right at the entrance to their camp in the middle of the Willamette Valley. On the other hand, I'd already concluded that they weren't very smart.

Zoller climbed out of the Jeep and trotted, almost pranced, up behind his two henchmen, careful to keep one of them between us and him the whole way. He was wearing suit pants and a wrinkled white shirt but without the coat and tie; his two companions were in khakis and tee shirts. He said something I couldn't hear to the guy who'd been driving, but it must have been an okay.

"Open your door slowly and come out here, then," called the guy. "Watch them, Al," he said to the man with the hunting rifle.

We did as we were told, both of us leaving our weapons behind us on the seats. I, for one, was grateful that none of the four men was in a position to see that we'd had our guns out already.

Once we were both standing in plain sight next to the hood of the Outback, our hands down now but all their guns still up, Zoller showed himself between his two men at the gate. This was a very different Gregory Zoller from the phlegmatic fellow I had first seen in Salem. He'd gotten a little jumpy then, when Jerry showed up, but now his eyes were bulging and breath shallow; he was unable to stand still, complexion even more ashen than usual. Apparently the guy could get very stimulated indeed by potential violence. I didn't know what the hell his men would do if the son of a bitch fell down in a fit right then. And I wondered again if this could possibly be the man Diane Austin asked us to find.

"You ignore the Lord's word at your peril!" Zoller cried, his voice near cracking. "He can exact a terrible price if you defy Him!"

This was not the opening gambit I'd hoped for.

"We didn't come here to defy anyone," I said as distinctly as I could. "We just want to talk to you for a minute. Tell your men to lower their weapons. You can see that we're unarmed." Just don't look in the damned car windows.

Actually I wasn't sure he could see us at all in his present state. Those eyes might have been seeing devils or even Satan himself standing in front of our vehicle. I found myself wishing that Devon hadn't come along, which I knew would really piss her off if I even hinted at it. So I just stood, looking at Zoller, hoping she was planning to hold still as well. We didn't have many other options at the moment.

The next thirty seconds lasted at least five minutes as all the rest of us stood immobile while Zoller twitched to a decision.

Finally he seemed to calm a bit. "It will be good for us to talk," he said, and gestured at his men to lower the guns— which in turn went a long way toward calming yours truly. He remained, however, a couple of feet behind his two henchmen. "I must make you understand," he went on, "that you cannot frustrate God's will."

Now I found myself presented with a dilemma. We had planned to stir the pot a little, ask a few provocative questions in the hope that Zoller would be disconcerted enough to reveal himself. It's a good tactic. Crooks are usually most vulnerable when they're actively trying to avoid revealing their crime; they almost always overdo it. In this instance, however, he was already 'way beyond disconcerted. Best to go with the flow.

102

"I'm sorry if I've offended your beliefs in some way," I said. "I wasn't aware that I was frustrating God's will."

He actually smiled—or, more accurately, the corners of his mouth lifted. There was no joviality in it. "You cannot," he said, "but the attempt will still bring the Lord's wrath down upon you."

Malone apparently was tired of standing silently by. "We're just doing our job, Mr. Zoller," she said as I winced slightly. "We were hired by a woman named Diane Austin to find her daughter Noelle. Ever heard of Miss Austin's old boyfriend, Paul Gregory? We're told he might have the kid."

Okay, maybe just a *little* stirring wouldn't hurt. Or maybe it would get us killed. Looked like a toss-up to me.

A slight twist of Zoller's mouth produced a smirk—not the reaction I had expected.

"Just doing your job. Yes indeed. I don't know who you are, woman, but you forget that the Lord God Almighty is omniscient. He knows all. He knows who those people are, for instance, even if I do not." Eyes beginning to bulge again. "He knows why you're here. He knows what will happen to you and yours if you continue to stick your nose into His business." He screwed his face into a frown as his body trembled with intensity. He focused back on me. "I'm doing my best to save your soul, Mr. McCall. You are going to have to save your own life by leaving here and never interfering with our mission again. Hear me!"

I quickly reached over and grasped my partner's arm. I just knew she was about to ask why only my soul was in play here. We did not need the grief at this moment. She glared at me but remained silent.

Long since convinced that Zoller was not in a mood to make sense, I assured him that we had heard clearly and moved warily to my driver's side door while Malone did the same on the other side of the vehicle. We eased ourselves inside, careful to sit on the guns lest they still cause a problem.

Zoller and his men just stood there looking at us as I started backing away.

I had to reverse down the gravel road nearly a quarter mile before I found a place to turn around—a minor inconvenience compared to being shredded by a couple of submachine guns.

Once I had the car pointed in the right direction, Malone finally spoke up again.

"What the fuck about my soul?" she demanded plaintively.

I laughed. She punched me.

CHAPTER TWENTY-EIGHT

We were back in the office by mid-afternoon, having tossed ideas about Gregory Zoller back and forth almost the whole drive from Salem to Portland. We reached no conclusions. It seemed highly likely that Zoller would turn out to be Paul Gregory but, if he was, he was the coldest customer either one of us had ever seen. He reacted to Malone's provocation, which should have been totally unexpected, with barely a twitch. And we hadn't seen anyone who could be Tommy Cling. So we had nothing, still.

Nevertheless, once we settled at the desk I felt obliged to check in with Diane Austin. The call did not go smoothly at first.

I'd barely gotten two sentences out when she interrupted with an excited stage whisper to someone on her end of the line, probably her well-to-do boyfriend: "He's found her! My God, he's found her!"

I raised my own voice to get her attention back. "Miss Austin! Diane! Calm down. We have *not* found your daughter yet."

She came back to me. "But...but you said you'd found Tommy Cling and he has...."

"I said we believe there's a man here in the Portland area who *may* be Tommy Cling. We haven't found him yet. We certainly don't know if he has Noelle or if he can even tell us where she is."

"He has to!" she wailed.

"There's no way to be sure, yet. I don't want you to be disappointed if...."

"I'm coming back to Portland. Right now." I could tell she was turning from the phone toward her companion even as she spoke. "You'll pay for the ticket, won't you, Poopsie?" came the muffled question. There was an answering rumble in the background—and another rumble from across the partners desk, where Malone was listening to the speakerphone. I glanced over and she rolled her eyes at me.

I had no doubt that Poopsie would pay, but we did not need any more complications right now—and Diane Austin would be a major one.

"Diane, this would not be a good time for you to be here. Let us find this guy and talk to him first. I promise, if there's any lead concerning your daughter, anything at all, we'll let you know right away."

"But I want to help!"

"Okay, there is something you can do for us."

"What?"

"You're on speaker and my partner is listening in. For both our benefits, go over the description of Tommy Cling again. Is there anything you were told about him that you might not have remembered when you were here? The smallest detail could make a difference in identifying this guy as the right person."

It was lame, I admit. All she had was the description her first investigator had gotten from a motel clerk with an unbelievably long memory. There was no way she could add anything to it, as she immediately confirmed.

"No, I'm sorry. I know I told you everything."

Something to help. Something to keep her in Alaska. There had to be something.

"Well, what about Paul Gregory? You certainly know all the details of what he looks like. If Cling is here, maybe he is too. Anything at all you haven't told us? Maybe if you dug out your old photos and letters, it would remind you of something."

There was a moment of silence. "We didn't have anything like that. That wasn't our life."

The brittle sadness of her voice made me suddenly very glad that she had someone now, no matter how old or frail, that she could call "Poopsie." My subtle attempts to keep her at home, however, were getting nowhere. Time to abandon subtlety.

"Then I'm afraid there isn't much you can do right now, Diane, except wait to hear from us. If you come back to Portland you'll just be in the way and make it less likely we can find your daughter. Do you understand?"

Sniffle. "Yes, I understand."

"Okay then, you sit tight. I'll call...."

"His teeth."

"...you in.... What?"

"Paul's teeth. Did I tell you about his teeth?"

I exchanged another glance with Malone, who was sitting a little forward now. "No," I said. "What about them?"

"He had ugly teeth. Yellow, crooked, kind of overlapping. I don't know why I didn't think of it before. I hated those teeth."

I felt a prickling on the back of my neck. Malone and I had seen someone with teeth like that: Gregory Paul Zoller of the True Christian Brotherhood. The sensation turned to mild excitement. Okay, so there are lots of people with bad teeth. But luck happens.

"You definitely did not tell us that, Diane, and it is helpful. Look, now I really need you to stay there. Today or tomorrow I'll be e-mailing you a photo to see if you can identify the person in it. Don't get excited. It's not your daughter. But you keep checking your e-mail, okay?"

"Okay. Who will it be? My God. Paul? I never saw Tommy Cling...."

"That's for you to tell me. Just stay put and wait for the picture."

"All right. I will."

We said our goodbyes and I was mentally checking surveillance supplies in the Outback as I hung up.

CHAPTER TWENTY-NINE

"So," Malone said, "you want to head straight back to Salem and get a photo of the guy?"

I looked at the time. It was ten after three. "Shit," I said. "I didn't realize it was quite so late. It would be nearly five by the time we got down there. Too much chance we'd miss him. We know he's not in that office all the time, but we can try first thing in the morning again. Or at least I can. It could be more useful for you to stay here."

She shrugged. "We'll see. What now?"

I thought for a minute. "I don't know about you, but I'm going to do a little further checking if I can on Hoke Moseley. I need to understand what's going on with him."

"Checking how?"

I picked up the phone. "Joy Castle again," I said with a slight grimace.

"Ah, the embittered old girlfriend." She grinned. "Put it on speaker."

I dialed Joy's office and she picked up the phone on the first ring.

"Records Division. Joy Castle."

"Joy, this is Clint."

No kink in the business-like tone: "Well, two calls in two weeks. I gather Moseley hasn't killed you yet."

"Actually I'm calling from the grave. Boo."

"Hmmm. Is it as hot as they say down there?"

Malone was grinning more widely all the time. Good that I could provide my partner with some entertainment.

"Nice and toasty," I told Joy. "Look, Moseley is the reason I'm calling again. I need to know something about his time in Snake River, what kind of inmate he was, the trouble he got

109

into, you know the drill. Can you get a copy of his record for me?"

"I could probably do that. They may even have inmate info online by now. I know they're working on it. And I have some contacts I could talk to. What are you really after?"

"I'm not sure. Just trying to figure out where he's coming from, I guess. What to look out for."

"So you haven't seen him yet?"

"I've seen him a couple of times. We've talked. Hell, once he warned me about a possible threat from someone else. He said it was from someone else. It doesn't *seem* like he intends to kill me, but he might be playing some game I don't understand yet. I need to know how cold he is. That's what I need to know."

"Hmmm. Okay, I'll do some checking. I'll find out what I can when I get the time," she said, still sounding a little reluctant.

"Good enough," I responded, and so it had to be. I was going to thank her, but she'd already hung up.

"That must have been some whiz-bang relationship," Malone said as I put down the phone.

"Let's just say it didn't end well."

"So it would seem. You know she's dating Harm Cluney now."

Detective Sergeant Harmon Cluney, an over-the-hill weightlifter and closet homophobe, was—ironically—a member of the Bureau's assaults and bias crimes unit. I knew he was a closet homophobe because of run-ins reported by my friend and fellow black belt, detective Mike Whitehall. Mike's the openly gay Lieutenant of the Bureau's Homicide Detail and apparently not one of Cluney's favorite people.

"Huh," I said. "I didn't know that, but it doesn't surprise me. Cluney's probably a much better fit than I was. Still, call me a sentimental fool, but I prefer to be at peace with old lovers. Especially when they have access to information that could be vital to my continued existence."

Malone reached across the desk and patted my hand. "You're a sentimental fool," she said.

I was about to make a sarcastic reply when the office door opened to reveal two very large bodies blocking any view of the hallway. I would have known who they worked for even if I hadn't recognized one of them as the driver of the Jeep from this morning. The other was apparently yet another Zoller minion, just as big, totally bald, and sporting a prominent bluish-red bruise on the side of his head.

CHAPTER THIRTY

Malone and I looked at each other, leaving the desk drawers closed for now. These guys definitely did not look like they'd stopped by for a friendly chat, but they weren't displaying any weapons.

"Good afternoon, gentlemen," I said. "What can we do for you?"

They stepped just inside the door and stood there for a long moment like two wax figures in some Gallery of Ignoble Goons. I think we were supposed to be intimidated.

Finally the new guy spoke up, his voice even deeper than Johnny Crew's, sounding like it came up from the bottom of a garbage can. "We came here to do for you."

"Oh wow," said my partner. "Do you watch The Classic Movie channel, too?"

The guy frowned at her, frowned at me, frowned at his companion, and then gave it up.

"Father wants you to know fear of the Lord," he went on. "He says you didn't really get it this morning." The corners of his mouth twisted upward. "Now you're going to get it." He and his buddy stepped slightly apart and forward.

"Well, crap," I said to Malone. "Do you even believe these guys?" We both opened our desk drawers, my top right and her top left, and simultaneously pulled out our guns. Which we then pointed at our visitors.

"You boys might want to re-think who's going to get what," she announced.

Normally when you point guns at two unarmed men they're going to do something like raise their hands and start breathing more shallowly. Clearly the followers of Gregory Zoller were nowhere near what you'd call normal. These two,

113

for example, immediately charged toward us with a mutual roar. Which, while unexpected, wasn't really that bad a move on their part. We couldn't shoot two unarmed men in our office and expect to keep our licenses. Malone and I both knew that.

So we dropped the weapons back in the drawers and stood to meet the charge.

The Jeep driver was coming at me while the other goon reached for Malone. Neither of them made it. My guy was already too close to handle with a kick, so I ducked under his first swing and landed a solid straight punch to his solar plexus. Meanwhile, out of the corner of my eye, I saw my partner knock her attacker's arm aside and punch him in the throat. Oh, ow.

Both guys went down thinking they couldn't breathe. I was afraid hers might be right.

So I went first to crouch beside the guy clutching his throat. He was bug-eyed and gasping, actually a good sign that air was still going in and out. He'd live. Meanwhile Malone had retrieved her gun, a sensible move since these two weren't going to be very happy when they recovered.

"I'll call the cops," I said as I stood up.

"No need," said a voice in the doorway. "My secretary already called them."

I looked over to see Sam Bitterly, our attorney from across the hall. A prim little guy with a perennially sour expression to complement his name, Sam views us as excellent clients but questionable neighbors. This was hardly the first time there had been violence in and around our office.

"Thanks, Sam," I said.

"You two okay?"

"We're fine," I replied.

"They're not," Malone added.

About that time we heard the *whoop whoop* of a patrol car pulling up outside on Stark. A minute later Sam stepped aside to admit two uniforms to the office, a young black woman and an older Asian guy. I didn't know either one, but they both exchanged greetings with Malone. She knew most of the Bureau's personnel, at least casually, from her years on the force before setting up as a private investigator.

We gave them brief statements about what had happened and they were escorting our two visitors, both handcuffed and breathing okay now, down the corridor when Mike Whitehall knocked on the frame of our still-open door. Sam Bitterly by that time had returned to his office.

"I was heading back from a scene when I heard this address on the scanner," he said as he stepped and surveyed the room. "I assume the trouble was in here? Those two with Gordon and Yukata?"

"Yeah," I said. "They had a message from their spiritual leader that they wanted to deliver. It didn't go well for them."

Whitehall's eyebrows went up. "Really. Well, I've got a few minutes."

Mike is extremely fit, as you'd expect a fourth degree black belt to be, six foot three of solid muscle with short-cropped brown hair. He's also way smarter than the average cop, so I welcomed the chance to get his take on our increasingly weird missing persons case.

We all took seats and Malone and I did a tag-team rendition of the case starting with Diane Austin and concluding with the two goons who were probably being processed at the Justice Center by then.

"Huh," said Mike. "And these two actually *told* you that this Gregory Zoller guy sent them to beat you up?"

"Clear as day and dumb as donuts," agreed Malone.

He looked at his watch. "I've got to get back but I'll do some checking on Zoller and this True Christian Brotherhood outfit, see if anything pops."

"That would be great," I said. He of course had information resources that went way beyond even those of our expert Internet researcher down the hall.

CHAPTER THIRTY-ONE

Devon Malone pulled into the Motel 6 parking lot at five after eight the next morning. McCall was already on his way to Salem to get a photo of Gregory Zoller and she wanted to get those notebooks from Sherry.

She'd thought about coming over last night. She probably should have, but she and McCall both were more than a little wrung out after the confrontation in the office. A massive adrenaline surge will do that to you.

And it hadn't helped that, as soon as all the police were gone, TV reporter Alison Roberts called to say she was on the way over for an interview. Like Whitehall, she had been listening to her scanner and recognized the address. The woman hosted her own little show on the local independent channel and seemed to depend on the McCall-Malone Detective Agency to maintain her ratings, such as they were.

Thus she and McCall had fled the office before Roberts could get there and gone to a restaurant they had never been to before just for good measure, in case she tried to track them down—which she had done plenty of times before. Luckily, she must have given up before they finally pulled into Clint's driveway around seven thirty.

All in all, there were plenty of good excuses last evening for Devon to put off having to face her mother again.

But no more. She turned off the engine and just sat in her Jeep for a moment taking deep breaths. Then, with a muttered curse at all the fates, she got out and strode up to Sherry's door.

She knocked, waited, and knocked again, harder, beginning to get worried. Finally she heard a kind of shuffling sound inside, then the snap of the lock turning, and the door opened to reveal her mother looking both groggy and grumpy.

Sherry was wearing what appeared to be an old housecoat and slippers. Her make-up had mostly worn off and she looked her age, older than her age. Even at a distance of three feet, her breath almost knocked Malone back.

Devon started to make a crack about Sherry drinking herself to sleep but then decided it would make no difference.

"I'm here for those notebooks," were her first words.

Her mother's expression had gone from irritated to almost a smile, but that now dropped away. "You want to take the notebooks? Why? Those are my leverage."

"They're my leverage now. I talked to Salazar and told him I had them. So I need to have them."

Wide eyes, a step back. "Marty's here? For real? Already? Oh shit. I'm dead."

"Not yet. That's why I need the notebooks. Let me in and get the damned books, all right?" Malone didn't even wait for a response. Sherry had already stepped back anyway, so she just barged on into the room.

Her mother stood for a moment as though confused, looking around the room. "Sorry for the mess," she said, and the room was indeed a disaster. "I guess it's a good thing I stayed put, though, if Marty is here." She lurched into motion, heading across the room toward a pile of clothes on the small round table. "You have to have the notebooks?"

"If I'm going to save your ass and get you out of my life again, I do."

The older woman pulled up and turned to look at Malone. "You really hate me that much?"

"Just get the fucking notebooks, all right?"

Sherry turned back to the pile of clothes and began digging through them. "You shouldn't hate me. I'm your mother."

Malone remained standing by the door. "Biologically, maybe. Not otherwise, not for a long time."

"I went to prison for you."

"You went to prison for you."

"I'm stuck here in this horrible room. I can't even go any-where." She was tossing clothes on the floor now. "They don't have room service so when I need to eat I have to run down the street to that hole-in-the-wall place for take-out, hoping no-body sees me before I can get back here." She apparently found what she was looking for and paused to frown at Malone over her shoulder. "It's a really crappy little café, that place. I'm pretty sure they spit in their food and piss in their coffee."

"For you, Sherry, I wouldn't be surprised."

The woman grunted and retrieved a battered old satchel from the corner, holding it out to Malone. "You're a terrible daughter. Here are the fucking notebooks."

"I'm the person who is keeping your ass alive. That's what you asked for and that's what you're getting." With that, Mal-one strode across the room, took the satchel from her mother's hands, and turned back for the door. "I'll be in touch," she said without looking back at her mother.

Which was a lucky moment of rudeness, since it meant that when she opened the door she was looking straight at the big guy standing right outside with a gun in his hand.

In a split second she recognized him as one of the men who'd been in Pioneer Square with Marty Salazar. In the same split second, she saw that he was caught off guard by the abruptly opened door and didn't have the gun pointed directly at her.

So she dropped the satchel and kicked him in the balls.

He lost his breath with a horrible groan as his body sagged and the weapon hit the ground, followed immediately by him falling to his knees. As he began to pitch forward, Malone caught him with a perfect haymaker in the jaw and he was out, sprawled headfirst across the threshold of the room.

She poked her head outside for a quick survey of whether there had been any backup or witnesses. No one in sight, at least no one looking in her direction. She reached down, grabbed the guy by the collar of his jacket, and pulled him inside the room, kicking the door shut as she dropped him again.

She caught her own breath and glared at her mother who was standing pale and sweaty against the far wall of the room, never having made a sound during the brief confrontation.

"So much for being in touch," she growled. "Hell and crap and fuck. Get your shit together, Sherry. We're out of here."

CHAPTER THIRTY-TWO

By eight-thirty in the morning I was settled in a parking space just off Lancaster about a quarter-block from the True Christian Brotherhood storefront. I had a clear view through the Subaru's windshield of the office door. At least the office appeared to be open; I wouldn't have to hazard the camp again trying to get a photo.

My disguise of newspaper, sunglasses and Seattle Mariners baseball cap was in place. The Smith and Wesson was on the passenger seat under a section of the paper and my Sony digital camera with three-power zoom lens rested in my lap. I do use a few high tech items. And, on the lower tech side, a wide-mouth bottle was available in case the surveillance outlasted my bladder. All was right with the world, if Zoller was inside there.

I thought he was, because I'd already seen Jerry come and go once and I suspected that Jerry stayed close to his boss. But I couldn't be sure. Come the end of the day, I might be re-reading *The Oregonian* for the twelfth time while pissing in a bottle for nothing.

It was a mystery, anyway, what Zoller would be doing in a bare office with Jerry lurking in the back room. Even my extensive research on cults back when I was a journalist offered no answer to that one—but I hoped he was in there doing it.

At 9:34 a stocky young woman with mousy purple-tinged hair hesitantly entered the office. At 9:41 she burst back outside and took off across the parking lot at a rapid, jerky pace. Whoever was inside, she had apparently not been pleased to meet them.

At 10:16 an old pick-up truck plastered with American flag decals pulled into the lot, rifle mounted prominently across the back window. The grizzled middle-aged driver wore jeans, white muscle tee shirt and camouflage cap. Classic.

He was in the office for almost twenty minutes before the door opened abruptly to reveal him struggling in Jerry's grasp. Jerry proceeded to heave Mr. Survivalist out into the parking lot where he retained just enough balance to keep from sprawling on his face. I got some great shots of the whole sequence.

Jerry stood filling the office doorway until their latest visitor had driven off. I wondered what he would have done if the guy had gone for rifle rather than the ignition. Shoot-out on Lancaster Boulevard? I was beginning to think that the big bruiser and his boss could use memberships in Brain Club for Men.

At least now I had little doubt that Zoller was inside.

At 10:50 an average-looking mid-twenties couple wandered across the parking lot, stood staring at the True Christian Brotherhood storefront for a few moments, and then went inside.

It was becoming pretty obvious that I was surveilling a recruiting station, though I could hardly believe four people would show up in one morning just from the web site. Maybe Zoller had his followers leafleting right-wing church congregations and survivalist groups. Whatever the source of the visitors, it appeared that up until now recruitment had not been going well. The Brotherhood's luck could be changing, however. These last two were still inside at noon.

It was almost twenty after when I finally got the shot I'd been waiting for. Zoller accompanied the two younger people out into the parking lot, followed by Jerry who locked the office door behind them and then disappeared around the corner of the building. The first three stopped, the young couple obviously excited, talking animatedly, and the pale, cadaverous Zoller making the occasional somber reply. So they remained for almost five minutes, until Jerry pulled up in an '80s-vintage Lincoln Continental with tinted windows. All three got in the back and the car pulled into the heavy rush hour traffic on Lancaster.

I had been able to get a number of good photos by then and I wasn't going to follow them. I'd called Malone, both at the office and on her cell phone, a couple of times during the morning and they had gone straight to voicemail with no call back. Worrisome.

So I put the camera aside, made sure the wide-mouth bottle was secure, and pulled out into traffic myself, heading for the freeway north.

CHAPTER THIRTY-THREE

I was getting really worried by the time I got back to the office, but I found our door unlocked and Malone sitting on her side of the partners desk.

"Why haven't you been answering your phone—or calling me back?" I hung up my jacket and walked over to my side of the desk.

"Another problem with Sherry," Malone responded as I stored the Smith and Wesson in its drawer. My partner was looking very grim.

"What happened? Is she all right? Did Salazar get to her?"

"One of his guys tried. He must have followed me to the motel when I went to get the notebooks."

"And?"

"I kicked him in the balls and left him unconscious in her room."

"Ookay. I assume you didn't leave her in there with him."

At that, Malone looked even more grim. Downright sour. "She's at my place now. I'm sorry I didn't call you back, but we were busy dealing with each other."

"Your mother is going to stay with you? I'll bet you're thrilled about that."

"Just fucking giddy. It's only until I can think of something else."

"Are you sure nobody followed you there?"

"I'm sure."

"Nevertheless, Salazar knows you're somehow related to her and he can find out where you live easily enough. Here's an idea. What if we put Johnny and Hap on your mother at your place while you stay at my place?"

She gave me a long look. "You want me to move in with you?"

I tried to look as innocent as possible. "Just temporarily, until your mother has another place to stay."

"Stop calling her my mother. Her name's Sherry."

"She's your mother. Hell, I've heard you refer to her as your mother."

"I can call her that if I have to, but I won't move in with you unless you call her Sherry."

"Oh, for Christ's sake. Talk about dysfunctional families. Okay. You got it. You stay with me until *Sherry* can move on. How's that?"

Her gaze moved from me to the window as she considered it. "I'll think about it," she said. "See if the old guys are available first."

"Oh, for Christ's sake," I muttered again as I picked up the phone. The irony wasn't lost on me that very likely Johnny Crew and Hap Harbaugh would both see my partner's apartment before I ever did.

Malone kept looking out the window.

CHAPTER THIRTY-FOUR

It was nearly eight that evening before we were settled at my place. Johnny and Hap were indeed available, no surprise since they were retired, didn't serve as backup for anyone else, and had wives who—I suspected—were happy to see them out of the house occasionally.

Johnny took the overnight shift, so we met him at Devon's apartment and introduced him to Sherry, who immediately did her batting eyelashes and décolletage routine. The old detective was not impressed and she was clearly disappointed. Malone was blatantly disgusted and packed up her essentials as quickly as possible, clearly having decided that anything was better than staying there with those two.

At least I got to see her apartment at the same time as Hap. It was unadorned but attractive just like my partner. I hoped to visit again someday—if I couldn't persuade her to stay with me.

So here we were, having fed the cats and dined on canned spaghetti ourselves, sitting together on the couch. Well, not so much together. More like, on opposite ends of the couch.

"It's not a lifetime commitment, you know," I said finally. "It's just until we get your...Sherry straightened out."

Malone shrugged. "What did your old girlfriend have to say?"

Okay, so she didn't want to talk about it. Her reference was to a call I'd taken from Joy Castle just before we left the office.

"She checked Moseley's prison record. It seems he settled down after the first six months and was a model prisoner for the rest of his stay. Got his GED. Even participated in an outreach program for kids with drug problems. She said the administration wrote him up as having gone pretty straight."

"That fits with what I've seen."

"It doesn't fit with the warning from his mother."

Malone made a humming sound. "You never know about mothers," she said.

Right then my cell phone beeped and I retrieved it from the coffee table in front of us. I didn't recognize the number but it was an Alaska area code.

"I'll bet this is Diane Austin," I said to Malone. The other thing I'd done before leaving the office was download the photos I'd taken of Gregory Zoller, then e-mailed the two best to Austin with a message to call me.

I hit the speakerphone button. "Clint McCall."

"It's him," came from the speaker. No greeting, no preliminaries. I felt a little surge of adrenaline.

"Diane? Are you sure it's Paul Gregory?"

"I think it's him. It is Paul. I know it is."

"It doesn't look much like the description you gave us," I cautioned her.

"He's changed his hair color. He's lost a lot of weight. He's older. But it's Paul. Those eyes. The teeth. It has to be. It just has to be."

Malone spoke up. "It sounds like you want it to be him but you aren't really sure."

"Miss Malone? No, I...I'm sure. Really. Mr. McCall, do you want me to come back to Portland to identify him? I should come back. Noelle must be there...."

"Diane, we already had this conversation. You stay put and let us do our jobs. I'll let you know when it's a good time for you to come back. Until then, stay put, stay safe, and think good thoughts. This is a big breakthrough, that Gregory Zoller is the man you knew as Paul Gregory. We'll go from there and keep you posted. Okay?"

"Okay," she agreed reluctantly. "Call soon."

"I will," I said, and we hung up.

"She's not sure," Malone said as I put the phone back on the table.

"No," I agreed, "but, with any luck, pretty soon we will be."

CHAPTER THIRTY-FIVE

The next morning I got the kind of call you never, ever want to get. Given that it was five a.m., I knew before I picked up the bedside phone that it wasn't going to be good.

"McCall."

The voice on the other end was muffled and low-pitched, speaking fast. "We have your daughter. You can have her back after it's done. Call the police and you don't get her back at all."

Then there was dial-tone.

I don't know how long I froze, propped up on one elbow with the handset to my ear. It probably wasn't more than a couple of seconds before Malone groaned, rolled over, and poked me. "Who the hell was that?"

I hung up the phone and swung my feet down to the floor. "I don't know," I said.

Whatever my voice sounded like, she went on alert, sat up, and put a hand on my shoulder. "Clint? What is it?"

"Somebody claiming they've got Colleen." The word "claiming" seemed to kick-start my brain again and I immediately punched the speed dial number for my daughter's cell phone. Which gave me a recorded message that the phone was not in service. Colleen's phone is never "not in service." It's the lifeline to her entire social circle.

Malone meanwhile had jumped out of bed and was already getting dressed. The two cats had fled the bedroom as soon as they picked up on the tension. "Any idea who it was?" she asked. "Was it Salazar?"

"I don't think so," I said. "At least there was no accent." I had a hunch, but it didn't really make sense. Nevertheless, I got up and started pulling on my own clothes. "It was a male voice," I told Malone. "He said they have Colleen and I would get her back 'after it's done,' whatever 'it' is. Oh, and of course don't call the cops."

Now Malone was strapping on her weapon. I still didn't know where she thought we were going. "After it's done? That's what they said? What the fuck?"

"I don't *know* what the fuck, Devon." I reached for my own holstered Smith and Wesson, still pretty much on auto-pilot. We really should go somewhere, I was thinking, at least check out Colleen's apartment to see if there's any evidence of what happened.

We were spared further pointless exchanges by a loud and sustained knock on the front door. I think we both jumped about a foot in the air and came down with our guns in our hands. A knock on the door at five-fifteen in the morning probably isn't good, either.

It had become a pounding by the time we got through the living room, Malone clicking on a table lamp as we passed, and I put my eye to the peephole. There wasn't enough light outside yet to be sure, but it looked like the silhouette of Hoke Moseley. If he had something to do with Colleen's kidnapping, he was a dead man.

"I think it's Moseley," I said to Malone and jerked the door open, leading with my weapon.

It was him, all right, but not quite as I expected. The light from the living room lamp behind me revealed blood streaming down the side of his face. His t-shirt was soaked red on that side. He looked pale as death otherwise and seemed to be swaying.

"Shit," I said as I lowered the gun and stepped forward to steady him, "what happened to you?"

He was even further gone than I'd first thought. He said just one word before pitching forward into my arms.

"Colleen," he gasped.

CHAPTER THIRTY-SIX

I dragged the semiconscious young man over to the couch and dropped him onto it, none too gently. I didn't know what had happened to Colleen or what was going on, but I had a pretty good idea now that Hoke Moseley was involved.

"I'll get some water," Malone said, and headed for the kitchen.

"Bring a wet towel, too," I yelled over my shoulder. Head wounds bleed a lot and I'd have to decide soon if the kid needed medical attention beyond what we could provide. I did not want to haul his ass off to the hospital before I got his story. I pulled up his shirt and could see there was no injury there; all the blood was from the gash on his head. So far so good.

Malone returned with the towel and a glass of water.

Moseley had come around enough by then to take the glass and sip the water while I sponged off his head wound. It wasn't really deep and his pupils looked okay, but he could still have a concussion or worse.

I set the towel aside on the floor and crouched down directly in front of him to see what his eyes looked like. They seemed to be clearing up; he was definitely looking back at me, more with fear than hostility.

"Moseley. Are you with us?"

He finished the water with a gulp and lowered the glass. "Yeah. My head hurts but I'm here."

"What happened? What do you know about Colleen?"

"Two guys took her. I saw it."

I resisted the urge to grab him by the shoulders and shake him. Probably not a good idea with a kid who was already woozy. "What guys? Where? When? Can you describe them?"

Later we'd get to why he was there at all. Oh yes, we'd get to that.

"I don't know who they were. It was at a club downtown, maybe...." He looked around. "What time is it?"

"Five-thirty in the morning," replied Malone.

"So...three or four hours ago. Four, I guess. Something like that. I followed Colleen to this club on Broadway...."

"You followed her?"

"Well, yeah. I didn't mean any harm. I wasn't going to do anything. I thought that maybe if we just ran into each other, you know, we could...."

Jesus. "Never mind that. What the fuck happened to my daughter?"

"I was still outside the club, trying to decide whether to follow her inside, when this van pulled into the alley right there. I saw these two big guys get out and go in the side door of the club. It looked like they jimmied it, so that got my attention. I didn't know what to do, or whether I should do anything, so I stayed put. Then all of a sudden they come out with Colleen. She was fighting like crazy. One of them had his hand over her mouth. I couldn't believe it. I yelled and ran across the street, tried to take them on, but the other guy, the one who didn't have Colleen, clobbered me with a tire iron or something just as I got there."

His hand moved up toward his cheek but stopped short, hanging in the air before him, curling into a fist. "The next thing I knew I was waking up in an empty alley. I might as well have just stood across the street and watched her being dragged away." He slammed the fist against his hip. "I didn't do any goddamn good at all."

"Why were you there?"

"I told you."

134

"Not good enough. You sure you didn't know the men who took her?"

"No, goddamn it! I was there to see Colleen. I tried to help her!"

"Why did you want to see Colleen?"

"I...I don't know. I guess.... It just makes me feel good to see her."

Looking at his face, I found I believed him—and I hoped a time would come when I could appreciate this very strange twist. This wasn't that time. "What about the van? What was the make and model? What year?"

"Shit, I don't know. I grew up ripping off old ladies, not working on cars. I don't know what the fuck kind of van it was. It was a white van."

"License plate?"

"Are you kidding?"

"You really are a big help."

Malone had, I guess, been standing right behind me this whole time and she spoke up again. "Close your eyes and picture the van," she said to Hoke. "Think hard. Was there anything? Lettering on the side? A decal? Anything."

He did as she instructed and meanwhile I stood up just because I couldn't stay still any more. Colleen was out there somewhere in the hands of somebody for some reason and I had no fucking clue.

"There was a decal," Moseley finally said, and I spun around to crouch before him again.

"What did it say? Do you remember?"

"It was...three letters, like a logo. "TCF? TOB? Something like that."

My whole spine went cold. We had a fucking clue after all and my first hunch had been right. "TCB? Was it TCB?"

He opened his eyes, which were perfectly clear now. "That's it. That's what it was."

CHAPTER THIRTY-SEVEN

In the next three hours a plan took shape. We would invade the True Christian Brotherhood compound tonight.

Why they had taken Colleen, I didn't know. What they meant by "when it's over," I didn't know. Whether the camp was where they had her, I didn't know, but it was a good place to start. The little Salem office was highly unlikely. And if she wasn't at the camp, someone there would know where she might be—and that someone was going to talk.

Malone checked with her mother and determined that Hap Harbaugh was now on duty, so I called Johnny Crew to provide us some backup. He was both grumpy and sleepy, having just come off his own shift with Sherry, but readily agreed.

I knew Mike Whitehall would be willing to join in without notifying the Bureau but if we ended having to shoot somebody he could get fired for that. I knew Reuben Keys was always up for a gunfight, but I didn't think I had enough credit with the justice system to save his ass if he injured anyone else on my behalf. The other black belts in the dojang were out of the question; they sometimes helped out, but invading an armed encampment? No way. So it was going to be me and Malone and Johnny. Tight, quiet, and clean.

And maybe Hoke Moseley, who insisted that we take him along.

To my surprise, Malone was on his side. She cornered me in the kitchen late in the morning and said straight out, "We should use the kid. He's here, he knows how to handle a gun, and he's got a vested interest. He walked all the way from that alley to here, bleeding and half-disoriented, to let us know what happened to Colleen. That's fucking commitment. Plus...he's a kid. A hell of a lot younger than Johnny." Or me, she didn't say.

137

I said I'd think about it. I also noted that we were lucky he didn't call the police himself.

"Calling the cops is probably not high on his priority list," Malone responded. True enough.

It was one o'clock now and I expected Johnny soon. He was stopping on the way at a storage unit where he and Hap kept some heavier weapons. I'd called Eleanor Ivory and given her an extremely edited version of what was going on, asking her to go online and find the best satellite photos of the Willamette Valley southwest of Salem, then e-mail them to my PC at home so I could print them out. I know everybody should be able to use Google maps or whatever by now, but I didn't want to take the time to figure it out today. Eleanor, as expected, had it down; the photos appeared within twenty minutes and they clearly showed the campsite and environs.

The whole time since the early morning call I'd felt a steadily simmering fury. Just when my daughter was in grave danger I had to forego most of the allies and backup I had cultivated over the years. This was going to have to be done with just the three—or four—of us and as many guns as we could carry.

Needless to say, I was still uneasy about the snot-nosed ex-con who appeared to have a romantic interest in my daughter rather than a homicidal one in me. But here he was in my living room with me and Malone, waiting for Johnny to show up. At this moment he was sitting on my couch petting Stella, who had finally reappeared. With all the activity and tension, I didn't expect to see Maxine until around Christmas.

Johnny arrived at one-fifteen, not bothering to knock before he bustled into the living room and grabbed me in a bear hug. "Goddamn," he boomed, "I can't believe they took the girl. We're gonna get her back, Clint."

He let go and I shook my head to stop the ringing in my ears. "Everything we'll need's in the trunk of my car," he went on at a more normal volume. "Hey, Devon. And who is this?"

Malone grinned. "Johnny Crew, meet Hoke Moseley."

Moseley was up and holding out his hand by then; I think Johnny was shaking it before he processed the introduction— at which point he practically jumped away from the kid. "You're...." A wide-eyed look at me. "Is this son-of-a-bitch...?"

"No, Johnny," I said quickly, "he tried to stop the kidnapping and then came here to tell us about it. It's because of him that we know it was the True Christian Brotherhood. For today, he's with us on this." And so that decision was made.

The four of us spent more than an hour examining the satellite photos and also an Oregon gazetteer that Johnny had brought in from his car. We thought we could see some kind of access to the TCB compound to the northwest, on the opposite side from the road Malone and I had come in on the first time. It was apparently not much more than a footpath through the woods...but that was enough. Better yet, there was a road near where the path began, giving us a place to park the vehicles.

We had a plan and a well-armed team, but it was going to be a long, painful wait until nightfall. Colleen was out there somewhere counting on me.

CHAPTER THIRTY-EIGHT

I don't know how I got through the next hours. Johnny took a much-needed nap. Moseley played with Stella and watched TV; I found it harder and harder to believe that he intended to kill me. Meanwhile, Malone and I mostly sat around waiting.

Maxine eventually appeared, hunger outweighing fear, and crept along the wall as far from everyone as possible toward the kitchen.

I desperately wanted to get going but a daytime incursion just didn't make sense. So I waited. We sat through a long evening of pops and bangs from neighborhood fireworks; I had completely forgotten it was the Fourth of July until we heard the first firecrackers going off and I had my gun out before I remembered.

We waited until after midnight, in fact, to minimize the chances anyone would be awake out at the camp. Maybe they had had a fireworks show of their own. Probably not, but who the hell knew?

Finally, we drove through the early morning darkness of the Willamette Valley, Malone and I in the Outback, Johnny and Hoke following in Johnny's Ford sedan.

Once we got off the freeway and main surface streets, there was little traffic—as you'd expect around one o'clock on a Sunday morning. Then there was none at all as we snaked our way deep into the rural terrain on a series of narrower and narrower farming roads and finally into a wooded patch.

It was one-twenty when I pulled over into a little clearing, really just a wide shoulder. The sky was sparkling with stars but lent no light to our pitch-black surroundings. Johnny pulled in behind me and the four of us met up between the two vehicles.

The air was dry and warm. I could hear an insomniac rooster crowing in the distance.

"I figure the path is a hundred yards back down the road," Johnny said softly. "I think we saw it as we went by." He opened the trunk of his car and took out two old Ruger Mini-14s, semi-automatic rifles with a 20-round magazine, pistol grip and folding metal stock. He and Moseley would be carrying those, plus I was sure Johnny also had a handgun or two on him. Apparently he'd already confirmed to his own satisfaction that the kid could handle the rifle.

I'd have my Smith and Wesson and Malone her Glock. If there was a chance to get into the camp before anyone awoke, I didn't want to be sneaking around carrying a rifle. Otherwise, we'd just be waiting and watching anyway. That was the plan.

We walked quickly back in the direction Johnny had indicated, he and Moseley holding the Rugers folded close to their sides in the unlikely event anyone drove by. No one did. After about a hundred yards we found an opening in the low brush on the right side of the road. It did appear to be a little-used path going into the woods.

"Best I can tell, this is it," Johnny offered in a hoarse whisper. "The camp should be about a quarter mile in, maybe a half."

"Well," I said, "let's go see."

He and Moseley unfolded the stocks of their Rugers. Malone and I drew our weapons. We moved in among the trees.

There was enough light by that time to make out the path a few feet ahead of us. We had timed our arrival perfectly. The trail was almost entirely overgrown with ground-hugging ferns, grass, and wildflowers but nevertheless well-defined by the mature cedar and pine that pressed in from both sides. We moved slowly in single file, Malone bringing up the rear, through the dim thicket. The sounds of our feet crunching the forest floor mixed with the rustle of the forest awakening around us.

I called a halt about ten minutes in because Johnny was beginning to wheeze a little. The hike was rugged going. "Let's take a moment to catch our breaths," I said.

"Sorry," he whispered as he stood taking long, slow breaths.

The four of us stood together in the dawning light, scanning the surrounding trees for any threat.

"You ever stopped to think," Johnny asked no one in particular, "that right this minute we got exactly so much time to live? Ten years, twenty days, six minutes, whatever. You don't know what it is, but it's there. Just so much life and no more."

I gave him a gentle punch in the arm. "Don't worry, my friend. With any luck it will be more than six minutes, at least."

From beside me came Malone's whisper. "You got any more cheery thoughts before we go try to take on God knows how many guys armed with automatic weapons?"

"Nope," Johnny responded. "I'm fine now. Let's go get Colleen."

"Okay," I said. "Let's move—but slowly—and no more talk." It was as if I could feel every muscle in my body and see the veins of every leaf as I led the way again, Malone on my heels now with Johnny and Hoke behind her.

Ten minutes later we came to the edge of a clearing. There were two tents in view through the last partition of green, but no sign or sound of life. My heart sank. The camp Reuben Keys had described should have contained a number of RVs and many more tents, probably some people sleeping out in the open in sleeping bags. I should have been seeing the Jeep we'd encountered two days ago and probably other, similar vehicles. There was none of that. This looked like an abandoned site.

I parted the leaves a little more and took my time examining the periphery of the clearing. There was no evidence of anyone lurking among the trees, no disturbance of the brush or branches to indicate someone had pushed through, no movement in the opening across from us where the access road began. Still, I couldn't be sure at this distance.

I hefted the Smith and Wesson, nodded at my partner, and we stepped into the clearing, leaving our two compatriots behind the curtain of leaves with rifles at the ready.

There was more light now, the sun having made its formal appearance somewhere over the horizon beyond the woods. A gentle breeze was rising to greet the growing warmth. The campsite was shrouded in the silence of abandonment. There was nothing to see but the two tents and a scattering of litter that told of recent occupation.

Both tents were oriented away from us, their entrance flaps toward the road that penetrated the clearing on the opposite side. We approached the nearer tent, the smaller one, carefully. I was striving to be as relaxed and open to every sight and sound as possible.

Motioning to Malone to hold up a second, I eased around to the front of the pup tent and found the flap already open. Inside I could see a small pile of dirty, ragged blankets. I eased through the opening and surveyed the space, seeing nothing besides the blankets except the partially crushed head of a small doll off in one corner. A young child had lived here. I shuddered and rejoined Malone just outside the tent flap.

"Nothing," I whispered. We moved on toward the larger shelter.

We were still a few feet away when I heard faint but clearly labored breathing. I knew from Devon's light touch on my arm that she heard it, too. There was someone in there and it was time to re-position our backup. Satisfied that no attack was coming from the surrounding trees, I motioned Johnny and Hap to join us.

As soon as they were in view I held a finger to my lips and then pointed at the tent; they got my meaning and silently spread out so that we would all four come abreast of the entrance at the same time. They were a dozen feet back, one on either side; Malone and I were on our bellies, creeping around the corner of the tent to peek beneath the hanging canvas flap. I was planning to tell whoever I saw that they were surrounded.

I raised the canvas a few inches and was immediately hit with a stench of chemicals and excrement. There was no movement in the dim half-light within but the breathing was louder, off to our left where there appeared to be another pile of dirty blankets. I waited a few seconds for my eyes to adjust further, then motioned for Johnny and Hap to approach as I fully raised the flap and Malone and I entered the tent.

The stentorian breathing came from a woman—I was pretty sure it was a woman—under the filthy blankets. I opened a flap on that side of the tent to get a better view and saw a severely wasted semi-comatose body with waxen yellowish skin, long and stringy dark hair, eyes swollen nearly shut, lips vibrating loosely as the air whistled between them. They hadn't even left her a pillow.

"My God," Malone said as she dropped to her knees beside the person. "She looks like she's on her last legs."

"Stay outside!" I yelled at the other two, and reached down to pull my partner upright again. "We need to get out of here and get her some help," I said. I urged her outside to join our two compatriots.

"There's an extremely sick woman in there," I told them, "and it's impossible to know if she's contagious, so we'd all better keep our distance."

Meanwhile I was checking my cell phone. There was not a bar to be had and Malone confirmed it was the same for hers. So we hiked back to the cars while Johnny and Hoke stayed with the sick woman and kept an eye out for anyone returning to check on her. I didn't think there would be. I was pretty sure the woman had been left to die.

I'm afraid I ranted as we walked. The camp appeared to be abandoned. Colleen wasn't there and there was no sign she'd ever been there. We'd wasted almost a whole fucking day and were no closer to finding her. Plus, now we had to involve law enforcement anyway.

"I might as well have called Mike and had him put out a BOLO," I muttered as I opened the driver's side door of the Outback. "I'm a fucking idiot, just sitting around the house, waiting for dark, planning the stupid invasion of an abandoned camp...."

"And I was with you all the way," Malone said as she settled in the passenger seat to look at me. "We couldn't just ignore their threats. We made a decision, all of us, and it could have been a good decision." She waved her hand in a helpless gesture. "But it wasn't. And now we have to try something else."

"First we have to get medics for that woman," I said, and peeled out toward the main road, looking for a signal.

CHAPTER THIRTY-NINE

My desperation had not lessened hours later as Malone and I sat in our office trying to imagine something constructive we could do on a Sunday to get closer to Colleen. We'd not heard anything more from the kidnappers. Neither Eleanor, working from home, nor Malone here on her office computer had been able to find any kind of home address for Gregory Zoller.

On our drive from the encampment that morning we had gotten cell service after just a couple of miles, then met the Sheriff's deputy and paramedics back at the trailhead to the clearing. We found the woman still alive but also still unconscious, clearly incapable of telling us anything about what had happened or where the others had gone.

At least the medics didn't seem worried that she was a vector for some terrible disease. That was a relief.

But we didn't know whether she was a member of the True Christian Brotherhood or another kidnap victim or what. Had they been abusing her? Why did they leave her behind rather than getting her to a hospital?

Maybe she would eventually wake up with some memories intact. Maybe the Sheriff's investigation would turn up something. I had told them we happened upon the campsite while following an anonymous tip about a missing person—not the sick woman—and that was all. I couldn't bring myself to bring law enforcement in on Colleen's kidnapping and maybe get her killed for sure. I wasn't that desperate. Yet.

"I hate this," I said. I paced back and forth beside our partners desk a couple more times, then stopped at the coffeemaker and poured another cup.

Malone eyed the cup as I took a good sip. "One more cup of coffee and you're going to be flying back and forth rather than tromping."

"I do not tromp."

"Whatever you call it, it's irritating as hell. Why don't you sit down? We'll come up with something pretty soon. We always do. Colleen will be all right. I know it."

Fear for my daughter was tearing at my insides like a claw hammer, but I had to be steady. I hoped my partner was right, on all counts. I was about to agree out loud when there was a timid knock on the frosted glass of our office door.

I exchanged a look with Malone. As far as we knew, we were the only people currently in residence on this floor. And a potential client was highly unlikely.

She pulled open her desk drawer. "Maybe it's more messengers from Zoller. At least that would give us something to do."

"We can only hope." Timid knock or not, I rested my hand on the Smith and Wesson in my own open desk drawer as I called for the visitor to come in. If it *was* more of Zoller's thugs, they were going to talk to us or die.

But it wasn't the bad guys. Nor was it someone I could send to the competition. It *was* just about the last person I wanted in our office at this moment.

"Mr. McCall?"

Her voice and demeanor seemed more frail than ever. She cowered in the doorway, doe eyes locked on me as if I were an oncoming car. My own expression, I realized, was not exactly welcoming.

I managed a smile, one not much stronger than her voice, as I closed my own desk drawer and stood up. "Come in, Miss Austin. It's good to see you."

She shufffshuffled hesitantly across the office, nodding to Malone, and settled lightly on one of our visitor's chairs, the one nearest me as usual. Her face was a mask of anxiety with only the eyes seeming capable of movement. They darted around the room as if looking for things that she might not want to see.

Far better than I would ever have wanted, I knew how terrified she was for her daughter...yet at the same time I was thinking, What the fuck am I going to do with this woman? Her presence was not going to make it any easier to help our kids.

"I'm sorry," she whispered. "I have to be here when you find her."

What could I say? "I understand."

She looked from Malone to me. "I can't believe I caught you in the office on a Sunday morning. I didn't know where either of you lived. You haven't...found her already, have you?"

"No," I answered. "We haven't even confirmed that she's with Zoller. There's a good chance he knows where she is, though."

"Have you talked to him? You know, questioned him?"

"We want to check out a few more things first." Like where the hell he is.

Her mask was crumbling into furrows of despair. "You aren't any closer to her than you were."

Malone leaned a little forward. "We know more than we did when you last talked to Clint, but it isn't adding up yet. You have to trust us, Diane. We will find her."

Austin sagged for a moment, then her shoulders straightened a bit and her lips set in a firmer line. "All right. Is there anything I can do to help?"

149

"The best thing you can do is stay out of the way," I said, as gently as I could. I held up my hand as she roused herself to protest. "I don't mean you have to go back to Alaska. It would be good if you were close by when we find Noelle. You might even be able to help us with Zoller when the time comes. But right this minute we need to be working on our own. You understand?"

A quick nod of affirmation. "Yes, okay."

Having achieved at least that much assent, I called the nearest motel to make sure they had a room available and sent Diane Austin on her way with assurances that we'd let her know the second we had any more information.

"It's got to be tough," Malone commented as soon as we heard Austin's steps receding down the corridor.

"I know it is," I said. "She wants to be here when we find her daughter. And, speaking of finding daughters, I'm going to call the hospital, see if our one possible lead is still alive."

CHAPTER FORTY

Fortunately I had a solid contact person at Providence Medical Center. Tyrone Gaddis had been a journalism student of mine at Portland State before he switched his major to nursing and he was on the staff there now. I just hoped he was working on a Sunday.

Tyrone and I had established a friendship beyond teacher-student while he was still in my classroom. I was apprenticing with Crew and Harbaugh at that time and some of those early cases were of course in the black community. Like most of my students, Tyrone knew about my moonlighting. Unlike most, he'd spent some time as a member of the Crips before deciding school was safer. He enjoyed offering me occasional advice about how to operate in his old environment. That inclination to help hadn't changed as he'd moved on in his new career.

Luck was with me and they called Tyrone to the phone. I explained what I needed and he said he'd call me right back.

Half a cup of coffee and more pacing later, he did. "You know I'm not supposed to be telling you any of this shit," he said when I answered, "but the staff was told to keep the detectives posted and you're a detective, right?"

He went on to report that they'd been able to identify the woman as Phyllis Turpin, last known address in Roosevelt, Washington, but had been unable to find any family or establish her recent history. She was near death due to a very aggressive and apparently completely untreated cancer.

"She should have been in a hospice long before now," he said, "but it's too late. They aren't going to try to move her. She's conscious, though, sort of. It's not really per the rules, but if you want to try to talk to her...."

I know I startled Malone when I jumped up from my chair. "Well, Jesus, Tyrone, save the lead for last why don't you? Yes, I have to talk her. Are there any cops with her? Have they already talked to her?"

"According to the nurse on duty, she just woke up. I don't know if they've notified the cops yet or not."

"I can be there in twenty minutes," I said, and hung up.

Malone was also on her feet. "The woman's awake?"

"And barely alive, apparently. Let's get going."

"If we don't get anything from her," Malone said as we trotted down the hall toward the stairway, "you've got to bring Mike and the Bureau in on this."

"I know," I said. And that could very well doom Colleen. I knew that, too.

CHAPTER FORTY-ONE

I drove like a son of a bitch and we hit the hospital lobby nineteen minutes later. Tyrone was waiting just inside the entrance. He was not a man to be missed, with the body as well as the name to be a pro football player.

He grinned briefly in greeting, then gave Malone a look. I introduced them and he escorted us to the nearest elevator.

"Nobody else is with her yet. You two are family if anybody asks," he said as the door closed on us. "Good thing there ain't three of you. Only two allowed in at a time."

The elevator door opened and we headed down the hall to the left. A bored-looking nurse at the station gave us a good stare as we entered Phyllis Turpin's room but being escorted by a nurse apparently made us okay.

I was relieved to see that Turpin had the room to herself, but otherwise the situation didn't look very promising. The woman lay with her eyes closed, breathing shallowly, pallid skin covered with a sheen of sweat. On the other side of the bed was an IV that snaked down into her arm. An oxygen tube ran up her nose, but she was free to speak if she could.

Tyrone quickly inspected various monitors to which she was attached and seemed satisfied. He gently nudged the woman's arm. After a moment I saw her eyes open.

"Ms. Turpin? There's some people here to see you."

I didn't hear her respond and he turned back to us with a slight raising of the eyebrows as if to say, "Take your shot for what it's worth."

"My break is over," is what he did say. "I still don't know if the cops have been notified she's awake. I'll keep an eye out while I go about my business. Find me before you leave. I'll be on this floor somewhere."

"Thanks, Tyrone."

"No problem."

Malone and I approached the bed. Sick as she was, Phyllis Turpin looked much better than she had when I saw her in the tent. Now it was possible to tell that she was probably in her mid-thirties. I think she had been pretty.

Her eyes were still open, glazed with illness in a death mask. She looked at me, then Malone, and frowned slightly with the effort to focus. Her first words, faint but clearly audible, shot up my spine.

"Do you know if my daughter is all right? Trisha? Is she all right?"

I don't believe I've ever focused on a lover or even Colleen as intimately as I did on Phyllis Turpin at that moment.

"I think she's okay, Phyllis, but I'm not sure. Do you know where she is? I could go check for you."

"She's with Father." Pause for breath. "So she must be all right."

"Do you know where Father is?"

Slight frown. She was working on it. "Why do you want to know?"

"My daughter is with him, too, and I want to check on her. Just like your daughter."

The corner of her mouth twitched. "She's lucky. It's such an honor to be his bride. I couldn't...."

His bride? I felt like I was watching myself from across the room. I had to learn everything without frightening Phyllis Turpin into silence. "You mean your daughter is married to him?" Could I be wrong about this woman's age after all? Don't push. Don't blow this.

"Oh yes. She is one of the Chosen."

Malone spoke from right at my elbow. "How old is your daughter, Phyllis?"

"Twelve. I was too old, but at least my girl...."

Twelve. Shit. "How many wives does Father have, Phyllis?" Malone again. I could hear the tension and anger in her voice. I'm not sure I could have spoken right at that moment.

Breath. "I don't know. Seven or eight. They're good girls. Your daughter will be happy."

Careful. Careful. I had to ask, to be sure. "My daughter is twenty-four. That's too old?"

The little frown. "Oh, I'm sorry. That is. That's too old." Breath. "But she can still serve. The others."

Oh great. "My daughter's name is Colleen. She just joined the group a few days ago. Did you see her before they left the camp?"

"No. I don't know Colleen. I wish I could see Trisha once more." Her eyes were glazing over again.

"Where did they go when they left the camp, Phyllis?" Malone asked. "We have to talk to Father. Maybe we can persuade him Colleen isn't too old. You know how important that could be."

It was a clever approach, but I know the look I gave my partner must have been close to a glare.

Breath. "I don't think you can do that," whispered the woman in the bed. Breath. "Father won't go against the word of God. Do you believe in God?"

This was not a time to get into the finer points of theology. "Of course we do," I said, having found my voice again. "Please, Phyllis. We have to try."

Breath. Breath. "The Hampton farm in...around Hood River somewhere...in the valley. That's where Trisha said they were going." Breath. Breath. "She came to say goodbye, you know. Father let her." Breath. "He is all kindness."

"Why did they leave you behind, Phyllis?"

"Part of the price." Just a faint whisper now.

"The price for what?"

Her voice surged, rasping with the effort. "For failing to stop the killing. For letting the new death into the world. Many of us will have to pay before Father can stop it."

"I don't understand."

Her eyes closed. "You will," she breathed and then drifted into unconsciousness. She still lived, but she wasn't going to say any more. I rested my hand on hers and wished her well. Then we went looking for Tyrone Gaddis.

Just two hours later Phyllis Turpin died with only a sheriff's deputy for company.

CHAPTER FORTY-TWO

He sat rigidly at his desk, grimly clamping down on the nausea that once again threatened to overcome him. Satan was not going to win! He knew that, knew that God would give him the strength to overcome the sickness and remove the new death from the world. It was his God-given mission and he could not fail.

"You okay, Father?" asked the scarred fireplug of a man standing in the doorway. That's how Gregory Zoller always thought of the man because he was almost as wide as he was tall: a dark-haired, fire-eating, God-loving fireplug, the best servant and follower that God's Avenger could have.

Zoller did his best to relax and smile. "I'm fine, Tommy, right as rain. God is with me."

"You was lookin' a little stiff and pale there, is all. I thought maybe you was upset we had to abandon the camp. I still don't know how that asshole detective found us."

"Language, Tommy. Satan has many tricks to help sinners like McCall. It was God's will that we leave the camp behind for now. We can use the property here for training our followers just as well."

The man stepped further into the office and shook his head, which looked odd since he appeared to have no neck. Gregory Zoller suppressed a smile, beginning to feel better as the nausea passed.

"I don't know, Father. We can't be doing a lot of shooting guns with other farms nearby...."

"Don't worry, Tommy. God will provide." Zoller paused. Speaking of providing.... "Did you confirm with Otto that he dealt with the trash we left behind?"

"Yeah, he swears that he made sure she was dead. And good riddance." The man named Tommy actually shuddered a little. "She was really a mess, a fucking zombie."

"Language, Tommy. She sickened because she was a sinner and without God's love." Unlike Father himself, who would prevail over his Satan-driven sickness. "Before that, though, she gave us one of the Chosen, so we should not speak obscenely of her. An eternity in Hell will be sufficient as her punishment."

Tommy shrugged. "If you say so, Father. You're the one with God's ear." He cocked his head as if he'd just had a thought. "But are you sure God has this McCall asshole under control, now? He knows where the office is and somehow he found the campsite. What if he finds this place?"

"Language, Tommy. Don't worry. As long as we have his girl, he knows better than to come after us."

"What are we going to do with her? She's too old for you, but for the rest of us...." His grin was without any humor.

"Tommy! That would be a sin. We need her healthy and unharmed until after the first step in our mission is complete. Then God will decide her fate and let me know. Is there anything else? Why did you come to see me?"

"Ah, I guess I just wanted to make sure you were all right. I'll leave you alone now."

Gregory Zoller smiled, a genuine and easy smile this time. The nausea was gone and he was feeling God's strength flow through his veins. "I'm never alone, Tommy. God is always with me. But, as long as you're going back downstairs, I think I'd like to have some human company as well. Bring one of the Chosen up, please. Young Maddy would be good, I think."

"Will do, Father," the man called Tommy said, and backed respectfully out of the room.

Gregory Zoller frowned even as Tommy disappeared down the stairs at the end of the hall. He had a feeling God was telling him that perhaps Satan *would* find a way to lead the detective and his whore-partner to the farmhouse, that perhaps it was time to leave here as well.

Tommy and the others could stay and deal with whatever God chose to provide. Zoller hated that he'd have to leave most of the Chosen behind. All the more reason to enjoy Maddy while he could.

Then, once he was sure it was God's will, he and Kimberly could easily find shelter with some of the followers out in the city. There would be enough manpower to complete the first step.

Of course Kimberly would have to come with him.

Even among the Chosen, Kimberly was special because she was also his daughter.

Sometimes God worked in mysterious ways.

CHAPTER FORTY-THREE

"We knew she was about gone," Malone said after I hung up the office phone and reported that Phyllis Turpin was dead.

"Tyrone said she never regained consciousness. Just slipped away."

"And left us with still another daughter to find."

"Yes," I said. "Damn it. Yes. And they all three—Colleen, Noelle, and Trisha, plus who knows how many more—could all be at this farmhouse near Hood River. So how do we find it and how do we go in?"

"You thinking it's time to call in the troops? Mike could locate the farm and coordinate with the police or the sheriff's office out there to take it on."

I jumped up from the desk and started pacing again. "Shit, I don't know. *I don't know.* I mean, I can easily see a bunch of small-town sheriff's deputies turning it into a Waco situation—with Colleen maybe in the middle of it."

"That could happen, but we can't sit here with our thumbs up our asses. We've got to do something. Call Mike. See how it feels. See how *you* feel once you're talking to him. You can at least check to see if he's got any new info on the Brotherhood. Hell, maybe he's already found the farmhouse."

"Okay. All right." I sat down and picked up the phone, determined to get a grip on myself. I wasn't used to being comforted and encouraged by my partner this way. Not that there was anything wrong with comfort and encouragement, but it was my daughter in jeopardy and I should be the proactive one here. I punched in Mike's number at the Justice Center and he picked up right away. It seemed that everybody was working this Sunday.

"Whitehall."

"Hey, Mike, it's Clint. I'm going to put you on speaker with Devon and me. We're wondering if you've got any new info on the TCB." I turned on the speaker and set the phone down.

"Hey guys. I've got a couple of pieces of news. One is that bomb-making materials were found at the abandoned campsite. Which is not good."

"No, it's not," I agreed. "What else?"

"Even worse news, maybe. The Bureau has opened an official investigation of the True Christian Brotherhood."

Which struck me as an odd way to put it—and I guess it hit Malone the same way. "What do you mean, an official investigation?" she asked. "You mean besides the questions you've been asking on our behalf? Why would you do that?"

"I didn't. Harm Cluney did."

Malone and I locked eyes for a long moment. What the fuck? Harmon Cluney was investigating the True Christian Brotherhood?

"Cluney?" I repeated incredulously. "What's his interest? For that matter, what's his jurisdiction? Their office is in Salem and the campsite in the Willamette Valley. They don't have anything in the Portland metro area that we know of, do they?" And I sure as hell wasn't going to mention the farmhouse or Colleen's situation if it might drag Harmon Cluney into the mix.

"I don't know of any, but his unit has opened an investigation and he's the lead detective on it. I heard that he pushed for it, but I can't exactly go ask him why. He's not big on sharing with yours truly, as you know. If I had to guess, I'd say he just wants to fuck with us. Somehow he found out I was helping with your case and he's trying to bigfoot the whole thing."

"Shit. You could be right. Between you being a nasty homosexual and me being his girlfriend's ex, he'd have motive enough in his mean-spirited pea brain."

162

"Well, look on the bright side. Maybe he'll find something helpful, however unlikely. He'd have to file paperwork on it eventually and then we'd know."

I was looking across the desk at Malone's grim smile as he spoke. We couldn't wait for eventually and she knew I'd have to leave the Police Bureau out of it now.

"Okay, Mike," I said with a sigh. "Let me know if you hear anything more."

"So," Malone said as soon as I'd hung up, "do we recruit the old guys and Moseley for another night-time incursion?"

I looked at my watch. A little after two in the afternoon. Jeez, it seemed like it should be mid-evening by now. But lucky that it wasn't.

"Get Johnny or Hap moving," I answered after a moment to think, "whichever isn't with Sherry. "We'll leave Moseley out of this one."

Again I was going to have to wait for dark. Again I would be taking people into potential danger without even knowing if Colleen was there to rescue. If we didn't have success tonight, I was going to have to admit failure and officially report the kidnapping.

Which would bring in Harmon Cluney and probably kill my kid...if she wasn't dead already.

CHAPTER FORTY-FOUR

It was actually early evening when our caravan—Malone and I in her Jeep, Johnny again following in his sedan—headed out. The town of Hood River is sixty miles east of Portland where the Hood River itself flows into the Columbia. The Hampton farm turned out to be about a dozen miles up the valley, just off the main highway leading to the Mt. Hood ski resorts.

Tracking it down had been easy enough. Johnny had a buddy he could call in the Hood River County Sheriff's Department and the guy knew the exact location of the Hampton property. He provided detailed directions on how to get there from the third Hood River exit off the freeway and told Johnny it hadn't been a functioning farm for years.

The plan was to drive up the valley and see if it was possible to at least scout the farmhouse before dark. We got there, looked things over, and decided to give it a try. This time we had walkie-talkies to stay in touch. Good thing, since the cell phones were just as useless here as they had been in the wilds of the Willamette Valley.

By seven-thirty, our cars were off to the side of the highway about two hundred yards beyond the farm entrance and we had moved up the short entrance drive, me to the south and beside the barn which was behind the farmhouse, Malone in front of the house parallel to the drive, and Johnny on the north side of the building. The two of them were currently concealed in tall grass. Between us, we could see all four sides of our objective.

It looked exactly like an abandoned farmhouse—a dilapidated old structure, gray paint peeling from the exterior, the land uncared-for, the barn that I was snugged against practically falling down. But there was an old school bus parked behind it, between the house and the barn, and inside the fragile barn were three relatively new vehicles, including what looked like the Jeep we'd seen at the campsite.

We were in the right place. But was my daughter in the same place?

No one had been spotted in the windows nor moving about outside. It was unlikely that any armed men would be posted where they might be visible to Monday evening traffic passing on the highway, so we were feeling pretty secure in our positions.

Now the challenge was to get inside and see if I could find and rescue Colleen without provoking a confrontation. What I had seen so far of the True Christian Brotherhood told me they were prime candidates for going out in a blaze of glory—and taking my kid with them. Much to Malone's dismay, I had insisted on going in alone. Two of us sneaking around were twice as likely to get caught, in my opinion—which she did not share, but acquiesced reluctantly.

She was right outside if I got in trouble. Johnny was instructed to go for his car and find a cell phone signal if we both got in trouble. And that was the best we could do.

We waited. It seemed like it took at least three days for night to fall completely, but finally it did.

I heard a click on my walkie-talkie and put it to my ear. "This is Clint," I whispered.

"I think the last upstairs light is out," Johnny returned softly. Malone had already reported no lights showing in front and I couldn't see any, either, so it was time to move. I glanced down at my watch. Eleven-twelve. I alerted the other two that I was going in, they both wished me luck, and then I turned off the walkie-talkie, leaving it behind on the ground. A single inadvertent click inside the house in the dark could alert the bad guys.

I gripped the Smith and Wesson tightly to compensate for sweaty palms and covered the ground between barn and house moving low and fast, skirting the bus as close as I could. For several hours I'd had my eye on a basement window near the southeast corner. I pulled up next to it and dropped lightly to my knees, holding my breath as I listened for any kind of alarm. Nothing.

I had a standard B&E kit on my belt, lock picks, glass cutter, etc., but I was hoping no one had bothered to lock the basement windows in a disused old farmhouse. My hope was almost too well met. The window gave immediately in response to a gentle push and the hinges nearly fell out of the partially rotten frame. I held the window in place as I slipped past it feet first into the basement.

CHAPTER FORTY-FIVE

More luck. There was nothing between me and the dirt floor. I stood for a moment in the dark, taking in the smells of ancient, damp soil and toilet overflow. With my free left hand I fished a tiny flashlight out of my pocket and clicked it on.

There wasn't much to see. It was more a hole in the ground under the house than a real basement, though the walls were loosely bricked. I could barely stand upright beneath the support beams of the first floor. Nothing was stored down here but wood scraps and some rotting cardboard boxes. For a moment I was afraid I'd already hit a dead end, but then the pencil beam of the flash caught some wooden steps at the other end of the open space, leading upward.

As I approached the steps I could see that they led to a trap door in the floor above me. I stopped at the first step, playing the flashlight beam over the raw, unpainted wood. I glanced back at the window, halfway expecting to see Malone crawling in after me, but apparently she had accepted that in this case I was better off on my own.

I got a firm grip on my breathing, tried to will a little extra strength down to my knees, and focused on thinking clearly about what I could see above me. A trap door leading where? Is there a heavy piece of furniture on top of it? Something light that will topple over and make lots of noise? A bad guy who can't sleep standing right beside it? Or maybe it opens into his goddamned bedroom. This had seemed like a pretty good plan until now.

Still, the alternative of sheriff's deputies surrounding the house and mounting an assault was even scarier than the idea of pushing up on that wooden slab. Maybe it would come to a storming of the house. It would come to that if I failed. But first I had to try making it quiet and clean.

I inched up the first three steps as slowly as I could to minimize creaking sounds; that put me in position beneath the door. I snapped off the flashlight and stowed it in my pocket, then pushed gently upward with my left hand.

No heavy weight pushing back, no crash to the floor, no clamor—but the door was almost fully vertical before I began to breathe again.

I held it there as I took the remaining steps and found myself in a small utility room in the back of the house, just off what looked like a main hallway. To my surprise, light shone dimly in through the open doorway. Had someone turned on a light while I was in the basement?

I steadied myself, eased the trap door down, and took a deep breath. Odors of rotting wood and mold now. This place was not in good shape.

A careful step to the doorway and a quick glance up and down the hallway revealed no one. The light was coming from bare low-watt bulbs spaced every ten feet or so in the ceiling. The corridor appeared to run the length of the house, with a couple of closed doors on either side and at the far end what was probably the stairs to the second floor. No windows, so it couldn't be seen from outside. The light had probably been on all the time.

There were two open doorways in sight, the one just across from the utility room revealing a full bathroom and the next one up apparently the kitchen.

Smith and Wesson at the ready, I turned right and began working my way toward the front of the house, checking each closed door to see if it was locked. I was looking for a locked one; that was where Colleen might be. As I tried each door I had to work at keeping my muscles relaxed enough to gently turn the knob and push just barely enough to sense that there was some give, then ease the door and the knob back in place. I was feeling as exposed in that long, dimly lit hallway as a raccoon in headlights. I'm pretty sure, though, that raccoons don't sweat.

The house around me was totally quiet and there was no reaction from any of the rooms I had tried, so I kept going.

The second door on the left was locked.

It was a standard tubular lock. Forcing a metal strip through the casing trim could make too much noise, but fortunately this type of lock can be defeated in a variety of ways. I crouched down and heard the click of success less than a minute after I inserted the first pick. I stowed the kit and softly pushed the door open, staying low and just poking my head into the room in case it contained a light sleeper with a firearm instead of what I hoped.

In the glimmer of hallway light that spread gradually across the bare wooden floor I could make out a bed against the far wall. There appeared to be no other furniture. Some food dishes were scattered in the middle of the floor along with a few items of clothing. I wasn't certain the bed was occupied until I saw a slight movement.

I was just bringing the Smith and Wesson up when I heard Colleen's voice, whispering weakly but recognizably: "What do you want? Leave me alone."

Relief rushed through my body only to be obliterated by what sounded like an echo of my daughter, a small voice behind me in the hall: "Who are you? What do you want?"

I fought an almost overwhelming impulse to ignore the distraction and rush to my daughter's side or at least call out some reassurance. Instead I took a step back into the hall, looking to my left and down.

A frail little girl with stringy blond hair and deathly white skin stood beside me. She was dressed in ragged green pajamas covered in smiley faces and held a small dirty glass in her right hand. Her eyes were big and getting bigger as she took in the middle-aged stranger dressed all in black and carrying a gun. Then she screamed.

My first thought was that I'd almost made it. My second was to hope the goddamned cops had learned something from Waco after all. If they came in shooting, kids would be in the crossfire. My kid would be in the crossfire.

I closed the bedroom door on Colleen's questioning voice, put the Smith and Wesson on the hallway floor, and was leaning with my hands spread against the wall even before the first armed man came running.

CHAPTER FORTY-SIX

I could feel blood trickling down the side of my face from above my left eye. I was hoping the blood was the reason I couldn't see out of that eye. Meanwhile, my lower back and right arm were in even more pain than my head—and the arm was nearly as useless as the eye. It hung at my side, throbbing and semi-paralyzed from what could be serious nerve damage.

I hadn't recognized either of the two bruisers who responded to the little girl's cry and they didn't seem to care who I was. The first one didn't even break stride as he drove a big, fat fist into my lower back. I sagged against the wall as a deep groan welled out of my throat. It felt like he'd shoved a branding iron clear through my kidney.

I was essentially helpless as he grabbed my right arm and twisted it up and behind me. He jerked my limp body away from the wall and toward his buddy who took the opportunity to smash the stock of his weapon against the side of my head.

My cooperative spirit in voluntarily assuming the position didn't seem to have generated much good will among these guys.

I was only vaguely aware of the next few minutes. One of the two men stopped to re-lock Colleen's door and then they half-dragged me through what was now a small crowd of crying and screaming children being comforted by a few adult women, all in nightclothes.

They forced me up the stairs at the end of the hall and into a room on the second floor, about halfway down the corridor. As the naked ceiling bulb flared to life it revealed a room entirely empty except for an old wooden straight chair in the center of the floor. Even in my woozy state I recognized an interrogation room and wondered why they felt the need to set one up in this place. My confused imagination flashed on an image of the little girl from downstairs sitting terrified in this stark bright light.

And now it was me in the chair, finding it difficult to keep my balance even though seated.

My captors either slept in their clothes or had been up keeping watch. They were both in old army fatigues—and both apparently wearing the same size, the mottled khaki stretched tightly on the ham-fisted one and hanging loosely on his shrimpy friend. Military-style crew cuts, mean expressions, and some very big guns completed the picture. Little guy had what looked like a semi-automatic rifle and big guy had pulled out a heavy pistol. I was not in any shape to identify the make of either firearm; I only knew that the barrels loomed large but slightly fuzzy in the vision of my one functioning eye.

A third man appeared in the doorway of the room. He too was crewcut and dressed in fatigues but with a difference: his outfit was clean, pressed, and the proper size for his extremely stocky and muscular body. He wore a field jacket in addition to standard-issue pants and shirt. The officer in charge.

He stared at me. A cruel smile broke slowly over the craggy features of his face. "Well, look who we have here."

I realized his were the first words I'd heard since the little girl screamed. I also became aware that my ears were ringing like crazy.

"You know this asshole?" asked the little guy.

"I sure do," replied Mr. Put-Together. "He's our new girlie-girl's daddy. You know, the detective." He pronounced it "DEE-tek-a-tive."

"We'd better call Father." That was the big one, in a voice ridiculously deep even for such a large man. It sounded like he was speaking from somewhere down in the dirt-floor basement.

174

Our new arrival gave him a sharp glance. "Do you want Father to know you let this motherfucker get in here with the women and children?"

"No, I guess not."

A wave of dismissal from the leader. "I guess not. You two check the rest of the house to make sure we don't got any other visitors. Be careful. Then get your asses back here. No calls."

"Okay, Tommy. We will."

Tommy. That punched a hole in my dark clouds of confusion.

He drew an automatic pistol as the other two scuttled from the room. He relaxed against the wall next to the doorway with the gun pointed loosely in my direction.

"Your name's McCall, ain't it?"

I risked raising my left hand to my face. Wiping blood out of the eye gave me some limited binocular vision. I sensed returning strength in the injured arm, as well. Maybe the damage wasn't so bad after all. "And yours is Cling," I said.

The evil grin again. "Not bad."

"You've got me now. Let my daughter go."

A dry, nasty chuckle. "Oh, I don't think so. You're not going to be nearly as much fun as she is."

"If you've touched her, I will kill you."

He stepped away from the wall and trained the gun more firmly on me. "You ain't killin' nobody, fuckhead. I'll touch the little bitch all I want and you ain't gonna do a thing about it." He smirked broadly. "It's God's will."

I have never been closer to going completely berserk. My brain was roaring with the tension in my body as I desperately held onto control and tried to clear my head enough to think. I knew that Devon or Johnny had to have seen the light come on in this window—with me still inside. They wouldn't wait much longer before calling for backup. I had to keep Cling's attention on me until the cavalry arrived.

"Zoller isn't here?" I grated.

"Father's off doing the work of the Lord. I guess." Again that smirk, along with a savage and bitter edge to the rhetoric. He didn't sound like the other Fundamentalist cult members I'd known.

I tried again to concentrate. "You're not a believer, are you?"

He glanced out into the hallway and turned back to me. "Do I believe Greg Zoller's the second son of God, a messenger from Heaven?" He shrugged. "Hell no. But I believe we're doing what needs to be done." Another glance down the hall. "And there's no harm in having a little fun along the way."

"So what *are* you doing?"

"You know what we're doing."

Mentally I took a very deep breath. Wow. Could that be what this is all about? They think I know their Big Plan?

"Humor me," I said. "I'm looking for some kind of explanation."

He took a step toward me, eyes narrowing, the gun—it was a Browning—very steady now.

"It ain't that hard to understand. We're takin' our country back from the kikes, niggers, fags, baby-killers, and the rest of the New World Order fuckers that run the so-called government in the District of Corruption."

His voice was becoming more fierce with each word. He took another step closer.

"We're the last true patriots and we're saving the world for your ass is what we're doing, you fuck, and you should be grateful."

Okay, so I could have guessed that much. It still didn't tell me what they thought I knew and I couldn't very well ask any more. Quite possibly my supposed knowledge was keeping me and Colleen alive.

"Gratitude," I finally replied, "is not what I have in mind just now."

CHAPTER FORTY-SEVEN

He lunged in and smacked the Browning against the already throbbing spot on my left temple. My vision was again obscured by blood before he'd fully retreated to his place near the doorway.

"You know," he said, "I figured you wrong. I thought sure the fake bomb and that other stuff would get you off our backs. You're an old guy. You oughta take care of yourself better. Must be somethin' about old detectives. You gotta use their families to shut them up."

What was this now? My mind was reeling again and I tried to focus. Something about Crew and Harbaugh?

"Who are you talking about?" I asked. I had to admit my voice was sounding like it came from an old guy—weak and rasping, barely more than a whisper.

"Forget it. A guy who was onto me for somethin' years ago. He about tracked me down, but then gave it up real quick when I got word to him I knew where his kids lived." He smiled as he apparently savored the memory and then his expression soured. "Me, I think it would be easier to just kill you guys but Father don't like killing cops—not even private. Too big a risk, he says. Maybe he's right. Gotta keep our eyes on the...bull's-eye or whatever the fuck."

Voices coming down the hall signaled the return of the other two men. I chanced wiping more blood out of my eye again, but it didn't help much. Both eyes were blurring now, a not uncommon result of too many blows to the head.

The bigger man led the way into the room. "The rest of the house is clear," he said.

"You want us to check outside?" asked the little guy.

Cling shook his head. "Nah. He'd have had a radio or somethin' if there was anybody outside, some way of signaling. Forget it."

"Okay."

Cling walked to the window and stood looking out into the dark. I sincerely hoped that the dark was looking back at him.

He turned away from the night and looked appraisingly at me. "Nah, I think the stupid fuck is here all by himself to rescue his little girl. Ain't that sweet."

"Yeah. Real sweet."

"*She's* sweet. That's for sure. What's your little girl's name, Daddy? She won't tell me. How am I supposed to make with the pillow talk if I don't know her name? That ain't very...."

The blur in my eyes went red and I was essentially blind as I launched myself across the room in his direction. It was not a move I would have approved in any of my students, but I was 'way beyond the trained-martial-artist state of mind. Mindless, vicious attack animal would more closely describe it.

Like most violent animals, all I accomplished was a few seconds of mayhem. I don't think I even got to Tommy Cling; it must have been the big man who intercepted me with that beefy fist of his. The blow took me off my feet and laid me out on the floor toward the chair. Oddly enough, it didn't knock me unconscious; it cleared my vision and even my head a bit. I was sharply aware that I'd added a split lip and loose tooth to my inventory of injuries as Cling's henchmen picked me up and slammed me back into the chair.

The new-found lucidity did not reduce my rage; it simply refined it. I glared my loathing across the room precisely into his eyes.

"There aren't enough guns in the world to keep me away from you, Cling."

180

He laughed but looked away. "We got plenty enough guns, McCall—and that ain't all." He waved the Browning in my direction. "We got your kid and we can take care of everybody else you know if we have to." He brought his eyes back to my face. "You get out of here alive and you're going to keep your fucking mouth shut or else. You got *nothin'* to threaten me with!"

At that moment I sensed a movement in the doorway and heard a familiar voice: "Maybe something, asshole. Drop the guns."

Devon Malone followed the barrel of her Glock into the room as my three captors froze in astonishment.

Cling's two cohorts dropped their weapons as instructed and turned slowly, hands up, to face Malone. Cling meanwhile leaned down to place his Browning carefully on the floor and, as he straightened up, sidled further along the wall from the doorway so that he could keep all of us in sight. His hands were away from his body but it didn't look like surrender to me.

He scowled at the other two. "You dumb fucks."

The smaller man shook his head, eyes frightened wide. "The house was clear, Tommy. I swear to God it was."

"Motherfucking dumb fucks."

My mental acuity was nowhere near crystalline, but it looked to me like Devon was leaving herself vulnerable. She had Cling on her left against the wall and the two henchmen right of center near the middle of the room. She must have seen the same thing.

She waved the gun at Cling. "Okay, you move over there with them. I want the three of you standing together. Right now."

But it was too late. The little guy apparently decided he needed to redeem himself for letting an intruder into the house. He let loose with a strangled shout as he suddenly charged Malone.

CHAPTER FORTY-EIGHT

It's almost impossible to describe being totally in a moment of violence; there is nothing in the universe but your moving body and what's before your eyes. No pain. No hesitation. Afterward, I can remember it as if it were a sequence of observations and events—but in fact it is as all-at-once as life ever gets.

Devon's attention turned entirely to the two on her right as she fired at the charging body. I was already diving at Cling as I saw his hand go behind his back under the jacket. Riding as I was on adrenaline and little real fitness, I knew I had one chance only; no choice but to do all I could with it. Just as his second pistol came flashing into view I hit his neck with a left-hand straight-finger thrust just below and to the left of his chin, all my weight and momentum behind the blow. I felt the larynx give way and his body go limp even as the impact of my body slammed it into the wall. The gun went flying and hit the floor at about the same time the two of us did.

I was lying half on top of and face to face with Cling as he tried desperately to get air through a crushed windpipe. I glanced up to see that Malone had the big man covered; apparently that one had never moved. The little guy was writhing on the floor at her feet, emitting weak half-screams as he pulled at his stomach trying to remove the bullet.

I looked back down at Tommy Cling. He was having no luck with that air, his lips bluing starkly against whitening skin. There was still awareness in the eyes as they met mine, awareness and raw hatred.

"I never knew anything about your plans," I said as slowly and distinctly as I could. "I was looking for that kid that you took from Alaska a long time ago. You had it all wrong, you dumb fuck."

His eyes widened even as they began to glaze over. Ever hear somebody try to laugh with a crushed windpipe? Be glad.

And then he was dead.

"You okay?" Malone asked.

I started struggling to my feet. "I'll live—which is more than I can say for this bastard. What are you doing in here? You were supposed to stay put outside. Did you call for back-up?"

"Johnny called them when we heard a scream. I decided not to wait. Does that really surprise you?"

I leaned against the wall above Cling's body trying to catch my breath and lose the dizziness. "No. It pisses me off. But thanks, anyway."

"You're welcome. Who screamed?"

"A little girl downstairs who got up in the middle of the night to get a drink of water and saw a monster all dressed in black and carrying a gun."

"Got ya."

I glanced down at the wounded man who had subsided into a series of faint moans. "He doesn't look good."

"You wouldn't either if you were gut shot."

I half-staggered over to my partner and put a hand on her shoulder. "Really. Thanks for having my back."

I felt her shrug. "I've always got your back."

We were still standing there together when I heard the crash of the front door breaking down. "Hood River Sheriff!" came a loud voice followed by a few faint screams of children and the same voice yelling, "Kids! There are kids in here! Watch your fire!"

Heavy boots came rumbling up the stairs. I stepped a little away from Malone and she timed it so that she was placing the rifle on the floor just as the first deputy stepped through the doorway. She straightened up carefully and we both raised our hands, although my right one didn't want to come up very high.

He took in the scene as he was joined by several other heavily armed deputies in flak jackets.

"My name is Clint McCall," I said, "and this is my partner Devon Malone. We're private detectives. Our associate outside is the one who called you."

There was a semi-automatic on me, another on the big man, a third on the wounded man, and a fourth on Malone. None of the weapons wavered. "Prove it," said the first deputy, who was covering me.

"I'm going to reach for my wallet," I said.

He nodded. "Very slowly."

My left hand was only halfway down, about level with the right, when Johnny Crew appeared in the doorway, followed immediately by another sheriff's deputy, a man older than the others I'd seen. "There they are," Crew said as he pointed to me and Malone.

"Okay, Jim," announced the older deputy. "That's McCall and Malone. They're good."

The weapon pointed at me, apparently held by Deputy Jim, was lowered abruptly.

I looked at Crew. "Colleen?"

"Medics are checking her out downstairs. I think she's okay. Shook up."

With that news my adrenaline level began to drop precipitously and I felt myself swaying. The headache and tinnitus came raging back into my awareness. The rest of my injuries had to be close behind.

"I've got to get down there," I hissed as Malone stepped to my side and took the good arm. "I have to see Colleen before I lose it."

"Let's go," she said as she moved me toward the door.

185

I went down the stairs and into the front room on pure will, held up by Malone and followed by Johnny. It was there the deputies had gathered the women and children, two adults and about a dozen kids ranging in age from five or six to thirteen or fourteen. There was no missing the blanket-wrapped figure huddled on the edge of the group.

"Daddy!" She threw the blanket aside, broke across the room, and caught me in a bear hug that reminded my injured back to hurt like hell. I would have gone down, I think, if Devon hadn't still been there.

I held my daughter with my right arm as best I could. "You okay?" I groaned as she buried her face in my shoulder.

She pulled back and stared at me. Her face was pale and drawn, her eyes glistening. "I'm okay," she said, "but you look like shit."

Malone snorted and let my arm go so that I could get both hands up on Colleen's shoulders, gripping hard. "Are you *sure* you're okay? They didn't...?"

She shuddered a little. "Rape me? No...but I'm pretty sure they'd have gotten around to it. There was this one guy named Tommy...."

"He's dead."

She collapsed against me again. "Good," she murmured faintly. "I shouldn't, but...."

I put my hand gently on her hair. "I know."

Over Colleen's shoulder I could see the little girl in the smiley-face pajamas who had originally raised the alarm. She had one arm around another little girl and was clutching a ragged stuffed lion in the other. She and her friend looked utterly lost. There was a huddle of older girls off in the corner. Maybe....

I called out, "Is Noelle here?" No response. Then, on impulse, "Is Trisha here?"

186

For a moment it appeared no one was going to respond to that call, either, but then from off to my left I saw a frail-looking dark-haired kid coming timidly toward us. She wore only shorts and a tee-shirt, spindly arms and legs seeming far too exposed.

She stopped six feet away, looking as if she might have simply run out of strength at that point.

"Trisha?" I asked. I did my best to smile. "I just wanted to see if you were all right."

"I'm Trisha," she said. "Do you know where my mom is? I want to see her."

My throat locked right up, no words coming in answer to the query I should have expected. I wanted to go to her, hold her as I was my own daughter, but figured that she didn't need a bloody black-clad stranger reaching out for her right now. I stayed put while Malone, reading my mind as usual, walked very slowly over to the girl and crouched down in front of her, putting them eye to eye.

"Your mother was at the hospital," she said gently. "She was really sick, but she wanted me to tell you she loves you very much."

Children are not stupid, especially not twelve-year-olds who have been through what this one probably had. She looked wide-eyed at Malone, processing what had been said—and not said. Then without another word she nodded and turned away toward a deputy who was just calling for everyone's attention.

Vans had arrived to transport the women and kids to Hood River and they were herded out the front door into the early morning darkness.

I was deeply grateful for the timing, as I'm sure my partner was. My daughter was found. Phyllis Turpin's daughter could have a few more minutes before she knew for sure that her mother was lost.

187

CHAPTER FORTY-NINE

Maxine was cuddled tight against my left leg, purring loudly, as I sat in early-morning zazen in a corner of the bedroom, my first opportunity to meditate in several days. Her steady hum confirmed for me that I had finally relaxed into the joy of having Colleen and myself both safely home. This was good considering that neither relaxation nor joy is easy to achieve when it seems that almost every part of your body is in some distress.

I sat quietly experiencing the gentle ache over my left eye, the soft ringing in my ears, the sting of my healing lip, the mild throb of a loose tooth, the tender stiffness in my right arm, and the enveloping soreness of my back. One thing I'd learned from years of training and sitting is that pain doesn't hurt; fear of pain is what hurts. Last night in the farmhouse I'd been unable to avoid the fear; now it was gone. Maxine and I were free to purr.

It was just past seven on Tuesday morning. Devon and I had crashed for four hours or so while Colleen snugged in on the couch with Stella for company. Malone was still asleep in the nearby bed.

We'd not been held at the scene in the farmhouse for very long, but the inquiry was not finished by any means. I'd killed one man and Malone had shot another who might die. In those circumstances, you don't just tell your story once and get on with life.

Meanwhile, we still didn't have Gregory Zoller or Noelle Austin, though Cling's story of frightening off another guy who was after him was almost certainly about that Alaska detective Diane Austin hired. If so, it was good evidence Austin's daughter could still be around Zoller somewhere.

My thoughts were interrupted by the phone ringing in the living room and it was time to see if my legs would straighten after thirty minutes folded beneath me. They did, but not with any pleasure in the process.

The caller was Diane Austin. "Did you find Noelle? Was she at that farm place? Where is she now?" Obviously Diane had seen the early morning TV news.

"She wasn't at the farmhouse," I said as gently as I could. "We haven't given up. We'll find her."

"You found your daughter. You got her back." Almost accusatory.

"Yes, Colleen was there."

I could hear her taking a deep breath. "I'm sorry. I'm sorry. Is she all right?"

"She was frightened, shaken up, but I think she's okay. She's here with me now."

"That's good."

"We *will* find your daughter, too, Diane. Try to be patient."

"Okay. I'll try."

"I'll let you know the second we know anything."

"Okay," she said again and hung up.

I was putting the phone down when I realized Colleen was awake, no surprise given the ringing phone and then the conversation. She was up on one elbow, looking remarkably perky considering her recent ordeal.

"You feeling okay?" I asked.

"Better. Who was that you were talking to?"

"A client. The client who got you into this trouble, in fact. We're looking for her daughter and we think the people who kidnapped you may have her. Obviously they don't want us to keep looking."

Colleen seemed to zone out for a moment, then came back. "I think I know who you're talking about," she said.

190

"Our client? How would you know her?"

"No, the girl, her daughter. I think I know who it could be."

"And I think I'd better make some coffee," a very tousled Devon Malone announced from the bedroom doorway.

CHAPTER FIFTY

Twenty minutes later we were all dressed and sitting around the kitchen table with the cats fed and our systems busily incorporating caffeine. It was time to hear what Colleen meant.

"The meanest one of the guys," she began, "the one they called Tommy, said something to me when I first got there, something about trading your daughter for Father's daughter. Father. That's what they called the head guy. His real name is Zoller?"

"His current name is Zoller," I said. "We believe it's an alias."

Colleen actually shuddered. "That Tommy guy was a real asshole. I should be sorry that he's dead, but...."

"No, you shouldn't," Malone said drily Colleen gave her a grateful glance.

"That's all, just the daughter for daughter comment?" I asked.

"Well, partly it was the way he said it, sort of sarcastic, like the daughter wasn't *really* a daughter."

"Which one of the girls was he talking about?" Malone asked.

"That's the thing. None of the girls that you guys saw last night. She must have left before you got there. I saw her with Father—Zoller, whoever—yesterday morning. Tommy brought him to my room, I guess just so he could see what I looked like. He had this young girl with him, eleven or twelve years old I think. She had long dark hair and he called her Kimberly. He and Tommy both treated her like she could be his daughter—different from how the other girls were treated, anyway."

"Kimberly," I said. "Not Noelle?"

"No, definitely Kimberly."

"Did she say anything?" asked Malone.

"She didn't say a word. She just stared at me. The leader guy said something to her.... He said something like, 'This creature'—he called me a creature; I remember that—'doesn't follow the ways of the Lord and she must pay for her sins.' He told her to remember that lesson. Then they went away. I guess they left entirely, since they weren't there last night."

"Anything else you can remember about her?" I asked.

Colleen paused to think about that for a moment. "Not much. She looked really thin and pale, kind of low energy. You know?"

Just then we were interrupted by a knock on the front door. I opened it to find Hoke Moseley standing there again.

"We have to find Colleen," he said. "Do you have anything new, any leads at all? Why are you just sitting around here?"

I stood back and gestured for him to enter. "She's in the kitchen," I said. "We found her last night."

First his mouth dropped open, then he grinned, and then he frowned. "That's great, but why the hell didn't you tell me? Where was she? Is she all right?"

"She's fine. I wasn't aware that I needed to keep you informed, but go on in and hear about the rest of it from her if you want to."

He stepped inside and took a breath. "Look," he said, "I know you don't have any reason to trust me, but I care about Colleen."

"Okay."

He locked eyes with me, his expression fixed in its intensity. "I told Bobby not to use a gun. I told him it would get him killed."

That was the last thing I expected to hear at that moment. "Okay," I said again, waiting to see where we were going with this.

"I guess it was the way he had to do it," Moseley went on, then paused for what seemed like a long time. "My mom doesn't want to hear me say that." He looked again at me. "You know how moms are."

"Yeah, I know. I'm sorry."

He heaved a deep sigh. "Me too. It wasn't your fault." Then he shook himself and looked toward the kitchen door. "You sure it's okay if I go talk to Colleen?"

I took a slow, deep breath but felt no need to sigh. It was as if a great weight had been lifted after a very long time. "Yeah," I said, "go ahead."

CHAPTER FIFTY-ONE

I had a touch of tinnitus again, this time from a phone receiver being slammed down in my ear. Albert Zualaga, grocery chain magnate extraordinaire, did not like being told to stick his store security up his ass. I had tried to be nice about it, explaining that a current case was going to take more of our time than we had anticipated, that of course I'd return his advance, and that I could recommend several good—if not equal—alternatives to our agency. It was about two minutes into his rant about irresponsible, low-class private dicks when I suggested the above-mentioned placement— at which point he terminated the conversation with a bang. Hell, I'd return his advance anyway. Later maybe I'd go shoplift at one of his stores.

I looked across the partners desk at Malone who seemed to be suppressing a grin.

"One less client to worry about," I said.

"I thought you handled that well," she responded with a chuckle. She'd have probably suggested something far more obscene than I had. "We have plenty to do, like you told him." She shrugged. "We may be dealing with yet another crazy person, as usual, but at least this time the client we do have is paying good money for it."

"True. So now we need to think of something productive to do for said client. We had three specific leads on the True Christian Brotherhood: the Salem office, the Willamette Valley camp and the Hood River farmhouse. We don't have a fourth. All we know for sure is that Zoller had a young girl named Kimberly with him, that Kimberly might be Noelle Austin, and that the Brotherhood has something big planned that they think we're onto."

"What about this Kimberly kid?" asked Malone. "I was poking around a little on the Internet while you were telling Zualaga to stuff it, but I couldn't find anything on a Kimberly Zoller."

I stood up. "Let me go see if Eleanor's got time to do a search."

"You invested in all the high-priced private eye search engines, databases, whatever, and they're all installed on your accountant's computer. Doesn't that strike you as strange?"

"She's *our* accountant and our computer expert. Do you want to learn how to do searches that require a dozen or more parameters? I don't."

Malone waved me off. "Ah, go see what she can do—if she's not busy cheating the government."

I had to laugh. "You girls really ought to go have a spa day together or something, get to know each other better, maybe even become friends."

My partner stared at me in obvious mortification. "A spa day? Are you fucking kidding me?"

I was still laughing as I walked down the hall to Eleanor's office.

CHAPTER FIFTY-TWO

I tapped lightly on the frosted glass of Eleanor Ivory Accountancy as I eased the door open and stuck my head into the room. Eleanor was alone, apparently deep in some client's financial records. Stacks of paper covered the top of her desk. Her lips were still pursed in concentration as she glanced up and waved me in.

She was wearing a simple white pullover knit shirt, hair pulled back in a ponytail and make-up more understated than usual. Definitely working-girl mode this afternoon.

There was something else different. I ran my eyes over the office as I settled into one of her comfortably padded visitor's chairs. The usual array of dolls filled the shelves behind her head...ah, she had changed her hair color. It was distinctly lighter than the full-bodied blond she usually favored, not as far toward the white end of the spectrum as Diane Austin's. In fact, it looked almost gray under the fluorescent light of the office. Probably better not to mention that.

I indicated her work surface. "Big job?"

She punched up a total on her calculator and sat back with a heavy sigh. "This guy has an audit scheduled tomorrow and I'm trying to come up with some explanation of why so much of his corporation's money found its way into his personal accounts and especially why the company has been renting a very, very nice penthouse apartment downtown."

"I take it he's lucky it isn't his wife doing the audit."

A quick grin. "Right the first time. I just hope you're smarter than the IRS."

I grinned back. "There's at least an even chance."

She got more serious. "You're looking a little beat up."

"I *am* a little beat up, but nothing too serious. I could use your help, though. Do you think you'll have any time today?"

"I wouldn't mind taking a break from this garbage. What do you need?"

"I need you to do one of your super searches for the name Kimberly Zoller. What are the chances of looking at school or medical records?"

Her eyes widened. "We can give it a shot but you have to hack into medical records and a lot of school records aren't digitized yet except at the college level."

"Forget the medical records, then. We don't have time for that. This would be more like elementary school. Do what you can. If you can't get anything using Zoller, try Kimberly Austin."

Eleanor picked up a pen and started making notes. "How young a girl are we talking about? This is the child you guys have been looking for?"

"That's what I'm trying to find out. If it is, she would be eleven."

"I'll check the major teenybopper chat rooms, too, then— the ones that will let me get at their visitor list."

I cocked a dubious eyebrow at that. "Okay, but I doubt this particular young lady is permitted to go visiting on the Internet."

"No harm in trying."

"No, there's not." I rose and headed for the door, then stopped with it half-open. She was already back at work on the promiscuous client. "I also need you to be extra careful for a while," I said to the top of her head.

She looked up curiously. "Careful about what?"

"Threats have been made that we have to take seriously, not only to me but to everyone close to me. That could include you."

"Those true Christian people?"

"Yeah."

She thought for a moment and then shrugged. "I'm not worried. You're just down the hall."

"Not always."

"Okay, I'll be careful. Don't worry about it. And I'll let you know what I find out before I leave today."

"Talk to you later then," I said. She lowered her head to her work and I closed the door behind me.

CHAPTER FIFTY-THREE

I returned to the office to find Malone staring glumly at the phone.

"Anything?" I asked.

"Just more calls from the media," she said. "I'm about no-commented out."

We'd found a number of voicemails from *The Oregonian* and all five local TV stations when we got in this morning and apparently they were not giving up.

"Does *our* accountant have time to do those searches?" she asked as I sat down.

I grinned. "She said she'd get right on it."

The office phone rang and I didn't even have a chance to check the Caller ID before my cell phone went off. I grabbed it out of my pocket as Malone checked our phone and picked it up. I'm pretty sure this was the first time since we'd joined forces that we had simultaneous calls. It was that kind of day.

Mine, it turned out, was from Hoke Moseley. He opened with, "You're not going to believe this."

"What? Is Colleen okay?"

"Colleen? Yeah, she's still right here with me in the coffee shop, but I just got a call from my mother."

"Okay."

"I think she's looking to kill you."

Immediate brain cramp. "What? Who's looking to kill me?"

"My mother. She finally figured out I'm not going to do it, so it looks like she's going to try. Typical parent thing. Kid doesn't clean his room, you have to do it yourself...."

"Oh give me a fucking break. You're kidding, right?"

"About the room, yeah. The killing, no."

"Now I have to watch out for your *mother*? Isn't there some way you can control her?"

"You don't know my mother."

"Sounds like I might make her acquaintance pretty soon. Hell, she already sends me postcards. Can I assume she has a gun?"

"It would be a good guess, but I don't know for sure what she has—or where she is. She didn't exactly give me any details but she was mad as hell that I'd helped you. Really, really dumb. I shouldn't have said anything."

"Okay, okay. I'll watch my back. Thanks for the heads up...I guess."

He paused for a long intake of air. "Don't hurt her, okay? She's a crazy woman, but she's still my mother."

And I've already killed your brother. I could hear the tremor in his voice and I took my own deep breath. "Believe me. There is no way I will hurt your mother, no matter what she tries. All right?"

"Yeah, that's good. I'll go see if I can find her."

"No, don't do that. You stay with Colleen."

"Ah. Shit. I guess that does make more sense. Okay, but you be careful."

He hung up.

Malone was still on the phone, looking no happier than I felt. My eyes wandered to the sunny sidewalks of Stark Street below my window, checking pedestrians for any older ladies staring up at me with gun in hand. Great. Just great. Now on top of Gregory Zoller and Harmon Cluney I had *another* demented person to deal with—and I'd just promised not to defend myself against her. Could the day get any worse?

As it turned out, yes.

My partner slammed the phone down as she stood up and opened the drawer where she kept her Glock. "That was Sherry. I've got to go see Marty Salazar and give him those fucking notebooks right now," she said.

What the hell? If it's not one mother, it's another.

CHAPTER FIFTY-FOUR

"What's happened?" I asked as I also stood and opened my own desk drawer.

An angry swipe of the hand. "Ah, she was looking out the window and thinks she just saw one of Salazar's people on the street outside my building. Shit. It's possible. I've given him plenty of time to track her down. I should have given him those notebooks already, but with everything going on...."

I hadn't even thought about Malone's mother in the midst of my concern about Colleen. "It's my fault," I said. "You could have done it on Sunday while we were just sitting around waiting for nightfall. I kept you with me instead."

Malone holstered her Glock after checking to make sure it was fully loaded, then clipped the holster to her belt. "Bullshit. You didn't keep me anywhere. I chose to have your back. I couldn't take time to deal with Salazar while Colleen was missing."

"Well, let's get it done," I said as I clipped my Smith and Wesson in place. "Do you want to call ahead and see if he's at the hotel?"

That stopped her for a second. "Yeah, I think there are a couple of calls I want to make. You go ahead. I'll be down in a few minutes."

"Okay." I wanted to ask, but I knew I'd learn what she had in mind if and when I needed to. Right now she was waiting for me to leave. So I left.

Six minutes later I turned the key in the ignition of the Outback as I saw her hurrying across 2nd to our parking lot.

She stopped first at her Jeep to retrieve an old satchel and then hopped into the passenger side. "He was there. We're going to meet him in the Park Blocks between Columbia and Clay."

I grunted. "I hope we can find a parking place."

"I think we'll be okay," she said as I pulled into traffic. That seemed strangely optimistic to me, but I still wasn't asking. Not yet, anyway.

The Park Blocks, formally divided into North and South, are Portland's own little Central Park—a dozen or so blocks of open space running through the heart of the city with lots of benches and artwork and fountains and the like.

We were heading for one of the South Park Blocks near the Portland State University campus. Thus my concern about parking. I took Clay to S.W. Park Avenue and turned right to parallel the park, creeping along with very little hope. I hadn't gone two car lengths when a black sedan pulled out of a space in front of us.

I looked over at Malone. "Tell me you didn't call to arrange that somehow."

Her mouth twitched. "Okay."

Unbelievable. "No, really. You got somebody, on that short notice, to save a spot for us?"

It was more than a twitch this time, more like a sly grin. "You don't know the half of it. Just park the damned car and let's get this over with."

I executed a perfect two-point parking job without another word, noting as I did so that Marty Salazar was already seated on a park bench mid-block, almost even with our spot. Two of the henchmen we'd seen before were stationed behind his bench.

We bailed out of the car, Malone clutching the satchel. I gestured at it. "I assume the notebooks are in there," I said.

"Of course." She started across the street toward Salazar—who couldn't have looked more out of place dressed as he was in a suit that probably cost more than my Subaru, every hair of his silver pompadour in place.

I followed closely behind, focusing my attention on the two behind the bench. Salazar himself was Malone's show.

She didn't pause for the opening credits. She stopped directly in front of him, held out the satchel, and said, "Here are your fucking notebooks. Are we good?"

Salazar smiled, entirely without humor, and took the satchel from her. He set it on the bench and opened it. All very leisurely, paying no further attention at all to Malone or me. He started to remove the notebooks, one by one, casually leafing through each before setting on his other side. He had a nice little pile in place before Malone finally spoke again.

"Really? You're really going to inspect each one before we're done here?"

Salazar leafed through the notebook he was holding, set it down, and looked up at Malone. He was no longer smiling. "We're not done then, either," he said. "Not unless I find thirty thousand dollars under the bottom notebook."

"The money's not there," my partner told him. "Sherry spent it trying to stay ahead of you. You get the notebooks and leave her alone. That was the deal."

His grim smile crept back. "That was the deal I said I'd consider. I considered it. I want my money."

The tension was going up with every word now. I could feel it in Malone, in the two thugs standing behind Salazar, and in my own body. Only Salazar seemed to be still completely relaxed.

"Not happening," announced Malone. "You'd be wise to settle for the notebooks."

The smile took on some genuine humor. "Or what? You two are going to take me out here in the middle of this piss-ant little park? Tell Sherry that she has twenty-four hours to come up with the money or it's her last twenty-four hours. How's that for happening, bitch?"

Oh, fuck, I thought to myself as I prepared to go for my weapon.

To my complete bewilderment, Malone raised her right hand instead of reaching for her Glock. I don't know what the other three were thinking, but it was damned hard for me to believe she was asking permission to speak.

Suddenly I was startled by a familiar voice coming from the street behind us.

"Hey there! This is a great day to enjoy the park, isn't it? All sunny and bright...."

I looked around to see Carl Gunther, Sr., of all people, heading toward us—smiling away, just downright jovial, wearing a suit even more expensive than Salazar's. It was then I became aware of several other men, about six of them in fact, who had appeared in the last minute and now effectively surrounded us at a distance of thirty feet or so.

And now I knew what Malone's other last-minute call had been. Clever, clever girl.

"Oh," Gunther exclaimed as he joined us, "and look here. It's my good friend from San Diego, Marty Salazar. What a coincidence that you should all be visiting here when I decide to take my daily walk in the park."

I'll give Salazar credit. He held Gunther's fake-sincere gaze for a long moment, then took his time on a 360 degree inspection of the other new arrivals, and finally brought his eyes back to Gunther.

"What is this, Carl?"

Gunther spread his hands in what may have been the phoniest innocent look I've ever seen. "This? This is me taking a walk in the park."

Salazar took another look around. "With a few friends."

Gunther abruptly dropped the joviality. "Yes," was all he said to Salazar. Then he looked at my partner. "Good to see you, Devon."

Salazar looked from one of them to the other, comprehension apparently dawning. Meanwhile, I was beginning to feel like the audience for a Pinter play. And right now was one of those dramatic moments of silent tension.

Marty Salazar seemed to reach a decision. He nodded, grasped the satchel containing his notebooks, and stood up. "Well," he said to Malone, "I guess we're done here."

Malone wasn't willing to leave it all between the lines. "We have a deal? Sherry is safe from you?"

He couldn't help his eyes darting up at the local crime boss currently looming over him, but he covered it well. "She won't have any problem from me or mine," he said.

"Good."

He started to turn, then almost grinned back at Malone. "But, knowing Sherry, there'll be somebody else looking for her pretty soon. Good luck with that."

He walked away with his two goons a respectful distance behind. I resisted the impulse to applaud.

CHAPTER FIFTY-FIVE

Malone and I both saw the Channel 11 minivan parked a block down from the office as I pulled into our parking lot, still savoring the memory of Salazar disappearing into the distance.

"Looks like your biggest fan is in the neighborhood," my partner observed dryly.

"Alison Roberts is not a fan of mine any more than she is of yours," I said. "She's a parasite. She thinks we generate ratings for her little local news show."

A chuckle emanated from the passenger seat. "She thinks *you* generate ratings. You were her favorite detective before I came along; she tolerates me only because I'm part of the package now."

"Huh," I grunted as I opened my door and got out of the car. "We can only hope she's in the area for some other reason."

Malone was also out by then and stood surveying the street, as did I. No video cameras or relentless reporters in sight. "Maybe." She scowled. "Or maybe she's upstairs already, waiting to ambush us in front of the office door."

We hurried across 2nd with the light, down Stark to our entrance, and up the stairs. I was more than half-expecting that Malone would be right, that we'd see Roberts and her big, ex-hippie cameraman Murray Kravitz camped out in the hallway in front of our office.

But they weren't there.

Melissa Moseley was.

She looked even worse than she had when I saw her at the Police Bureau years ago, just after Robert's death. At one time she had probably been attractive in a slatternly way, but she was long since over the hill from drinking, drug use, and general hard living. Her body under a plain gray muumuu (possibly hand-sewn) appeared to be barrel-shaped and her hair, probably once the ginger now sported by Hoke, was hopelessly streaked with past attempts to become a blonde. She looked at least twenty years older than I knew her to be. There was a revolver in her pudgy right hand. Looked like a .32. Old. Pointed square at us.

Needless to say, Malone and I came to an abrupt stop. I was silently kicking myself. Hoke had warned me, after all, and here we were with Mama Moseley having the drop on us. I hadn't even gotten around to telling my partner about it. Too late now.

The face-off continued for several beats. My focus was entirely on the tension in Melissa's right arm.

"What did you do to my boy?" she suddenly asked, her voice cracking and forced. She wasn't moving her eyes off of me, which was good; maybe it would offer Malone an opportunity at some point. Not yet. At least twenty feet of hallway separated us from our dowdy, gun-slinging visitor at the moment.

Then her question really registered. Shit. Was she so far gone that she didn't remember I'd killed her son? Now she just wanted to kill me on general principle? I was speechless for a moment. Meanwhile her lower lip had begun to tremble. Her right arm had not.

"I'm sorry," I finally said softly.

"He should be here doing this. I shouldn't be here doing this." Her voice was modulating oddly between a nasal whine and the rasping growl. "I told him to do it and he said he would. Then you did something to him and now he doesn't care about me anymore. You've taken both my sons, you bastard."

214

She was talking about Hoke. So maybe she wasn't totally nuts, but hanging onto sanity by a fingernail. Either way, she was not going to understand that her remaining son had apparently decided for himself murder wasn't a good idea.

Considering what an easy target I had made of my partner and me, I was pleased to hear that Melissa Moseley was at least grumpy about having to do it herself. Mixed feelings are always a plus in someone who might kill you.

During these exchanges, Devon Malone had been absolutely still beside me. She was, at least for now, leaving it to me to deal with my past—very wisely, I thought, since there was no telling what an interruption from another party might do to Mrs. Moseley's fragile stability.

I was also thinking that I didn't want my partner hurt by this and that I had to do something pretty soon. I took a step toward Melissa Moseley, which left only about fifteen feet to go. The pistol looked a lot closer than that.

"Hoke is a fine young man," I said. "He loves you very much. You haven't lost him at all." Another step.

A tear, black with mascara, rolled down her cheek. "You don't know anything," she said.

Another step, while I was hoping that Malone continued to stay put behind me. Maybe twelve feet now. Moseley wasn't going to pull the trigger unless I moved too fast. I was betting my life on it. Our lives.

The woman seemed to gather herself together, her lips compressed firmly. "You killed Bobby," she croaked.

Just when I was thinking I'd made a bad wager, I saw a door opening down the hall behind her. A young man emerged from the telephone survey office, moving casually, with no idea what was going on of course. All he could see of Melissa Moseley was her back. He ambled down the hall in our direction.

215

Clearly she had heard the door open and close, then the approaching footsteps. I was moving again even as she started to turn; I knew I had only a second before she caught herself and brought the gun back to us.

Two more steps and I launched myself into the air, a large middle-aged missile seeking one very small moving metallic target.

CHAPTER FIFTY-SIX

I landed just close enough to bump Melissa Moseley off balance, grabbing the pistol with both hands to wrest it away from her. She staggered back a few feet, a yowl exploding from deep in her throat. The young man let out a hearty scream of his own as he registered that there was a gun loose in the hallway.

Without further ado, I pointed said gun firmly at Mrs. Moseley, hoping to hell she had the wit to stand still when I told her to. By this time Malone had joined me with her own weapon leveled. Moseley shuddered a little with the impulse to do otherwise, but didn't move forward. Apparently she wasn't as stupid as she was crazy.

The young man meanwhile had retreated quickly to the telephone survey office, asking over his shoulder if he should call the police.

"No," I said. "It's under control now. I'll escort this lady downtown. You can relax." Remarkably, no one else poked their head out into the hall. Maybe they were getting used to armed attackers hanging around our office.

The young man disappeared back through the door, leaving just the three of us eying one another. Hoke's mother was semi-crouched like a cornered wild thing, panting as if we'd just finished two minutes of sparring. Her glaring eyes darted back and forth between her revolver, now in my hand, and Malone's Glock.

I didn't see any choice but to take her down to the Bureau. No way could we just let her go; we had too many reasons to watch our backs already. If we took her in, I would have some control over whether she was treated as a criminal or a woman who needed help. I preferred the latter and I imagined that Malone had no opinion either way.

"Take it easy, Mrs. Moseley," I said as gently as I could. "We're not going to hurt you." I waited for her breathing to slow a little. I went on, relaxing my own posture as much as I could to project calm and reassurance.

Malone spoke her first words since the confrontation had begun, her voice quiet and soothing but firm. "We're not going to let you hurt us, either. There's been enough hurting. You understand that?"

Finally, Moseley nodded her head slightly. She was standing a little straighter now.

I went on, "We're going to take you to the police station"—she started to tense again—"but you won't have to stay there very long. Just a time out, to calm down a little. Okay? Hoke will meet you there. It will be all right." I caught Malone's eye as I spoke and got a little nod of agreement.

Mrs. Moseley gasped as if I'd just announced the Second Coming. "Hoke will meet me?"

"Of course he will," I said. "He loves you. I'll call him as soon as we get there."

A tear rolled down her fleshy cheek. I was beginning to feel like I was on an afternoon TV talk show, except that they hadn't quite reached the point of holding their guests at gunpoint. Time to get moving while we had our own guest's reasonably stable attention.

"I'm going to put the gun away now," I said, glancing over to get another nod from my partner. I slipped Moseley's weapon into my pants pocket as Malone holstered hers. If our erstwhile attacker went bonkers again, the two of us could certainly subdue her without using the guns.

We finally got her moving down the stairs, a little ahead of us, and I was beginning to think our problems were momentarily over. Then we came out into the bright sunlight and I immediately caught the glint off a camera lens across the street.

I took a firm hold of Momma Moseley's arm and brought her to a halt as Alison Roberts and her cameraman started across the street toward us. Shit. I'd forgotten all about them. This was going to take some serious creativity and fantastic luck.

"Melissa," I whispered fiercely, "you've got to believe me on this. These two will be bad news for Hoke if they find out who you are. Let me do the talking. You don't say anything. Just go along. For Hoke."

Roberts was talking as she hit our side of the street, the camera covering her all the way, her narrow features flushed with the joys of ambush journalism, focused exclusively on me as usual. "Mr. McCall, we have some more questions for you about...."

Malone abruptly stepped in front of me and Melissa Moseley so that she and Alison Roberts were nose to nose. "We're in the middle of something here and it has nothing to do with you. Put it on the air and you're going to end up looking very bad." Malone didn't look away from Roberts as she addressed her companion. "Turn off the camera, Murray. Isn't that your name? Murray?"

I held onto Melissa Moseley while he hesitated. "Alison?" he asked querulously.

"Okay, let's give them a minute," Roberts finally said.

I love my partner.

I stepped up beside Malone and gestured at Mrs. Moseley, whose arm I still held tightly. I leaned forward and said softly, to Roberts, "This woman is the mother of a client. She's having a breakdown and we're taking her to get some help. The client's very wealthy and he will sue the bejesus out of you and your station if his mother ends up on TV in this condition."

I glanced over at Melissa Moseley to ensure that she was going along with this shtick. She was pale and sweaty, her eyes beady and skipping from one to the other of us in a kind of ocular Brownian motion. Playing the part pretty damned well.

Apparently Alison Roberts agreed. She stepped back with a frown. "You win," she said. "For now."

"Thank you very much," I said, and we guided Mrs. Moseley across the street to our parking lot.

The short trip to the Justice Center actually passed quietly with no outbursts from our passenger, no fender benders, and no drive-by shootings. I could hardly believe it. Mrs. Moseley remained submissive as I got us past the front desk and up to the Detective Division.

We checked in with Mike Whitehall and I left it to him to find the right detective to finagle her some psychiatric help without any charges being filed. That would keep her—and me and Malone—safe for only twenty-four hours, but it was better than nothing. Maybe a shrink could do some good. Multiple doses of very strong drugs sounded like a plan.

I called Hoke from Whitehall's desk to tell him what was happening. He wasn't thrilled to hear that he had to come see his mother at the Police Bureau, but understood that we'd not had much choice. He promised he'd work with the psychiatrist and do his best to keep her off the street for the time being.

I hung up and was about to take my first halfway relaxed breath in a while when I realized that Mike Whitehall had disappeared while I was talking. A quick glance around told me why. Detective Sergeant Harmon Cluney was looming right behind Malone with an unfriendly smile playing over his skinny lips.

"You two come on in my office," he growled. "You've got some explaining to do."

Oh boy. Yesterday was beginning to look good by comparison.

CHAPTER FIFTY-SEVEN

Cluney's office occupied a corner of a squad room two floors below. It was cramped and dusty and managed to smell of stale cigarette smoke even though smoking had never been permitted in the Justice Center.

His appearance was exactly what you'd expect of a guy who'd spent decades lifting weights and smoking two packs a day—a type I like to think of as a "fitness butt" rather than "fitness buff." Now that he was nearing sixty and had given up the lifting, his muscle was going to fat as quickly as it could get there and he was a little shorter of breath every day. He was about my height and totally bald, not a hair anywhere above the eyebrows. And he was slovenly. His white, short-sleeve shirt looked like it had been slept in—as did the loosened, solid blue tie.

I found it disturbing that a former girlfriend of mine was now with an overweight, elderly asshole who resembled a badly organized closet. I hoped it meant that her taste in men had drastically declined since we were together.

He offered us a couple of ratty vinyl chairs and settled in behind his gun-metal gray desk. All things considered, I thought he appeared way too pleased with himself. He leaned forward, elbows on the desk and fingers interlaced.

"I talked to the survivor of your little shoot-out in Hood River," he began. "I know it didn't go down the way you said. You two could lose your licenses, lying that way about a scene involving fatalities." He leaned back with a big, empty smile. "But I could help you out with that if you give me the details. I want to know *exactly* what happened out there."

Right. Just looking to help us out. No doubt that's why he apparently drove all the way to Hood River to interview a suspect who had committed no crime in the Portland jurisdiction.

I exchanged a glance with Malone who was about as impassive at that moment as a human being could get. So we'd just play dumb for a while. It's a standard interrogation technique to pretend you've already pinned down most of the story and just want "the details."

"I don't know what you're talking about," I said. "Devon, do you know what he's talking about?"

"Not a clue."

It was just a flicker of disappointment, a slight crinkling of the broad forehead, but it was enough to tell me my instinct was right. Harmon Cluney might have a hunch that there was more to the farmhouse scenario, but he didn't actually know shit.

He leaned forward and I could practically hear him gritting his teeth as he attempted to look concerned and sincere. Already shifting to another tactic. The poor guy wasn't very good at this.

"Okay," he went on, "I hate to admit it but we need your help. Why did those guys have your daughter, McCall? What did they want from you? What do you know about them? Come on, guys. Be good citizens."

Good citizens? This was becoming pathetic.

I adopted my own frank and open demeanor. "I wish we could be of service, Harm, but I don't know why they had her. Maybe they wanted money. Maybe they needed a new recruit. They never had a chance to say." I couldn't resist. "Didn't the guy you interviewed tell you that while he was telling you everything else?"

Standard interrogation techniques one and two having utterly failed, Cluney reverted to type. He sat back abruptly, once again the self-righteous Officer of the Law.

He put both hands palm-down on the desk, elbows locked. I'd seen the same pose on TV many times. "One thing I do know," he said coldly, "is that a couple of two-bit private eyes aren't supposed to be in here using one of our homicide detectives as support for their own business."

Lucky for us and Mike that Melissa Moseley had been out of sight, on her way to a holding cell, by the time Cluney showed up.

"Gee, we just stopped by to say hello and use the phone." I reached in my pocket. "You want reimbursement for the call?"

"Cut the crap. I know something was going on and, when I find out what it was, I'm going to file an official complaint against Whitehall."

Having had plenty of time for the "two-bit private eyes" line to sink in, Malone suddenly sat forward. "You can sling bullshit at us all day, Harm, and file all the complaints you want. It won't do any good because everybody knows you're an incompetent asshole."

My partner, making friends and influencing people as usual.

He jerked forward as if to jump over the desk at her. The tension in his body was so great that I could almost see muscles in his flabby arms. "Get the fuck out of here," he said fiercely.

We got.

"That went well," I said when we hit the sidewalk outside the Police Bureau.

"I'm hungry," was Malone's only response after glancing at her watch. I checked my own and saw that it was indeed a little past lunch time. No wonder she was snippy.

Rather than driving back to the office right away and grabbing our usual hamburgers at the Home Run, we strolled down
the block to a Chinese place we liked.

After we were settled in a booth and had ordered
(Szechuan double-cooked pork for me and stir-fried shredded
beef for Malone, with egg drop soup for both of us), I
checked the office voicemail and found a message from
Eleanor.

"We need to visit the Summit Christian School," I told Malone as I hung up.

She frowned. "Why is that?"

"Because Eleanor's latest research turned up a Kimberly
Ann Zoller who attended Summit Christian School three years
ago. Parent listed as "G." Zoller. The girl was eight at the time
and her home address in the school records was phony, an un-
developed lot on the periphery of Lake Oswego."

"Sounds promising—but you'll have to check it out on
your own."

"Oh?"

"Now that Sherry is off the hook, I need to go get her on
her way."

I didn't want to even try to imagine that conversation and I
certainly didn't want to step in anything, so "okay" was all I
said and about that time our appetizers arrived.

CHAPTER FIFTY-EIGHT

Ninety minutes later I found Summit Christian School near the corner of Twenty-First and Glisan in Northwest Portland, in a neighborhood referred to as Nob Hill. It was housed in a converted Gothic Victorian home across the street from a high-end bicycle shop, the latter being one of the many specialty stores and boutiques that make the area a shopaholic's paradise.

As I stood on the front sidewalk and surveyed the immaculately tended yard and glistening windows, I concluded we were talking about some very well-to-do Christians here. Zoller had not struck me as such an upper-class fellow, but this was a lead too good to be ignored. I strode up the flagstone pathway and knocked firmly on the oversized, ornate front door.

While at the restaurant I had found the number and called for an appointment. I was right on time for a three o'clock with headmistress Charlotte Borden to do some reminiscing about old students.

A wiry little woman with a soft-looking helmet of white hair, sparkling blue eyes, and a wide smile of greeting opened the door. She identified herself as Borden. Although probably in her seventies, she obviously had an energetic kid bubbling just under her prim exterior. I'd never seen a sprite before, but this might be one. I couldn't help grinning back at her as I confirmed that I was her appointed visitor and she invited me in.

The entrance hall gleamed with polished dark wood, every surface in sight immaculate. A wide stairway led upward to floor-to-ceiling windows on the landing. There were open double doors on either side of us, one leading to a sitting room and the other to a library. A hallway directly ahead led to the back of the house. The overall impression was remarkably light and airy for an old Victorian.

Borden invited me to follow her down the hallway. We passed several classrooms on the way to her small office at the end of the hall. The students that I saw were elementary school age and working quietly at their desks. The one teacher I glimpsed was a young woman benignly surveying her kids from an old-fashioned wooden desk in the front of the room. Our footsteps echoed on the polished floor in the absence of any other sound. It appeared that Summit Christian School was quite serious about schoolwork.

Charlotte Borden's office was as neat and spotless as every other part of the school I'd seen, but unlike the other rooms it was bursting with a colorful and eclectic assortment of furniture and decoration. Dressed in a simple cream-colored blouse and tan skirt, the headmistress seemed almost translucent against the motley background.

She motioned me to sit on a paisley-covered loveseat against one wall as she settled lightly on a nearby bright yellow ottoman. A well-cared-for mahogany table apparently served as her desk. The walls were covered with the artwork of students and the shelves filled with books. A conventional picture of Jesus hung prominently above and behind the desk; a large bronze statue of the laughing Buddha sat with equal prominence in a corner opposite me.

"I appreciate your taking the time to see me, Mrs. Borden," I said, "especially on such short notice."

"It's perfectly all right. And it's 'Miss' by the way."

"Excuse me. Miss Borden." I indicated the far corner. "That's a nice statue of Hotei."

She glanced back over her shoulder, smiling fondly at the seated-Buddha image. "He's a very cheerful presence." She looked more closely at me. "Are you a Buddhist, Mr. McCall?"

I pursed my lips, trying to decide how to answer. "That's a good question. I study Buddhism. I do zazen. I try to live by the Buddhist precepts as I understand them. I'm not part of an organized group."

She laughed. "I study Christianity and pray and try to live by the commandments and *I'm* not part of an organized group either. If you aren't a Buddhist, I'm not a Christian." The laugh settled into that delightful smile again. "And, I suppose, some would indeed say I'm not a Christian."

"Gregory Zoller, for instance?"

She frowned briefly. "The name is familiar."

"Three years ago you had a student named Kimberly Ann Zoller, eight years old...."

"Of course! Kimberly. Yes, her father is one who would say I was not a good Christian. He did say that."

Gotcha. "Is that the reason she wasn't here for a full term?"

Charlotte Borden nodded. "That, and also because she was ill."

"I'd be grateful if you could tell me everything you remember about Kimberly and her father. It's vital that I find her. I assume there was no mother involved?"

"That's correct. Just the father. I understood that her mother was dead."

"What kind of illness did the child have?"

She looked into the distance, her face softening into a mask of remembered concern. "I don't know. It might have been emotional rather than physical. She was tired all the time, down and draggy. Almost like some kind of fatigue syndrome."

"And you had trouble with Zoller himself?"

She carefully placed her hands together on her lap. "His beliefs were, ah, more rigorous than ours."

"I suspect that's a very nice way of putting it."

229

She smiled. "You're probably accustomed to relying on your suspicions, Mr. McCall...as a good detective should."

I spent another half-hour so at the school but I learned little else to assist in the investigation. Zoller's "daughter" apparently believed she had been born in Seattle; Borden remembered her talking about that.

She also rounded up two older students who had been at the school when Kimberly Zoller was there. The two girls remembered Kimberly as a bright but reclusive classmate, not really a friend but more a "project." Their little group had apparently adopted her in an attempt to draw her out, get her gossiping and giggling, turn her into more of a "regular kid"...all without success. They remembered nothing of substance about the girl or her family circumstances.

As she escorted me to the front door, the headmistress told me all about how progressive and "totally wired" Summit Christian School was, obviously very proud of their technological savvy. I made a point of determining that she was not, on the other hand, familiar with the term "firewall." I gently advised that it would be a good thing to learn about. Wouldn't want strangers hacking into the student records. Shocked at the very idea, she assured me she would look into it.

I gave her my card in case she remembered anything else that might be helpful and we parted with a handshake that somehow felt like a hug.

As soon as I hit the sidewalk in front of the school, I realized that I had company. One of the men from the Willamette Valley campsite was leaning against my Subaru, a young guy holding a gun low at his waist where it couldn't be seen from the street.

I stopped and tensed, but there was nowhere to go, no immediate cover. My first thought was, *Twice in one day? Really?*

Then he raised the gun.

CHAPTER FIFTY-NINE

This is what someone like Sherry can do to you, thought Devon Malone. *You feel uncomfortable going to your own damned home.*

She hadn't been back to the apartment since she installed her mother there with Johnny Crew and Hap Harbaugh taking turns standing guard. She knew that Hap had the current shift, which might make things a little easier. It was hard to imagine Sherry getting very drunk or being too bitchy in front of a man so fundamentally decent—or so very large. Still, you never know....

Devon resisted the urge to knock on her own door. Instead, she unlocked it and stepped inside with clenched jaw and stiffened spine.

Hap was sitting on the couch facing the door, eyes alertly watching her entrance, doing his job as she expected. He immediately relaxed but didn't even have a chance to say hello before her mother charged into view from the direction of the kitchen.

"Devon! Sweetie! You finally came to see me!"

Malone had to straight-arm Sherry at the shoulders to stop her before she could get within range of a hug. At least the woman seemed relatively sober and as well put-together as she ever was: heavy make-up, low-cut top, and too tight jeans on this day, no surprise given that she had constant male company.

"I came to tell you that Salazar has the notebooks and he's satisfied," Malone said firmly, still holding her mother at arm's length. "You don't have to hide here anymore."

It took a moment for it to sink in, then Sherry took a step back, putting her hands together prayerfully. "Satisfied? Really? But the money...."

"You're off the hook for the money. He'll leave you alone from now on." Thinking back on the San Diego crime boss looking up at the Portland crime boss and turning noticeably pale, Malone was certain it was so.

"You don't have to stay here anymore," she repeated, taking a sour look around the usually neat apartment that was strewn with clothes and fast food boxes. "And you," she said to Hap who was on his feet by his time, "can go home to your wife, with my thanks. Tell Johnny thanks for me, too."

"I'll do it," the big man said, already heading for the door with remarkable speed given his size. Apparently he'd had more than enough of Sherry Malone.

Suddenly Devon found herself wondering if anyone liked her mother—and then wondering why she would give a shit. She turned back to Sherry after watching the door close behind Hap. "Well...," she said, at a momentary loss for words.

Meanwhile, her mother had clearly accepted the fact that Marty Salazar was no longer a problem. Her hands had gone from prayerful to gleefully rubbing together. "I can't thank you enough, Devon," she said. "I'm free of that asshole! Time to go looking for the next adventure!"

"You could stick around here for a while." Malone couldn't believe she'd said it and Sherry looked equally shocked.

"Oh, I don't think so," she said. "This is a pretty small place—and your TV doesn't even work. Did you know that?"

Her brain still trying to catch up with her mouth, or maybe it was trying to catch up with her heart, Malone said, "I didn't mean that you'd stay *here*, with me; I meant...staying in the Portland area for a while. Where else do you have to go?"

Sherry spread her arms with a grin. "Anywhere. Everywhere! Thanks to you!" At that, she scurried into the bedroom where Malone could see an open suitcase on the floor next to the bed, oddly with a greasy pizza box half in and half out of it. Sherry tossed the box aside and hefted the suitcase onto the bed, grabbing a nightgown that was readily to hand and dropping it where the box had just been.

The tiny bit of warmth Malone had momentarily felt for her mother went back into hiding. She stepped up to the bedroom doorway and leaned against the door frame. She watched Sherry continuing to pack.

"So what is your plan?" she asked casually. "Go looking for the next guy to fuck up your life?"

Sherry paused in folding a pair of red Capri pants and then slowly finished the task, thoughtfully dropping them into her suitcase. She turned to her daughter.

"Devon, I love you. I want you to know that. I've been a crappy mother, and I know *that*. I didn't protect you when I should have and we both paid the price for it." She picked up a cream-colored blouse but did nothing further with it. "You hate me. You have good reason to. Part of me would love to stay and try to get past that, have a real mother-daughter thing, but...it's not the biggest part of me. I've been inside for a long time and it nearly killed me. I need to move, to keep going even if there's no Marty Salazar on my tail. I need a wide open life and all the adventures I can find. And, yes, another man. And maybe he'll fuck me up, too, but that's an adventure, isn't it?"

She finally looked down at the blouse, carefully folded it, and placed it in the suitcase.

Malone took a deep breath and pushed herself away from the door frame. "I understand, Sherry. It is what it is. I hope you find what you're looking for."

Her mother paused again. "Have you?" she asked without really looking at Malone. "Have you found what you're looking for?"

"Maybe. Probably. Yes, I think so. I think I have."

A small nod, a little smile, then back to the suitcase. "He seems like a good man."

Malone jolted. "Whoa. Wait a minute. Why do you think I'm talking about McCall? I could be talking about my career, this apartment...."

Sherry just gave her a quick glance and continued packing. "Call it a wild guess," she said drily.

"Huh. Well, I've got things to do," Malone responded finally, suddenly feeling even more uncomfortable. "Make sure the door is locked behind you when you leave."

"I will."

And, with that, Devon left the apartment. Once on the sidewalk she gave the street an empty stare, let out a breath that was more of a sigh, then pulled out her cell phone. Time to find out where her partner was and what he'd been doing. She needed to see him. Needed to get back to work.

But he wasn't answering his phone.

CHAPTER SIXTY

The young man eased away from my car and brought the gun up awkwardly, keeping it close to his body so that it wouldn't be easily seen by anyone else but was still pointed at yours truly. At least he didn't pull the trigger. Instead, he gestured with the other hand for me to come closer. Having not much choice, I complied, necessarily ignoring the vibrating of my cell phone in my pocket.

I wondered how Malone's meeting with her mother was going. Very likely better than my day right now.

The guy was even younger than I'd first thought. At the closer distance I could see the fine peach fuzz covering his cheeks. "Mr. McCall?" His voice was soft, almost timorous. "Father would like to speak with you. If you'll just get in that car over there...."

I looked across the street where he was pointing and found myself staring at the barrel of a large gun that was pointed at me from the window of a gray mid-size sedan. I guess they wanted to be sure I was well and thoroughly covered.

My legs were aching to run and my arm twitching toward the Smith and Wesson under my jacket, but I knew I wouldn't have a prayer.

Oh well. I wanted to know where Zoller was and this would answer the question—hopefully with me living through it. With any luck Daddy-o still harbored a healthy paranoia about harming minions of the law.

"Please, if you'll just come with us...." my polite companion urged and I crossed the street with him, surveying the area to see if anyone noticed. There was one passing car, unfortunately not a patrol car, and the driver kept her eyes on the road.

I got in the rear seat of the sedan as indicated and my companion slipped in beside me, holding the gun on me more openly now. The interior of the car smelled of sweat and stale coffee. Suddenly I found myself aware of the residual pain and stiffness in my body, the aching eye and tender arm and sore spine. All those recent injuries were complaining that they didn't need company.

The driver twisted around as I got in, apparently just to give me the evil eye. He was older, late thirties maybe, and looked oddly familiar; I couldn't put my finger on why. I noted that his weapon was an old-fashioned double-action Colt .45, probably with twice as many years on it as he'd been alive. Must have been passed down from a gun-slinging great-grand-father.

He brought said weapon around the seat and leveled it at my navel. "Search him," he harshly ordered the younger man, who put his own gun away and moved to do so.

I submitted to an awkward pat-down—more like a grope—and of course he came up with my gun immediately. At least he had the sense to check if it was loaded before pointing it in my direction. After favoring me with a final glare, the driver turned away, laid his own weapon on the passenger seat, and started the car.

On TV, the bad guys always drive the captured good guy a long way, out into the boonies. Makes for attractive scenery tracking shots. Creates tension. We drove for less than ten minutes, into the northwest industrial area of Portland, and pulled up in front of a nondescript warehouse. That was okay with me. I was making my own contribution to the sweaty smell in the car without benefit of long tracking shots.

I did wonder how many different properties the True Christian Brotherhood had access to.

The driver again took over covering responsibilities as the younger man, ever polite, stepped out of his own door and leaned down to look in at me. "This way, please."

I scooted across the seat and got out to the right of the car. I could hear the driver's door open and close at the same time and had no doubt his .45 was trained on my back across the car's roof. I saw some workmen loading a semi a block to my left but the area appeared to be uninhabited otherwise. At least no bystanders would get shot if I tried something now. The way these guys were positioned on opposite sides of me, I might be able to drop and get them to shoot each other.

But I'd already decided to play this out, so I let them escort me to the warehouse door.

It was hot and stuffy in the big, nearly empty building. Sunlight filtered dimly through high, filthy windows and the floor was thick with dust, littered with fragments of a white material that looked like plastic. Whatever had been stored here either came apart easily or had not been treated well in its last days.

The interior expanse, maybe three hundred feet by three hundred, was open except for a walled-off portion in the far corner that had apparently served as an office with the outward-facing wall mostly of glass. We headed in that direction. The light was so bad that we were halfway across the room before I saw that there were four figures waiting in there. That made six of them and one of me. The odds were not looking good.

The news got worse as we reached the doorway of the office and I registered that three of the four men were carrying Uzi 9mm machine guns. Very nasty. Very illegal. Probably not inherited from their grandfathers.

The fourth, Gregory Zoller, was unarmed.

CHAPTER SIXTY-ONE

He looked just as he had in the Salem True Christian Brotherhood office: slicked-back greasy hair, bad teeth, cheap suit. Maybe a little thinner and a little more sallow. Again I was struck by how extraordinarily he had changed if this really was the muscular, blond Paul Gregory who'd taken Diane Austin's daughter Noelle.

The office was bare except for the dust on the floor, a busted light bulb in the ceiling, and the seven of us. The glass wall let in what light was available from the rest of the warehouse, but it wasn't much. I realized that the only color in the whole place was my blue shirt with tan pants and jacket. Zoller and his men were all dressed in gray and black. I felt like I was standing in the middle of an old gangster flick.

The elder of my two escorts, the one with the .45, moved past me and took up a position on Zoller's right. That put two armed men on each side of him, a nice symmetry. My younger captor, the one with my own weapon, stayed behind me; at least I assumed he was back there.

"Good afternoon, Mr. McCall," Zoller said finally. "There's someone I'd like you to meet. This"—he gestured to the goon with the .45—"is Tommy Cling's cousin Leroy." The man flinched slightly, apparently at the name. "We call him Cowboy," Zoller added quickly, "because of his unusual choice of weapons. He and Tommy grew up together, almost like brothers. Cowboy here would like nothing better than to blow your head off right now. He won't do it because I've asked him not to...but I could easily change my mind...or direct his anger elsewhere, at someone close to you."

Great. Just great. I made a mental note to kill only people without close relatives from now on.

Meanwhile, time to get to work.

"What do you want, Zoller? If you don't want me dead, what are we doing here?"

He bristled. "Oh, don't think for a second that I don't *want* you dead, Mr. McCall, but in the Lord's work you can't always have what you want. What I *need* is for you to stay out of our way and let God's will be done. If you do not, we can find your daughter Colleen again—or perhaps that dyke you call a partner. Devon? Isn't that her name? Or the old detective, the one who helped you kill Tommy and enslave other members of my family. John Crew, I believe, based in Gresham. Nice house."

I would have sworn I could see spittle gathering at the corners of his mouth. If he started to drool, I was going to become nauseated.

"You see," he went on, "there are many dear ones to be lost if you try to stop us. You can't protect them all forever."

My gut was twisting a little more at each name and detail. This guy knew far too much about me and I far too little about him—even though he seemed to think it was the reverse.

"What about the girl?" I asked.

Zoller blinked in surprise. "Kimberly? Drop it, McCall. She's of no real interest to you. Let's focus on reality, here." He smiled slightly. "That does remind me, though. You should take a lesson from the detective who was looking for her. He went away quite nicely after a little chat about *his* family."

"The guy in Alaska?"

He blinked again. "Yes, of course."

Ah, so this had been worth it—assuming I lived. That *had* been what Cling was talking about. Kimberly Zoller was Noelle Austin. Keep Zoller blabbing long enough and he might give me the rest.

"Okay," I went on, "say I agree to stay out of your way. Then you leave me, my family and friends alone, right?"

"Exactly." His eye did a little flick toward Cowboy. Some uncertainty there, but that was not my problem at this moment.

"And you really think what you're doing is God's will?" I had spent enough time with right-wing fundamentalist nuts in my days as a journalist to know the answer to that one, but I also knew it was likely to buy me a rant. Rants can be revealing.

I won't even try to reproduce most of the verbal poison that assaulted my ears for the next quarter-hour. (Another thing about rants is that they are rarely short.) I heard all about the "real" terrorism—economic assault against true Americans, social assault against true Christians, genocidal assault against the unborn...all of which the True Christian Brotherhood was bravely opposing in its struggle to bring God to the ungodly and divine reckoning, preferably violent, to the sinful.

As Zoller raged on, the Four Henchmen of the Apocalypse remained quiet, their three Uzis and one Colt .45 pointed reverentially at my gut. No doubt the young fellow at my back was equally attentive.

Speaking for myself, I was having to bear down to prevent an eruption of my last meal. The anger and revulsion that I wanted to throw in his face were instead backwashing into my stomach.

This was no time, though, for the sort of smart ass remarks I'd offered Zoller in our first meeting at his Salem office. I didn't know then that I was talking to a guy capable of hurting my kid. I kept as quiet, if not as reverential, as the others. He hadn't given me anything else I could use yet, but I wasn't going anywhere with five weapons trained on me.

Then he somehow got from baby killers to talking about young girls...and "the sickness."

I thought I'd heard it all back when I was researching that newspaper series on cults. Apparently some purported members of the human race had devolved significantly since then. I had a hunch that the only sickness he and his followers had to worry about was the one in his head. Not that that wasn't scary enough.

"We're at war with the baby butchers," he said, "because every one of the unborn has the potential to serve God and we cannot allow the murderers to deny God His servants. We will destroy the perverts and blasphemers in the fires of hell." He paused and screwed up his face into what he must have thought was a fierce expression; in fact, it just looked like a screwed-up face. "As for you and yours, I'm not going to forget that you denied God some of his servants when you attacked our sanctuary in the Hood River Valley. After we've done what we must do, there may yet be a day of reckoning for that.

"You took away part of my family, McCall,"--his voice was cracking—"sweet and tender young wives, beautiful virgin girls who could have borne even more of the blessed to serve God." Now I couldn't tell if he was going to cry or drool on himself. His eyes were gleaming with what might have been tears of zeal...or maybe lust.

I could feel sweat beading on my forehead and I really was very close to throwing up. He wasn't talking about the adult women I'd seen in that house. I clamped down even harder on my own murderous impulses; I was not going to get myself killed in this lousy warehouse.

"Do you know how important it is to protect the pure and holy vessels of God's future servants, McCall? No, of course you don't. You're an unbeliever, a pagan atheist collaborator. I'll *tell* you how important it is!" He gestured to either side. "Do you see these men? Do you see *me*? We are being punished by God! Punished because we too were collaborators through our inaction! A sickness has been visited upon our whole family and the only cure is to act! That's why I cannot let you stand between us and our goal. We've spent many months preparing, gathering materials, rehearsing, making sure our plan will work —and it *will* work, it is a *grand* plan, and it will show the world that the so-called government has declared war on unborn babies, is slaughtering God's children, and must pay the price!"

By this time, Zoller's face was mottled and he seemed to be running out of breath. There was a long pause, then he peremptorily motioned that I be taken away. He'd not asked for a response and I'd not dared offer one.

"Cowboy" and his more well-mannered partner escorted me to their car and drove me back downtown. My Smith and Wesson was returned, unloaded, and I was let out a half-block from the office. The only words spoken on the entire trip came from Tommy Cling's cousin as I was exiting the sedan: "I'll see you again, McCall."

CHAPTER SIXTY-TWO

Devon Malone was on her side of the partners desk when I opened the office door at quarter to five. She rose halfway out of her seat, then settled back and gave me a glare.

"Where have you been? And why the hell haven't you been answering your phone?"

I realized then that I'd actually felt my phone vibrating several more times during my confrontation with Zoller, but I'd been too concerned about surviving to pay attention.

"I'm sorry," I said as I hung up my jacket. I sat down and retrieved a box of bullets the drawer to reload my weapon before stowing it. "I was tied up listening to Gregory Zoller rant about perverts and baby killers."

That almost brought her out of her seat again. "What? You talked to Zoller on your own, with no back up? How did you find him?"

I closed the drawer, beginning to relax for the first time in what seemed like a long while. "He found me, or a couple of his goons did, and I was escorted into his presence—in a warehouse in Northwest this time. I wasn't literally tied up, but at one point I was covered by five guns."

"Shit. How did you get away?"

"I didn't. He gave me a good talking-to and then let me go."

Malone squinted at me for a moment as if she were doubting my sanity—not for the first time, probably. "A talking-to? What exactly did he talk about?"

"Oh, you know. Un-American deviants who are somehow making him and his people sick, perverts and baby killers like I said. God. He mentioned Him several times. Threatened me and everybody I care about. Still seems to think we know all about his plans." I paused. "Honestly, I don't know what the fuck he thought he was talking about or why he had me brought before him just to repeat himself."

"Here's an even better question. If he has all these big important plans and he thinks we're such a threat, why doesn't he try to kill us? Or maybe he figures he can talk you to death?"

"That is an excellent question. There was that one 'bomb' under the car, but it wasn't big enough to really count. So I don't know. He's crazy. Maybe there isn't an explanation, or at least one we could understand."

"Or," my partner said thoughtfully as she took in the street scene through our window, "maybe there is an explanation we can understand. Maybe it's all misdirection."

"What do you mean?"

She looked back at me. "If you had to guess what Zoller was planning, what would you guess?"

I didn't have to think long about that. "A bombing. There was the firecracker under my car, the residue of bomb-making materials found out at the campsite, a reference he made this time around about subjecting his enemies to the fires of hell...."

"And you remember a week or so ago that a bus shelter was blown up for no apparent reason?"

"Yeah, I do. I think you mentioned it before."

"That could have been a trial run."

I considered it. "Okay. But where does the misdirection come in?"

"What if it's not going to be a bombing but he wants everybody to think it is? That would be a good reason not to kill the private detectives who believe he's planning a bombing. We pass it on to all our contacts and then he goes another way."

I sat back. "Huh. So your theory is that, for once, we *aren't* dealing with a crazy person."

"Oh, he's crazy, all right—as a shithouse rat. We're not that lucky. But crazy doesn't mean dumb, doesn't mean he couldn't be clever and devious."

I thought about it some more. "That gives me an idea of my own," I said, and picked up the phone. I punched in Eleanor's number and put it on speaker, hoping she hadn't yet left for the day.

She picked up on the first ring. "Eleanor Ivory, accountancy for the masses. How can I help you?"

I knew she'd seen our number on her Caller ID, so I just launched right in. "I need you to check all the local news websites for references to abortion, birth control clinics, pro-choice events—anything happening right now or scheduled to happen soon. Something that would attract a lot of media attention."

"Ookay. Having to do with those Christian Brotherhood, I would guess, right?"

"And our missing person's case, maybe."

"What's it got to do with the little girl?"

"I'm not sure. It's got to do with the guy who has her, though. I heard from him again and it sounds to me like he's planning some kind of anti-abortion protest, possibly involving explosives. You remember reading a few weeks ago about that bus stop being blown up? The homeless guy was hurt?"

"I think so."

"We're betting that was one of their practice runs."

I heard a little gasp. "Really? Okay, I'll see what I can find out."

We hung up.

"So you still think it might be a bombing," Malone said.

I shrugged and took my own look out the window to watch the traffic. "You could well be right, but it could also be that he's trying to confuse us because it *is* a bombing that's planned. Remember that he doesn't want to kill law enforce-

247

ment people, not even private ones, because it would draw too much attention. As long as we don't figure out what he's going to bomb, he's okay."

She nodded. "And you think you may have just figured it out."

"Maybe. Let's see what Eleanor comes up with."

She nodded again, offering me a little grin. "We'll get that son of a bitch and save the kid one way or the other."

CHAPTER SIXTY-THREE

We left the office a little after five. It had already been a long day, what with Salazar and Mrs. Moseley and Charlotte Borden and Gregory Zoller. Malone was not forthcoming about her visit with her mother but had agreed to stay at my house one more night before moving back to her apartment.

It was a mostly quiet evening, thank goodness. Devon finally started talking about her mother's decision to move on now that the threat was lifted. I could tell she was disappointed, but there was no way in hell she was going to admit it even though she actually referred to Sherry as "mother" at one point, just in passing. I don't think she even realized it.

We went to bed around ten, and settled down to sleep an hour or so later.

Then the next thing I knew I was groggily awake in the dark, listening to a sound I couldn't immediately identify. I looked at the luminous numbers of the clock. 3:12 a.m. By then I'd awakened enough to realize I was hearing a growl. That brought me wide awake.

Of the two cats, only Maxine growls. And she only growls when someone is outside the door. She doesn't like any humans besides me and, more recently, Malone. In this case, the growl was coming from the kitchen—which meant the back door.

I clicked on a bedside lamp and shook Malone, who apparently was not bothered by cats growling. She stirred. "What?"

"There's somebody out back," I whispered.

She sat up, shaking her head as if to clear it. "How do you know?"

"Maxine told me," I said as I bailed out of the bed and into a pair of jeans.

I looked back at my partner, who was squinting at me. "You expect me to get out of bed because your cat thinks there's something out back? It's probably a squirrel."

"She only growls at people." I shrugged on a shirt and picked up my Smith and Wesson.

Malone looked at the gun in my hand and threw back the covers. "Well, shit, if Maxine says so...."

It took only a few moments for her to don pants and shirt, then retrieve her Glock. We headed on bare feet for the kitchen from which feline growls were still emanating.

The first thing I saw was Stella on alert in the kitchen doorway. Obviously she'd also heard her sister's warning. Then, beyond her, I could see Maxine in the middle of the floor staring at the back door, still growling away. There was definitely somebody out there—which meant somebody who had come over the high wooden fence that surrounded my small back yard. Probably not somebody who had the wrong house.

Malone and I both paused. Simply going to look through the screen door was out of the question; a silhouette against the living room light would make either one of us a perfect target.

"I think the cat is right," Malone whispered.

"Why don't you keep an eye on this door while I go out the front way and around the side?" I whispered back.

"Sounds like a plan. Be careful."

I hurried through the living room, eased out the front door, and made my way down the side of the house opposite the gate leading into the fenced area. My plan was to go through my neighbor's back yard and over the fence at a point that would put me behind my solitary tree. That would either give me a chance to survey the yard or put me right on top of an intruder already hiding there. One way or the other, I'd soon know if Maxine was just being paranoid.

250

The fence was five feet tall. I grabbed the top with both hands and bent my knees for a good jump, then swung up and over in one motion, landing lightly on my feet in the grass. No one in sight, but it struck me that the sound of my landing in the silent darkness of the back yard was an almost-certain give-away. If anyone else was in the yard, they were thinking right now that they had company.

The tree was a thick-trunked old oak, plenty big enough to initially conceal my presence. I moved softly to my right a couple of feet, giving me a view of the yard. There was no moon, but my eyes had long since adjusted and I could see well enough by the dim light filtering through the screen door from the living room.

Starting from my right, I scanned the area slowly as I edged carefully around the tree. Nothing...nothing... something.

The lower portion of the far, shadowed corner to my left was a little darker than it should be. There was no motion, no light reflection...but there was light absorption. Someone or something was crouched in that corner.

CHAPTER SIXTY-FOUR

I held my breath as I eased back behind the tree and around to the other side where I had a better view. I could see no glint to indicate a gun but that didn't mean there wasn't one. On the other hand, from where he—assuming a male intruder—was positioned, he should have been able to see as well as hear me come over the fence. There would have been a chance to take a shot then—and another when I first stepped around the tree far enough to see him. Either he didn't have a gun or he wasn't eager to use it.

So here we were in our two dark corners, each aware of the other and waiting for a move. Not being a particularly patient person, I decided to break the impasse and also give Malone a heads up: "So," I said loudly, "I can see you in that corner and you know I'm here behind the tree. What do we do now?"

After a few seconds, a vaguely familiar voice came back across the yard. "You got a gun, McCall? I didn't bring mine. I'm gonna kill you with my bare hands the way you did Tommy."

Interesting. He'd spoken only a couple of words when I met him before, but apparently I had a pissed-off Cowboy Cling in my back yard. Either Zoller had changed his mind already or he was losing control of his troops.

If Cling was lying about being unarmed, I'd be an easy target when I stepped out from behind this tree, as would Malone if she came to the back door. I found it hard to believe that "Cowboy" would leave his .45 behind. Time to find out.

"I do have a gun, as a matter of fact," I said, "and my partner is right inside with another one. So you probably should come out with those bare hands up. We won't be fighting tonight."

253

"Ah, don't be a chickenshit, McCall. Let's get it on." He stepped into the light, such as it was, and his hands were indeed up—but in fighting stance rather than above his head. He was looking right at me and my tree. "You're gonna have to shoot me if you're afraid to fight," he announced dramatically. "You afraid to fight, asshole?"

Well, crap. I took a deep breath and joined him out in the open.

As far as I could tell in the faint light, he was dressed entirely in black--pants, shoes, shirt, ski mask, gloves. The American version of a Ninja uniform rather than anything Western. Must have been hot as hell, but what do crazy people care about being overheated?

I could see him getting ready to charge and my mind was racing. I couldn't shoot him if he really was unarmed. In low-light conditions like this, there was too much danger I'd kill him even if I was trying not to. And killing people was maybe becoming too much a habit of mine.

"Did Zoller send you?" I asked, just by way of trying to give myself time.

He paused, at least. "Father wants me to leave you alone. You heard him. No way I'm going to do that. If Father's not happy about it, then fuck him. Fuck God. I don't give a shit. I'm going to kill you the way you killed Tommy, with these hands."

I could tell by his stance that this would be the real deal. He'd been trained in some martial art, hopefully one I was familiar with.

Because it appeared that if I couldn't shoot him I'd have to fight him.

I held my gun up for him to see it more clearly. "Okay, Cowboy," I said. "I'm going to toss this gun—but keep in mind that if you're lying and you've got a weapon concealed somewhere on that outfit, my partner still has you covered. Isn't that right, Devon?" I could see in my peripheral vision that she was at the back door.

"You bet," came her response. I heard the screen open and close as she joined us in the yard. I tossed my gun and that was all it took. Cowboy Cling charged me with a howl.

He was pretty good. He came in fast with a circular punch, bringing his back foot around at the same time, spinning into the air on that front foot. It seemed like everything was moving at once. If the maneuver had worked it would have taken me out right there.

But, of course....

There was an instant as his foot and arm came around that his back was to me. I planted myself solidly at that split second and, as he came further around, I knocked the punch down with my left foot, throwing him off balance. Then I pivoted to slam my other heel into his stomach. It stopped him like he'd hit a wall. He grunted and sprawled away from me.

And that was it. These things have to be choreographed by a Hollywood martial arts advisor to last longer than a few seconds.

He lay on the ground, arms spread wide and mouth open, struggling—successfully, unlike his cousin—to breathe.

"That was disappointing," my partner said as she picked up my gun and handed it to me.

CHAPTER SIXTY-FIVE

By the time Cowboy Cling got his breathing under control, we had bound his hands and feet with some rope from the utility room. It seemed like a necessary precaution given that he'd tried to take me on barehanded even knowing that Malone had him covered.

Then we all stood (or lay) around the back yard for about forty-five minutes before a couple of patrol officers showed up to trade the rope for handcuffs. Luckily, Malone knew one of them from her days on the force so there was no problem about who the bad guy was.

We made it back to bed finally but then speculated at length about Zoller and his crew, spent some quality time releasing the left-over tension, and ended up with only about two hours sleep—which made us two hours late to the office.

I was just checking for messages, hoping there were none, when someone knocked on the frosted glass of our door and started to come in. I tensed and reached for the drawer, but relaxed when I saw it was Eleanor Ivory.

Nodding a greeting to Malone, she crossed the office and placed a copy of *The Oregonian* in front of me. The headline on the lower right of the front page read, "State's Largest Family Planning Clinic to Open."

"Wow," I said, "you got an actual copy of the paper rather than doing a print-out."

She leaned over and pointed at the masthead. "Actually it was delivered to me this morning, right up against my front door in fact. It's today's paper," she said—a little smugly, I thought.

"So I see."

She straightened with a big grin. "I got this hit over break-fast. Didn't even need a computer."

I hate uppity assistants. "Yeah, well, I appreciate all your ef-forts."

The grin got even bigger. "No problem."

"What the hell are you two talking about?" Malone in-quired grumpily. "Is there something we need to know in the paper today?"

"Clint asked me to check on things like birth control clinics and there's an article about one opening this week. Just doing my job," Eleanor concluded a little snippily and then flounced out of the office.

Malone got up and came around to my side of the partners desk as our accountant closed the door. Together we read the article:

> PORTLAND - The national abortion controversy comes to Portland this week when the state's largest women's health clinic opens its doors just down the street from Providence Medical Center Wednesday af-ternoon.
>
> Women's Hope Clinic will provide counseling and a full range of maternity health services, including early termination of pregnancy.
>
> The facility is the long-time dream of Portland Mayor Beverly Rand and State Senator Arlene Clem-mons (D) of Gresham, Oregon's two most well-known women's rights advocates. Both will be in attendance at the opening ceremonies.
>
> Rand and Clemmons first proposed such a clinic nearly a decade ago when they were freshman state rep-resentatives. The two women, life-long friends and for-mer neighbors, have endured conservative criticism and

even death threats over the years as they gradually found support and funding for the project.

That isn't all they have endured. Rand lost her husband to cancer eight years ago and Clemons lost hers to complications from diabetes five years ago. They each have a single child.

"It hasn't been easy," Rand says. "There have been some discouraging and sad days, scary days as well, but Arlene and I have always been able to support each other. We knew each other as children and our political careers have developed together. Our families are incredibly close."

"We always knew we would reach our goal in the end," adds Clemons.

It will probably not be a quiet victory. The opening ceremonies, well-advertised and to be attended by supporters from all over the West and perhaps even the nation, are set to begin at 1 p.m. this Wednesday.

The clinic, which will be open 24 hours a day, 365 days a year, is located on the 5200 block of N.E. Glisan.

A number of pro-life groups have already made known their intentions to demonstrate during the ceremonies. The Portland Police Bureau, citing security concerns, will say only that adequate preparations have been made. They note that Glisan will be blocked off in the immediate vicinity of the clinic.

There was more, mostly where the funding was coming from and how the two old friends had managed to maintain successful political careers in the face of many obstacles.

"Well, that sounds like something that would ring Gregory Zoller's bell," Malone said. "We should give the folks down the street a heads up." Referring, of course, to the Justice Center.

I agreed and picked up my phone as Malone returned to her side of the desk. I put it on speaker, punched in the number of the Police Bureau, and asked the sergeant at the front desk if he knew who was in charge of security for the clinic opening.

"Yeah, sure," he said. "Detective Cluney's on that."

I saw my partner wince and knew just how she felt. But I guess it made sense that it would be somebody from the bias crimes division. If only it had been somebody *else*. "Cluney?" I whined into the phone. I couldn't help myself.

The desk sergeant chuckled. "He volunteered. What can I say?"

So I was going to have to deal with Harm Cluney whether I liked it or not. At least I could take care of both the True Christian Brotherhood investigation and the threat to the clinic ceremonies in one phone call. "Well, transfer me then," I said to the sergeant.

"Sure thing."

After a few clicks and another moment: "Cluney."

"Sergeant, this is Clint McCall."

"What do *you* want? You ready to tell me what happened in the farmhouse? If not, I'm busy."

"You're running the security for the women's clinic opening on Saturday?"

Silence, then a "Yeah" drawn out with suspicion.

"I think there's a good chance the True Christian Brotherhood is planning to bomb the ceremonies."

"What? Bullshit. I haven't heard anything like that."

If you look up "exasperating" in the dictionary, you'll probably find a picture of Harmon Cluney. "There's no reason you would hear it, Harm. I imagine it's supposed to be a secret. But Gregory Zoller said some things that make me think that's what he's planning."

"Zoller? You've been talking to him?"

"We had a little chat, at his invitation, yes."

"Then why the fuck didn't you bring him in?"

"Five reasons I can think of, all of them armed."

"Humph."

"What about Saturday?"

"We've got it covered, McCall. I've got plenty of guys and a good security plan. It's just two dykes opening an abortion clinic, for God's sake. I've even assigned officers to them for the next couple of days. It's not a big deal."

"It could be a very big deal if...."

I let the rest of my sentence go when I realized I was talking to a dial tone.

CHAPTER SIXTY-SIX

"That man gives bigotry a bad name," Malone said as I hung up. "Next time I see him on the street, I think I'll kick him a new asshole."

I was just savoring that image for a moment when the phone rang again. Johnny Crew, according to the Caller ID. I picked it up. "Hey, Johnny."

"I heard something about them brotherhood people," he said immediately. "It don't make sense, but it's something."

I held up a finger to Malone and then used it to punch the speaker on yet again. "Okay," I said, "what exactly do you have on the True Christian Brotherhood?"

"One of my old informants says that they're out on the street recruiting."

"Recruiting? You mean, converting?"

"No. Well, yeah. Sort of, I guess. But it's not like they're standing on the corner preaching to just anybody. They're going after players, the guys who know how to use guns and their fists. It don't sound like they care much whether you're all peace and compassion, if you know what I mean."

"They've lost some of their goons, lately." That was Malone, to me. "Looking for replacements?"

"Could be. Anything else, Johnny?"

"One weird thing. I don't know if my guy got this right, but he was one of the ones they approached and he said part of the pitch was this whole thing about mothers."

"Mothers?" Again, that was Malone.

"Well, you know, I guess there was the whole anti-gay, anti-any-fucking-body-who-isn't-us crap, but they were really on about abortion and the sins of the mothers. My guy said that was almost like a slogan, the sins of the mothers."

An ice-cold shiver washed down my back and into my legs. Sins of the mothers. I glanced over and could see that Malone was making the same connection.

"Anything else?" I asked Johnny.

"Nah. I don't know if it means anything."

"I think it does," I said. "Thanks for the tip."

I hung up. "This is sounding bad," I said to Malone.

"We can't leave it to Harmon "Mr. KKK" Cluney, can we? That could be a fucking disaster."

"No," I said, "we can't." And I picked up the phone once again, this time to dial Mike Whitehall's number.

He answered immediately and I gave him a quick update on our latest information, which led me to a repeat of the same suspicions I'd offered Cluney, and Cluney's response.

"Well, I don't blame you for figuring he'll blow you off," Whitehall said. "He blows off everybody he doesn't like—which is pretty much everybody. There's not a lot I can do about it, though. I'm still strictly working homicide. You can bet he's not going to ask me to help out with any extra chores. Oh, and did you hear? It seems that Cluney and your old girl-friend Joy Castle are thinking about moving in together."

"No, I hadn't heard that. I don't know which of them to feel sorrier for, but I'll think about it at another time. If you get a chance, at least pass along the possible threat to some of the guys he is working with, will you?"

"Sure."

"You have any idea why they'd stick Cluney with security for some anti-abortion protests? He'd more likely be carrying one of the damned signs."

Whitehall laughed. "Yeah, but you gotta remember he keeps all that right-wing shit under wraps here in the Bureau. Everybody knows, except maybe Joy come to think of it, but nobody knows officially. I heard he asked for the assignment, if you can believe that."

"I heard the same thing from the desk sergeant. I don't understand it, but it seems to be true."

"Huh. Well, I'll pass the word along that there could be a real threat, for what it's worth."

"Thanks. Talk to you later."

CHAPTER SIXTY-SEVEN

"It probably won't be worth much," Malone offered after I hung up, "not unless Cluney also takes it seriously. He is the guy running the show."

"Yeah, that's a problem all right."

"So, what do we do? And how do we get back on track to find Diane Austin's kid?"

"And that's a problem, too. I don't know. The next time Zoller comes after one of us, if he does, we need to get him. If we have him, we probably have a way to get the girl. I'm sure he's abandoned the warehouse location, just as he abandoned the camp and the farmhouse, so capturing him might be the only way."

"What about the office in Salem?"

"We can't keep an eye on it and there's no reason for the Salem police to do so. Zoller's not been charged with any crime —yet. I'm guessing he wouldn't go back there right now, anyway. He seems to be committed here in Portland until he's achieved whatever nutty goal he has."

"Yeah, you're probably right. We haven't heard from Austin since yesterday morning," my partner said then, apropos of nothing in particular.

"You think we should give her a call? See how—or what— she's doing?"

"No, I...."

She was interrupted by our phone ringing, the main office line. She picked it up. "McCall-Malone Agency, Devon Malone."

I saw her frown. I glanced at the Caller ID which was "unknown caller" and wondered if it might be her mother. But then she said, "He's here. Just a moment." She muted the phone. "It's Zoller. Keep him talking as long as you can. I'll try to get a trace going." She put her handset back in the cradle and picked up her cell phone, standing and moving away from the desk as she punched in a number.

I picked up my own handset and unmuted the phone.

"What do you want now, Zoller?"

"I'm calling to apologize for the actions of my disciple last night, Mr. McCall."

"Really?"

"Yes. Leroy acted contrary to my explicit orders and he will be disciplined," he went on in the same business-like tone. He could have been talking about a misdirected telemarketing call.

"He's in custody. You're not the only one who expects him to pay a price."

"True, but God is even more exacting."

Huh. Maybe I should suggest to Cowboy that he assault a few officers, try to get a longer sentence. Anyway, I could see that Malone had gotten through to someone. I needed to keep Zoller talking.

"So, how about all your other plans? You have any better control over those than you do your own people?"

"Ah, Mr. McCall. How transparent of you. You want me to let you know if you've caused us a real problem, perhaps made us change our plans. A faint hope indeed. A mere mortal such as yourself can't interfere with God's plan."

He paused and I was afraid he was hanging up. I was about to try another tack when he continued.

"I will tell you this. You have inspired me to focus on what I feel more comfortable with. But you won't be happy with the result." At that, he hung up.

I put down the phone and looked inquiringly at Malone. She listened for another moment and shook her head, returning to her side of the desk as she punched off her cell.

"Didn't quite make it," she said. "The call was definitely coming from within Portland city limits, but that doesn't help a lot. What did the asshole have to say this time? More threats?"

"He claimed he was calling to apologize for the attack last night, but really he was just playing more games. Ended up saying that he was going to focus on what he feels more comfortable with, whatever the hell that means, and that we wouldn't be happy about it. So, yes, more threats."

Malone looked thoughtfully out the window. "Huh," she said.

I waited awhile. Nothing. "I can see your brain churning," I said.

She surveyed the street one more time and then brought her eyes back to me. "I'm just thinking about what Gregory Zoller seems to be most comfortable with."

"Yeah?"

"That article we read about the clinic. It said that Mayor Rand and Senator Clemons each have a child. They're both mothers. I wonder if those children would happen to be young girls."

"Oh shit," I said, and picked up the phone yet again.

"You're not going to call up and ask them, are you? That would sound pretty weird. Why not just look them up on the Internet?"

"Public officials usually have info about their kids well protected. I'm going to see what Eleanor can find out."

Malone's mouth took a grumpy twist. "Okay," she muttered, singsong, "let Eleanor do it." I ignored her further muttering about my Internet ineptitude as I punched in the number.

269

Eleanor answered on the second ring and I explained what I needed. She told me to hold on. I heard the keyboard clacking and she came back with the answer almost immediately. Which was somewhat embarrassing.

"Okay, okay," I said after I'd hung up, "you were right. I could have done it myself."

My partner chose not to rub it in, but instead raised an eyebrow inquiringly. "And the answer is?"

"Two girls, one ten and the other twelve."

"Bingo."

CHAPTER SIXTY-EIGHT

Malone swallowed another big bite of double cheeseburger and ticked off the points on her fingers: "We only have speculation. We know Cluney is not going to take the possible threat seriously. Mike can't officially do anything. And we sure as hell can't spend the next twenty-four hours surveilling two little girls because we have yet another kid we need to find." She lowered her hand to the table, palm down. "So what the hell do we do?"

I'd been thinking about that as we ate. We were sitting in a corner booth of the Home Run Sports Bar, surrounded by the noisy lunch crowd and big screen TVs showing every known sports channel.

"What about the black belts?" I asked, knowing that my partner would immediately frown with distaste. "I know you don't like the idea of amateur friends of mine backing us up, but Bobby Brewster is a big-time corporate lawyer and Daisy Mansfield is an independently wealthy heiress. They both probably already know the mayor and the senator, or at least run in the same circles. They could track down the girls easily enough and keep an eye out, maybe even share with the parents that somebody out here thinks there's a threat. And Bobby could keep Mike clued in as well, since they live together."

She had indeed been frowning through that whole speech, but by the end of it her expression cleared a little. She took another huge bite of her burger and chewed thoughtfully. I took the opportunity to do likewise on a slightly smaller scale.

"It's not a terrible idea," she finally said. "Better than using Crew and Harbaugh, I guess—as long as your friends call us about any suspicious activity rather than trying to deal with it themselves."

"Agreed."

"Are they even going to remember who you are? You haven't been doing your every-evening workout with them lately."

I grinned. "I prefer our workouts, but they'll remember me."

Her lips curved in a half-smile. "See if you can set it up."

"As soon as we get back to the office. Speaking of our evenings, are you moving back to your apartment now that your mother is leaving? Is she gone, do you know?"

"I'm sure she is—and, yes, I'll be moving back. Whatever that means, since I spend most of my time at your place anyway."

"I guess it has symbolic importance."

"I guess it does."

I had to say it: "I'm sorry your mother didn't stick around for a while. Maybe you could have resolved a few things."

Malone tried to shrug it off. "She is who she is. And so am I. There probably aren't any resolutions to be had."

We finished our burgers in silence after that, then my partner gave me a look over her last French fry. She must have been mulling it over the whole time. "You're not going to move on, are you?"

It took my breath away, it was so un-Malone-like. "You know me," I answered carefully. "I never go anywhere. You can count on it." I reached across the table and took her hand. "On me."

She gave my hand a gentle squeeze and let it go.

"Good," she said, and picked up the check.

CHAPTER SIXTY-NINE

We spent most of the rest of the afternoon in the office.

It turned out that Bobby knew the mayor and Daisy knew the state senator, plus both were available for surveillance duty, so it was settled that they each would have a talk with their friend and help keep an eye on the kid for a day or so if the mother agreed.

After those calls were done, Malone and I did some paperwork and talked to a couple of potential clients on the phone, the normal business of a detective agency. I called Diane Austin just to be sure she was staying put and staying safe, even though it meant admitting that we were currently marking time because we had no further leads on Zoller or his plans.

At least the afternoon gave my poor beaten up body a few more hours of rest and Malone some more time to process her mother's departure.

By four o'clock both Daisy and Bobby had checked in to say they had eyeballs on the girls and were also set for tomorrow.

Daisy had told her friend Senator Clemmons the straight-up story that a private investigator friend heard there might be a threat to the family and she was volunteering to spend some time with twelve-year-old Natalie as a precaution. Apparently, the Senator considered that sufficient in the face of a vague concern from some local P.I. she'd never heard of.

On the other hand, Bobby gave Mayor Rand some tale about needing to get a ten-year-old girl's perspective for a case he was working on, so he'd be hanging out with Maria for a while. I guess he thought the Mayor might panic even if the threat was vague and not reliably sourced.

I ended the call with Bobby and related his story to Malone. She shrugged, looking a little sour. "Whatever works, I guess. Considering the progress we've made on finding Kimberly Zoller, namely none, we might as well be watching the kids ourselves."

"Something's going to break," I said. "Reuben will hear something or another one of Johnny's informants will come through. Or Zoller will make a mistake that tells us where he is."

"Or he will try to hurt those kids—or blow the fuck out of that clinic or both of the above—while we sit here pushing papers and soliciting new business we can't focus on anyway."

"Look," I responded sharply because I was beginning to feel exasperated, "I'm more than happy to do something besides sit here on our asses. So what's the plan, partner?"

She stood abruptly. "How about we get out of here so I can get my stuff from your house and move back to my place now that Sherry is on the road again?"

Uh oh. I stood, as well.

"You're not going to move *all* your stuff back there, are you?"

She hesitated, but then her shoulders relaxed a little and her mouth twitched almost into a smile. "No, just the extras that I brought over while Sherry was using my apartment. We're still hanging out. Don't worry. But..." She pointed a finger. "...we are not living together." Pause. "Not yet."

And there we had another tiny step. That was plenty good enough for me, for now.

CHAPTER SEVENTY

Malone and I caravanned to the office from my house the next morning.

Yes, she had moved some of her stuff back to her apartment and even stayed there for a few hours, but—I'm guessing—didn't enjoy dealing with whatever feelings her mother had left behind.

I was moping around my living room, trying to explain to Maxine that I really didn't want to follow her into the bedroom and give her another belly rub on top of the one fifteen minutes ago, when there came a sharp knock on the door.

I wondered who would be coming by at ten-thirty in the evening, though of course I had a hope. And it was fulfilled.

"You have a key, you know," I said as I opened the door for my partner. I didn't want to appear overly enthusiastic.

"I just moved out five hours ago," she muttered as she swept past me and almost tripped over Stella. "It didn't seem right to walk in on you. Excuse me, cat."

"You want some coffee? Wine? Beer?"

"No, I'm done with today. I just wanted the company."

So I didn't mind going to the bedroom after all, though it wasn't Maxine who got the belly rub.

At the office by eight the next morning, the pleasures of the night and commute behind us, we were both acutely aware of the clock ticking down to the clinic opening this afternoon.

"The security is Harmon Cluney's job, for better or worse," I said as I unlocked the office door, continuing the conversation we'd started in the parking lot. "We told him there's a threat. Mike said he'd pass it on to some of Cluney's people. Daisy, at least, was straight with the Senator about needing to keep an eye on the kid and Bobby is hopefully back at it this morning under his false pretenses. There's not much else we can do on those fronts."

Malone hung her light jacket on the hall tree and was unhooking her holster as she crossed to the desk. "I know, damn it, but what do we do if we're still fucking nowhere at one o'clock this afternoon? Listen to the news and hope we don't hear anything?"

"No." I sat down across from her after stashing my own weapon in the drawer. "We attend the opening and keep our eyes peeled for anyone we recognize. Meanwhile, though, let's go back over everything we know, starting from the beginning. I used to do that with notecards when I was here by myself. Maybe something will click."

Remarkably, we got in a solid hour of fruitless review before the phone rang for the first time of the day. I glanced at the Caller ID. "It's Bobby," I told Malone as I picked it up. "Maybe he has something.

"This is Clint. What's going on, Bobby?"

"Just checking in. We're at the mall."

"We? You and the kid?"

"Me and Daisy and both kids, actually. The girls wanted to get together and go skating at Clarion Mall this morning. Since Daisy and I are buds, that worked out great as far as the mothers were concerned, so here we are."

"There's no other security on them?"

"I guess mall security is around here somewhere, but nothing special besides me and our society girl."

Cluney right on the job, as usual. "There have been no problems? No sign of a threat?"

"Not a one. I...." I heard a sharply indrawn breath. "Wait a minute. What...? Daisy! Look out!" I heard what sounded like the cell phone hitting the floor and then dead air. Nothing.

"Bobby? Bobby!"

I slammed the phone into the cradle. Malone was already on her feet. "What happened?"

"Something, probably a bad something," I said and also jumped up, grabbing my gun out of the drawer. "Bobby was just telling me there'd been no threats when suddenly he yelled at Daisy to look out and the line went dead."

She was retrieving her own weapon. "Yelled at Daisy? They're together?"

"With the two girls, at Clarion Mall."

"Shit. Should we call Cluney? Or Mike?"

I hesitated. "We have to give Cluney a heads up, but I'll bet it does no good. All we can tell him is that something might have happened somewhere in a retail space bigger than a small city, but we don't know where or what. It might or might not be directly related to the clinic opening, but we don't know that either." I eased back down onto the edge of my chair and started punching in the main police number. "The fucker will blow me off again," I muttered. "I know it."

"Call Mike instead?"

"It's Cluney's job," I answered as the desk sergeant picked up. He confirmed that Sergeant Cluney should be in the building and transferred me once again.

Cluney picked up the phone and I interrupted his greeting. "This is Clint McCall and I have to be quick about this, Sergeant. We think the daughters of Mayor Rand and Senator Clemons may be in trouble at the Clarion Mall, possibly threatened by the True Christian Brotherhood."

I got dead air for a couple of seconds and then: "Oh, really? Why do you think that?"

Here we go, I thought. I didn't have time to explain about amateur detective black belts watching the girls and a cell phone going dead after a shout. It sounded lame even to me. "We have our reasons to believe it," I said. "You've got the responsibility for security on the families, so I thought you should know."

"My responsibility is the security for the opening this after-noon but, what the hell, I'll certainly take your fucking paranoia under advisement." And he hung up on me. Which was just as well, because we needed to get going.

"Dumb prick," I said as I tossed the handset back into the cradle, not sure whether I was talking about him or me, and we headed for our parking lot as quickly as we could.

CHAPTER SEVENTY-ONE

About five minutes later we sped across the Burnside Bridge and jumped on the Grand Avenue entrance to the Banfield Freeway eastbound. That would take us to Interstate 205. I accelerated the Outback as fast as the late morning traffic would permit.

Malone, meanwhile, had tried both Bobby's and Daisy's cell phones with no response and now was on the phone with Clarion Center Mall security. I could tell she wasn't having much better luck with them.

"Damn it," she said. She punched the phone off and stuffed it in her pocket. "They don't have a clue. No disturbances have been reported, as they already told the Portland police."

The latter information surprised me more than the former. "Cluney actually called to see if something was going on?"

"Or more likely had one of his minions call. They didn't say who it was."

We were both silent for a few minutes as I got us onto 205 and headed toward the Clarion Mall exit. I was dealing with some sizable pangs of regret that I'd put my amateur friends in possible jeopardy. What was I thinking, making them responsible for the safety of two young girls?

"Maybe it's nothing," Malone finally offered. "Maybe someone ran into Daisy and Bobby dropped his phone."

"And now they're not answering their phones because...?"

"I said maybe, didn't I? It's lame, but possible."

I held on to that possibility as I accelerated past the drivers with less at stake.

It was eleven sixteen when I pulled into a parking space as close to one of the mall entrances as I could get.

Clarion Mall has about a million and a half square feet of retail space on two levels. It's not one of the more original designs, basically a vast box containing a great many smaller boxes. There are four or five anchor department stores, a twenty-screen movie theater, ice rink, food court, a branch of the county library, and about a hundred more modest retail outlets. There might be fifteen thousand shoppers inside the property at any one time on a good day.

I hoped Bobby and Daisy had made it to the skating rink before he called. Even if so, it was not going to be easy finding our needles in that haystack.

We exited the vehicle and hurried toward some entrance doors on the north side of the building.

We burst through the entrance into the women's lingerie section of one of the major department stores. Easy listening music and aerosol scents filled the air. Women and children and the occasional adult male filled the aisles. We got some strange looks as we rushed through to the mall's vast open pedestrian hallway.

Where we stopped to survey the area. It was mid-morning, not prime shopping time, but there were probably two hundred people in sight and who knew how many others inside the storefronts we could see. I calculated that we were about dead center along one side of the complex with the central food court somewhere to our right.

"Fuck me," said Malone. "How do we find anybody in this?"

"You know where the skating rink is?" I asked. "That's where Bobby said they were going. It's a place to start."

Malone gave me a frown. "Do I look like I'd know where the skating rink is? Let's find a fucking directory for this place."

I couldn't see anything like that in our immediate vicinity, so I gestured to the west. There would surely be a directory and probably a layout map in the food court if we didn't come upon one sooner.

Two hundred yards further along, we found ourselves at the edge of the food court. It was an immense space surrounded by maybe forty small food outlets, ranging from sushi to ribs, many of them still closed. There were little round tables filling the central area, seating for many hundreds of people, but the current population numbered in the tens—most of them seated near a fragrant donut and pastry shop.

Right in the middle was what looked like a free-standing mall directory and map. We quickly made our way among empty tables to the colorful display and learned that the rink was still ahead of us, at the end of the next stretch of retail stores.

Without a word we headed in that direction. I was glad Malone hadn't inquired what we were going to do when we got there. I assumed we would not immediately see Bobby, Daisy, the girls, or Zoller.

And I was right.

CHAPTER SEVENTY-TWO

It was a medium-sized skating rink taking up one corner of the mall with a single figure on the ice, a boy maybe five or six years old who was currently sliding around rather than actually skating. Three tiers of bench seating formed a semicircle on the other side of the rink. One woman, presumably the child's mother, sat there. No one else was visible on or around the rink itself.

We'd seen nothing suspicious on the way and didn't see anyone of interest in the shoppers who continued to flow behind us as we stood there.

"Well, shit," I said. "We've got one and only one potential witness. Let's go talk to her."

We worked our way around to where she was seated. She looked a little uneasy by the time we got there, probably spooked by our hasty approach and tense expressions. She was already calling for the boy when we reached her.

He skated/slid up to us as we showed her our credentials.

"You're private eyes?" she said as she gathered in the young boy. "What's going on? What do you want?"

"Nothing to worry about," I assured her. "We're looking for a group of four people who were planning to skate here this morning: two adults, a man and a woman, and two little girls. Have you seen anyone like that since you've been here? Seen anything unusual at all?"

She shook her head. "No. We've only been here a few minutes and I've been focused on David. He's just learning, you know."

Damn. That left us with an almost hopeless task.

But then the little boy spoke up. "I saw something," he said. "There's two grown-ups asleep over there." He pointed toward the far end of the bench seating.

"I don't see anybody," I said. I glanced at Malone and she indicated that she didn't either. "Where did you see them, exactly?" I asked the kid.

"Over there. They're over there. You can't see them because they're laying down."

That didn't sound good. I surveyed the ice more closely. Still nothing. "Where?" I asked again.

"Up where people sit."

"Between the benches?"

"Yeah, I guess. You can see them if you get close."

He must mean from the ice, if you skated close enough. Assuming he wasn't just telling a tale.

Malone stepped past me, already heading in that direction around the semicircle. "Let's check it out," she said. I thanked the mother and son and followed right along.

"There," my partner said a few moments later. When I caught up with her I could see that there was someone down between the second and top tier. Then, a few feet later, another someone. That one with long blond hair. Daisy.

I had fucking done it. I'd gotten my two friends killed. I pushed past Malone and ran the last ten or fifteen yards as best I could on the narrow bench.

When I reached them I saw to my great relief that Daisy, at least, was stirring. "You check Bobby," I said to Malone who was right on my heels. "Daisy's still alive."

I dropped to my knees on the bench just as her eyes fluttered open. "Take it easy," I said, and helped her sit up. I didn't see any blood or even bruising so I held off on calling for help. I still wanted to avoid creating a big scene if I could.

She looked at me like I'd just arrived from Mars. "Clint? Where did you come from? What happened?"

"That's what I was going to ask you," I said. Then I looked over at Malone who was crouched beside Bobby. "Is he alive?"

"Yeah, but he's still out. I don't see any injuries." She leaned closer to him. "I do smell chloroform. That's old school."

I leaned down to Daisy. Yep. She smelled faintly of chloroform as well.

She grabbed my arm, looking around a little wildly. "What happened?" she asked again. "Where are the girls? Is Bobby okay?"

Clearly she wasn't entirely with us yet. I took her by the shoulders and tried to maintain eye contact, which wasn't easy with her pupils jumping around. "Daisy, I need you to focus. You and Bobby brought the two girls here to the skating rink. Bobby was on his cell with me. Do you remember anything about what happened then? Anything at all?"

She frowned, actually gritted her teeth, and after a few seconds began to look a little less wonky. "We just got here," she said slowly, as if she were having to search for the words, "and I was with the girls, about here. They just sat down to put on their skates." She looked around and pointed. "Bobby stepped away, a little over there, to make his call." Another frown. "There was a guy coming up behind him. I remember wondering if I should say something. I was about to when Bobby looked at me and yelled. I don't know what he said.... And then it all goes fuzzy."

I looked over at Malone, who was helping Bobby to sit up. He looked even more out of it than Daisy had. "You heard all that?" I asked my partner.

"I heard it," she said. "So a couple of Zoller's people chloroformed two adults and walked off with the kids right here in the open, where anybody passing by could have seen it, and no one raised an alarm. No one saw fucking anything." She surveyed the shoppers currently walking past as if it were their fault. Maybe it was, some of them.

Malone checked her watch. "And all this happened, what, more than a half-hour ago now? They're probably long gone. Hell, they could be in another state." She looked at Daisy. "You said it went fuzzy. You weren't entirely out? Are you sure you didn't see what they did with the girls? A direction? Anything? Think hard."

Daisy slowly surveyed the shopping area beyond the edge of the rink and finally settled on staring off to our left, down the next hallway of shops along the west side of the mall. "There," she said. "I think they went down there. I sort of remember them starting out that way, but I'm not sure. And then you guys were here."

"Better than nothing," Malone said. She looked at me. "Maybe they're closer than I thought."

CHAPTER SEVENTY-THREE

I could see that Bobby was still out of it. He could barely sit up and his eyes were totally glazed. He hadn't said a word yet and he probably wasn't going to be coherent for a while. Meanwhile, Malone and I needed to move.

"You stay here with Bobby," I said to Daisy. "You have your cell phone?" She did a quick check and nodded. "If he isn't back among the sensible pretty soon, get ahold of mall security. They probably have medical staff right here on site. But don't try to explain what's going on. Just tell them Bobby passed out. I don't want a bunch of amateur cops on our heels. Not yet, anyway. If it looks like we need backup, I'll call you and then you can point them in our direction. Okay?"

"Sure. I hope you find the girls. I'm sorry we lost them."

"Not your fault." *My fault for giving you the responsibility in the first place*, but I wasn't going to say that and make her feel even worse. "Just take care of Bobby and listen for your phone."

By this time Malone was already at the far edge of the rink in the direction Daisy had indicated. David and his mother were long gone. I hurried to join my partner and we headed off into the retail space again. It was late morning now and the pedestrian traffic was noticeably heavier than when we'd arrived. We speed-walked toward the next corner of the mall, keeping an eye out for anyone we recognized or any hint of unusual activity. We both knew it was probably hopeless and I, for one, was totally stumped about what to do next.

Then, suddenly, I saw the very last profile I expected to see appeared ahead, a man casually strolling among the crowd. I grabbed Malone's arm as I pointed across the open space and ahead of us to our left.

"I don't believe it." I said.

"What?"

"Zoller. Look over there. The son of a bitch is walking along like any other shopper with a cell phone in his ear."

"I'll be damned. What the hell is he doing?"

"Let's hope he's talking to whoever has the girls and that he leads us to them. He's not here to buy socks, that's for fucking sure."

We immediately dropped a little further back, staying on the opposite side of the big hallway from him. I was torn between feeling exhilarated that we had him in sight and bewildered about what the hell he was doing.

He was just about at the end of this side of the mall when he paused for a moment, put the phone in his pocket, and disappeared around the corner. We broke into a trot. It wouldn't do to lose him now.

We immediately slowed as we rounded the corner so that we wouldn't attract his attention. Then we abruptly stopped.

"Do you see him?" I asked Malone.

"No."

"You think he ducked into one of these shops?"

"Not unless he made us. And he didn't."

"Well, what then?" We moved slowly ahead. Where the hell was Zoller?

Just past the first storefront on our left was an EMPLOY-EES ONLY door that wasn't quite closed. I nudged Malone and pointed to it. "You think?"

"It's more likely than he was shopping for socks after all."

"Agreed. Be ready for anything," I muttered, and stepped forward with one hand on my Smith and Wesson. I grasped the knob and slowly pulled the door open.

We were looking at a straight, brightly lit corridor that extended back along the way we'd just come, behind the retail outlets on the west side. There was no one in sight. I breathed a sigh of relief and heard a similar one from my partner.

We stepped through the door, I closed it behind us, and we both drew our weapons. I squinted down toward the far end. "Is that another exit down there?"

"It has an exit sign and a panic bar, so I would guess that it is," she said a little smugly. Okay, so her younger eyes could see better than mine. The sides of the damned mall were very long.

"Could he have gone that far, that fast?" I wondered.

"I doubt it, not even if he was running. We need to check it out, but there are all these other doors, too."

"Agreed. Exit first. What are the odds that he went into one of the commercial spaces?"

It took us probably four minutes to make it the full length of this portion of the mall, down the corridor to the exit. None of the doors we passed, one for each of the retail shops apparently, opened suddenly to reveal a gunman. Or a clerk taking a break. Or anyone else.

Once we were at the exit, I carefully pushed the panic bar down and opened the exit door. Nothing there but a delivery dock. There was a small van parked right in front of us, back doors open, empty and abandoned at the moment. Public parking began just to the right of this delivery area. If Zoller had come out here, he was already gone.

But where? And why?

"I have a thought," Malone said suddenly.

"That's good," I replied, "because I sure as hell don't." I gave her an inquiring look.

"Did you notice as we were following Zoller that there was one retail space not being used? The windows were covered with cardboard and signs advertising the next occupant. It was next to a shoe store, I think."

"Yes, I do remember that. Shoe store on one side, bookstore on the other, right?"

"It's possible...."

I spun around and headed back the way we'd come. "Damned right it is," I interrupted. "Better than looking at an empty loading dock, anyway. Let's check it out."

CHAPTER SEVENTY-FOUR

"Just what I was going to suggest," she hissed at me as she hurried to catch up again.

Fortunately, each of the doors here in the hallway was labeled with the name of the retail outlet. We quickly hit Smith's Shoes, followed by Tacos and Stuff, and Carson Books.

"I don't remember a Tacos and Stuff," I whispered. "That has to be the one that's getting a new tenant." I reached for the doorknob.

"Careful," Malone whispered.

I turned it slowly, pushed gently, and it started to open. I paused with it open just a crack but didn't hear anything inside. We both had our guns out and ready. I mouthed a "one...two...three" at Malone and on three pushed the door open and we stepped inside, her covering right and me left. The door banged against the wall and what I saw before me looked very bad.

Zoller and two men I didn't recognize stood halfway across the big open space; at their feet were two small, sprawled bodies. My heart sank. Were we too late? Had they already killed the kids?

My immediate impulse was to simply blow the three men away, but I somehow found the strength to restrain myself— and I held my free hand out toward Malone to encourage her to do the same.

"Nobody move!" I yelled.

Three heads jerked in our direction. None of the men appeared to have a gun in his hand and none of them made a move to draw one, which was somewhat disappointing.

I was finding it very difficult to keep my own gun hand from shaking. Relief that we had found the children swirled around the growing fear that we were too late to save them.

There was still hope, though. I observed that one of the men standing over the bodies had a cloth in his hand.

"Step away from the girls, slowly," I said. I gestured with the gun that they should move to our right. "Zoller, if those kids are dead...."

"They aren't dead. They'll wake up and be fine once they've accepted their new purpose." He did take a few steps back, along with his men, but he sounded just as matter-of-fact as he had when he called us yesterday, which was more frightening than anything else. This was his endgame.

"I have to admit," he went on in that surreally calm tone, "that I'm surprised to see you here. I thought we'd done a better job of misdirecting you. But I'm glad. Now that our mission is almost complete, I don't have to worry about attracting attention. Attention is what we want now. You've saved us the trouble of tracking you down."

Malone spoke for the first time since we'd entered the room. Her voice was shaking with rage. "You chloroformed those girls?"

"Yes. They'll be fine," Zoller reassured us again.

"And what is their purpose?" asked my partner.

He actually smiled. "They have a glorious destiny."

"Which is?"

"To serve as my new daughters."

That didn't sound good, for a variety of reasons. "What happened to your old daughter?" I asked.

Bigger smile. "Kimberly shall, once and for all, demonstrate to the world that God is just. The sins of the mothers, McCall, will come down upon their heads for all the world to see. It is a lesson that must be learned if man is to have salvation. It must be done to remove the curse on true believers like us who should have acted before now. We have been sickened by our failure to act but we will be cured by our coming success!"

"What the fuck are you talking about?" exploded Malone.

His smile disappeared and he stared at her for a long moment. "You are an ungodly slattern and a foul-mouthed whore," he said finally.

"She's a former police officer who has a very large gun pointed at your belly button," I interjected before she could shoot him. "Answer her question. Where is Kimberly and what kind of demonstration are you talking about?"

Meanwhile the other two men stood on either side of Zoller, their attention on him rather than us. They were probably waiting for a signal, probably willing to die for the son of a bitch. We had to be ready for that, if it came to it.

"You'll know soon enough. She will fulfill her purpose, as will these new daughters. As will I. Because God will not allow us to fail."

"Yeah, well, God may let you down this time." Malone had her cell phone out as she spoke, still holding the gun steady in her other hand. "I'm going to call for backup and medics. We will get answers to our questions and find Kimberly." She punched the first number on the phone but didn't get any further.

"Drop it, Malone," came a ragged voice from behind us. I jumped and glanced back. Harm Cluney.

He was standing in the doorway, flushed and breathing hard. He looked even less put together than usual. I started to ask how they had found us when it sunk in on me what he had just said. Then I noted three other salient facts: He'd closed the door behind him, he was alone, and his weapon was pointed at us rather than Zoller and his men.

CHAPTER SEVENTY-FIVE

"Cluney?"

Malone had kept her eyes and gun straight ahead rather than looking back. She winced when I said his name. She hadn't dropped the phone but was holding it away from her ear.

"Sorry about this, asshole," Cluney said, the words coming among deep breaths. "I'm the only backup you're going to see and"—gesturing toward Zoller—"I'm his backup, not yours. Malone, I want you to shut off your phone and then both of you put your guns down on the floor real slow and stand with your hands up. Do it or die."

My arm didn't want to move. Nothing wanted to move. "You're kidding," I said finally.

He took another step into the room but kept his distance. "Do I look like I'm kidding? Put the guns on the floor!"

I carefully laid the Smith and Wesson at my feet and Malone did the same with her Glock, setting the phone beside it, and we straightened, facing halfway between Cluney and the other three, hands above our heads as requested. Meanwhile, Zoller's two thugs had drawn their weapons.

Malone was staring a hole through Cluney. I guess she still couldn't believe it. "You're a follower of this fundamentalist nutbag?"

"I'm a believer in making America godly and great again, yes."

I can't even describe the noise she made in response to that.

"Now I understand," I said to Cluney, "how you knew something went down at that farmhouse—but why did you ask me what it was? Your great leader wouldn't tell you? Is that it?"

"Fuck you, McCall."

And there was an opening.

"That's a big yes. So maybe he didn't trust you? You are a cop, after all. Maybe not the best cop in the Bureau, but you've got a lot of years on the job." I took a tiny step toward him. "Come on, Cluney. You can't be on the same side as this child-fucker. He turns little girls into sex slaves, for God's sake. His own daughter included—and now it sounds like she might be in even bigger danger. Is that what you believe in?"

"Stay put!" he yelled at me and then glanced hard at Zoller. "I don't know anything about that."

Malone took a step to pull even with me. "This piece of shit is that sick and you don't even know it? He's disgusting and sick, Harm. He's going to make these two little girls his 'daughters.' You know what that means? That means his *wives*. That's who he is, Harm. That's your spiritual leader right there. And he might have something even worse planned for the girl who has been his so-called daughter up to now. You can't let him do it. You can't. You're a police officer, Cluney."

He frowned and looked at Zoller again but his gun didn't waver. "We're just using these girls to draw attention to our cause. They aren't going to be sex slaves. That's crazy talk. And Kimberly will be okay. I'm sure she's somewhere safe."

Zoller himself, meanwhile, was listening to our exchange with the smug smile of the self-anointed. He didn't care what I said about him; he knew his actions were God's work.

Harm Cluney, however, might be another story and I followed up on Malone's approach with full force.

"Jesus, Cluney! Do you know these fuckers at all? Are you a member of the True Christian Brotherhood or what? Do you even know what this crazy child-abusing motherfucker is planning?"

His eyes were flickering back and forth between us and Zoller. "I believe in the same things they do...."

I kept on the attack. "You sure about that? What, you think you're just lending a hand to some radical political group? You're fucking nuts, Cluney. This man uses little girls for sex! He believes he's some kind of Messiah. Just like in Waco. Only worse. That's what you want to be part of?"

He was looking more flushed and agitated now than when he first arrived. "That's bullshit! Bullshit!" He took a couple of jerky steps in my direction as he spoke, almost as if unaware of what he was doing. He wasn't speaking to me. He was looking at Gregory Zoller.

"Of course it's untrue," Zoller finally said calmly. "There's nothing crazy about doing the will of the Lord—which has been revealed very clearly to me. To all of us. We have been sickened by our failure to act. We have permitted unborn children to be killed and it is killing us! My own daughter will redeem us just as the son of God redeemed us. Kimberly's sacrifice, even the sacrifice of the two men with her, will live in world history as a glorious moment of truth." His voice reverberated in the empty space. "Her death will bring us back to light and purity!"

Harmon Cluney's mouth slowly sagged open. "You are shitting me," he rasped.

Zoller pointed in my direction. "This devil knows! He is trying to poison your faith, to prevent us from achieving our holy mission. He is a force of evil! That's why he's here!" Back to Cluney. "And stopping him is why you're here. You are doing the work of God, Harmon."

"You're going to kill your kid?"

"I'm not going to kill her, Harmon. She's doing God's work. She's at the opening of the baby killing clinic, in the care of two of our followers. She has a backpack full of C4." He smiled a little. "She's going to be right up front and she's supposed to call me when the evil women, the politicians and baby killers, are at the podium. Punching in my number on that cell phone will set off the explosives and God's work for today will be done." He gestured at the two unconscious girls on the floor. "That's why I need new daughters. It's God's will."

CHAPTER SEVENTY-SIX

We all were silent for a long moment. Finally Malone voiced what we must have all been trying to comprehend. "She doesn't know? You've tricked her into being a suicide bomber?"

The son of a bitch shrugged. "God sometimes works in mysterious ways."

Cluney hadn't said another word, but suddenly there was a cell phone in his free hand.

"Harmon! What are you doing?"

"I can't go along with this. You said a counter-demonstration, not a fucking suicide bomb carried by a kid."

"Traitor!" Zoller howled. "It will do no good. I also told Kimberly to call me if anyone approached her and tried to take her into custody! Your treachery will only mean that these sinners die sooner!"

Cluney looked down at his phone, hesitating, but at the same time turned his weapon away from us toward Zoller—whose two followers didn't wait to find out whether he was going to make a call or why the gun was coming around.

Zoller's last maniacal scream was still echoing as the empty space surrounding us exploded with the deafening sound of a gunshot. Cluney jerked back, dropped the phone, then rapid-fired twice in return. The henchman who had shot him yelled and spun sideways, falling to the floor as his buddy shot Cluney again.

Harm was going down even as I realized his gun was flying through the air toward me.

I saw in my peripheral vision that Malone was focused on reaching down for her own weapon. Meanwhile, the guy who'd just shot Cluney, the one still standing, could see as well as I could that I might be able to catch the gun that was in the air.

I dove toward the falling gun, my arm seeming to swim through molasses as I reached out. I caught it awkwardly by the grip and was trying with both hands to get my finger on the trigger when I hit the floor hard. At that same instant I heard another explosion and the ricochet of a bullet near my head.

I had it. I rolled fast, heard another shot and ricochet, slammed my left arm on the floor to stop my momentum and, lying flat on my back, fired twice at the second man. Malone had come up with her own weapon at that same moment, but she didn't need to fire. The guy staggered backward, his chest already blossoming red, and fell. No question he was dead before he hit the floor.

"Don't do it!" I heard Malone yell.

Gregory Zoller was dashing with an odd, stiff-legged gait toward the first fallen man. His normally pale skin was red, almost flaming, like a man literally possessed by demons. He reached the body and—ignoring Malone's command—stooped down, going for the gun that lay beside it.

I saw I was holding a Colt .45 automatic that should have seven bullets in the clip. And I had an idea. "Hold your fire, Devon!" I yelled. "I've got him." Still on my back, I put the last three into his upper body before the son of a bitch could raise the gun from the floor. He dropped to his knees, looking straight at me, eyes blazing wide, and then toppled over without a sound.

Thirty seconds, maybe less, beginning to end.

I sat up and looked around, gasping for air as if I'd been holding my breath. Maybe I had been. I could hear faint screams coming from the mall retail area.

"You hit?" I asked Malone.

"No. You?"

"No." I stood quickly. "Check on the girls while I make a call. Then we've got to get out of here." I put the gun I'd been using down beside Cluney's outstretched hand.

CHAPTER SEVENTY-SEVEN

Malone nodded and hurried over to where the two kids were lying. Meanwhile I punched in Daisy's number and she said hello before the first ring had finished.

"How's Bobby," I asked. First I needed to know whether she'd contacted mall security.

"He's fine," she answered, "not even woozy anymore."

"So no medics?"

"No. We tried following you guys but didn't see you. We heard what sounded like gunfire, though, and a bunch of security guys just passed us going in that direction. It didn't involve the kids, did it?"

"Nobody was shooting at the kids—and we aren't hit, either. Three bad guys are down and.... Hold on a second." I lowered the phone and looked over at Malone who was just standing up from examining the girls. "Are they okay?"

"Looks like they're uninjured but I'd guess they're going to be out for quite a while longer."

I surveyed the carnage surrounding them. "That's a good thing. I wouldn't want them waking up to see this." I pointed at the shooter nearest Malone. "Check to make sure he's dead," I said, and I stepped over to do the same with the other guy. I was absolutely sure about Cluney and Zoller already.

"He is toast," she said after checking. "Same here," I confirmed, and put the phone back to my ear.

"Here's the scoop," I said to Daisy as I motioned Malone to follow me into the corridor. "There are four dead men and two unconscious children in a currently untenanted retail space on the west side of the mall, where something called Tacos and Stuff used to be. It's the only space with the windows covered. We will not be there by the time security finds it." The corridor

303

was still empty and I was heading for the loading dock exit as I spoke, Malone right beside me. It was the quickest way to reach the car, plus we could avoid whatever panic the gunshots had generated among the shoppers.

"You follow along to identify the kids," I continued with Daisy, "but don't mention us. Tell security about the kidnapping and that's it. They're going to discover that one of the dead guys is a police detective named Harmon Cluney. It's going to appear that he killed the kidnappers and died from their return fire."

"He didn't?" Daisy asked and at the same time I heard a gasp from my partner. We hit the exit door about then. The loading dock was still deserted. I held us up for a second, just to finish the call.

"I'll fill you in on what really happened later," I said, "but right now I want you to call Mayor Rand and Senator Clemons. They're going to be hearing about all this as soon as the kids are identified and I need for them to hear from you and Bobby first. Tell them both that the their kids are fine, not hurt, just unconscious. Assure them that you should be able to bring the girls back home as soon as they're awake. We don't want them postponing or cancelling the ceremony and rushing down here." That would probably trigger a call from Kimberly to her father, to get new instructions. "Is that clear? And call me right way if it sounds like they're going to cancel or postpone anyway. A lot of lives could depend on it."

"Well crap. I can't wait for this explanation. We'll do it. Stay safe, Clint."

"We'll do our best," I said, and broke the connection. We headed for the car, running as hard as we could.

"Call Mike?" asked Malone between deep breaths as we piled into the Subaru.

"Only if it looks like the ceremony is going to be post-poned or cancelled." I responded between gasps, turning the ignition. "In that case they'd *have* to try to get to Kimberly before she makes a call."

"Do you really think they'll stay at the clinic and proceed with the ceremony after they hear about what's happened?"

"I hope so. They're professional politicians, which is a lot like a professional actor: The show must go on."

"They're also mothers."

"I know. I know."

"Speaking of mothers, how about calling Diane Austin? It is her daughter."

"Yeah, but her daughter doesn't know that."

"The kid's not going to know us, either. Maybe there would be some kind of connection."

I kicked it around for a few seconds as I backed out of the parking spot, "Okay, if you can reach her, tell her to meet us there. It gives us another option, at least."

She started punching numbers on her phone.

"What time is it?" I asked as I concentrated on getting us out of the parking lot and onto the freeway as quickly as possible.

She lowered her phone from her ear to glance at the screen. "Twelve oh eight," she answered and then raised it again.

Quick calculation as I pointed the car south on the interstate. "That gives us fifty-two minutes before the ceremony begins. I hope traffic isn't too heavy. If we get stuck, we're going to have to call Mike and let the cops take their chances."

She was focused on the phone. "Hello, Diane, this is Devon Malone."

I pressed the accelerator even harder. I wasn't a praying kind of guy, so all I could do was hope.

CHAPTER SEVENTY-EIGHT

Malone had just finished her short conversation with our client as I transitioned to the Banfield heading west.

"She's going to meet us there," she told me as she stowed away her phone, "in front of the Providence building just down the street from the ceremony. She's very excited."

"I didn't hear you say anything about a bomb."

"I thought it would be best to save the bad news for when we're all together. Excited is better than frightened for getting her there in a hurry."

"And we have to do it without her if it takes her too long."

"That we do."

We were both quiet for a few minutes as I concentrated on getting us through the traffic as quickly as possible. Luckily, it was not at a complete standstill anywhere along our route.

Malone spoke as we approached the Halsey exit. "You're really going to let Harmon Cluney get credit for rescuing the girls?"

"Have you got a better idea? We had to get going. And we'd probably lose our licenses for leaving the scene of a crime, not to mention being responsible for more dead bodies. Cluney was an asshole and an idiot, but you saw his move; he was a cop at the end. That's good enough for me."

"And it will make your old girlfriend feel better."

The connection took a moment. "Huh. I honestly hadn't even thought of that, but yes. Joy won't have to think she's been let down by another man. She can believe her boyfriend was a hero."

I had taken the Halsey exit to 47th during this exchange. Malone said nothing more as we headed south to Glisan. There I turned left and we very soon encountered a barricade with a cop redirecting traffic and holding back a small group of pro-testers. We had to find a parking spot on the side street and trot back.

I stopped to ask the cop at the barrier if she'd heard any-thing about the ceremony being postponed or cancelled. She hadn't. So far so good.

By the time we reached the Providence building where we were supposed to meet Diane Austin, it was 12:35. Twenty-five minutes before the mayor and the state senator stepped to the microphone. At least, I assumed that they would. We hadn't heard from Daisy or Bobby, so that was further evidence the ceremony was still on time.

The waiting crowd filled the street in front of the clinic building, on the other side of the street from us. Diane Austin was not in sight nor did I see Kimberly. Zoller had indicated there were two men escorting her here and I assumed that they hadn't been warned about the bomb, either. They should still be with her, but I didn't yet see anyone who fit the bill. All I could see on this side of the crowd from our current location was a lot of happy looking citizens, mostly female. There were a few uniformed officers spaced around the periphery but no evidence that a specific threat was anticipated.

I looked at my partner. "We can't wait for Diane," I said. "We've got to get in there and find Kimberly. Rand and Clemons still might call this thing off at the last minute if their kids aren't awake yet."

She was nodding when I caught sight of Diane Austin hur-rying up the block behind her. "Wait one," I said. "There she is."

Austin saw us and broke into a halting run, arriving a cou-ple of moments later completely out of breath, looking older and more frail than when she'd first visited our office.

"Is Noelle here?" she gasped. She wasn't even looking at us; her eyes were scanning the crowd.

Malone stepped closer to her. "We believe she is, in the company of two men, and that she's in danger. We have to approach her carefully and not let her make a call. That's very important. She has a cell phone with her and we don't want her to use it."

Austin tore her eyes away from the gathering and frowned at my partner. "Why? What's so important about her making a phone call?"

"We've been told there's a bomb and that the phone might set it off."

Good move, I thought, to not say exactly where the bomb was supposed to be. Nevertheless, Diane Austin instantly went deathly pale.

"A bomb? Oh my God. Noelle!" We had to restrain her from charging into the crowd.

"We'll find her in just a minute," I said. "But first we need a plan. We expect to find her accompanied by two of Gregory Zoller's men, as Devon just explained. You have to remain calm and strike up a conversation to distract her. Remember that she doesn't know who you are or that her name is Noelle. As soon as you have her attention, Devon and I will quietly take out the two guys. Then we have to get the phone away from her." I was holding eye contact with Malone as I said all this to make sure she didn't have a problem with any of it. Apparently she didn't. "Once we've done all that," I concluded, "everybody should be safe and you'll have your daughter back." Not that I expected any of it to be quite that easy.

Diane Austin took a deep breath and firmed up her thin lips. "How do we do this?" she asked. So maybe she wasn't quite as fragile as she looked.

I again surveyed the crowd, which had continued to grow, both in number and density, as we were talking. Still no likely suspects visible. I had a hunch Malone and I would recognize the two goons the moment we saw them. If there were a young girl with long dark hair between them, that would be our target.

I glanced at my watch. We now had twelve minutes if the ceremony were precisely on time. The spectators had already begun to focus more on the still-unattended podium that sat on a temporary platform. Behind it was a fairly typical two-story family dwelling. Extra privacy was provided by large trees and shrubs in the front yard. A handicapped ramp had been added from the side driveway and a sign indicated that there was extra parking in back. There was no obvious signage about the purpose of the building, no big ABORTION CLINIC RIGHT HERE with a pointing arrow. Probably something discreet up on the porch, behind the foliage.

The platform was set up on the sidewalk next to the front steps. Several official-looking types were already standing near the podium, looking out over the crowd. I suspected that the mayor and senator were just inside, getting ready to appear.

"Let's go," I said, "We'll work our way to the front. That's where Zoller said they'd be, as near to the podium as possible."

We plunged into the crowd.

CHAPTER SEVENTY-NINE

I immediately felt like I was in the middle of an overcrowded PTA meeting, hemmed in on every side by young and middle-aged women. There were very few men, which was going to make this much easier.

In fact, within a few seconds of starting our push toward the platform I could see two close-cropped male heads right in front of the podium, standing just far enough apart that they probably had someone between them.

"There," I said to Devon and Diane, pointing.

"I see them," Malone responded. She tapped Austin on the arm and also pointed. "You go around so that you approach your daughter from the front," she said. "We'll be behind the men." She caught my eye. "You take the left and I take the right?"

"Sounds like a plan." We started to push ahead.

But then we were suddenly stopped by a familiar voice right behind us, calling our names. I glanced back to see Mike Whitehall pushing through the crowd.

"What's happening?" he asked as he joined Malone and me. Diane Austin had already moved on, per Malone's instructions. "I came down to check it out because you got me pretty damned worried. Do you know more about the supposed threat? Is that why you're here? And do you have any idea where the hell Harm Cluney is? He's supposed to be in charge of the damned event and I can't find him."

We didn't have time for this, certainly not for any lengthy explanations. "Okay," I said, thinking fast. "New plan. Mike takes the guy on the right and I take the one on the left." I gestured to Malone. "You follow Diane and make sure we get that phone before any buttons are pushed."

"Gotcha," she said, and moved off.

Mike Whitehall, meanwhile, was frowning as me. "What the hell are you talking about? What guy? What phone?"

I leaned in to whisper, hoping no one in the crowd would overhear me. "We believe the threat is a bomb in a kid's backpack." I pointed over the heads of the women in front of us. "You see the two big guys up front? The girl should be between them. We move up behind them, wait until Malone and another woman are talking to the girl, and then we take out the men quickly, quietly, and cleanly."

He began moving with me but wasn't quite buying it yet. "In the middle of this crowd?" he asked incredulously.

"No choice. Trust me." I couldn't explain further because I hadn't decided yet how we knew about the bomb given that we hadn't been at the scene in the mall.

We separated as we came up behind the two men and settled in position. Just as I expected, a young girl wearing a backpack stood between them. She was small for her age of eleven or twelve and her hair was pulled back in a ponytail that rested on her backpack. It was hard not to focus exclusively on that backpack, bright red and cheery looking, probably carrying enough explosives to replace all of us with a very large crater.

Both of the men we were targeting were big. I couldn't see their faces, of course, but I guessed they were mean-looking as well. Gregory Zoller had a type when it came to followers. I knew how I was going to handle my guy, and in my peripheral vision I saw Mike easing a Taser out of his pocket. Good choice. Be nice if I had one, but my approach should work as well.

I realized, looking past the right shoulder of my guy, that the door of the house had opened and the two politicians had started down the steps toward the platform and podium. We needed to act now.

Luckily, by the time I had registered all this, Malone and Diane Austin had worked their way up beside and slightly in front of the girl and her companions. In what was clearly (to me) a rehearsed move, Diane looked over at her daughter. "Hey, don't I know you?" she asked brightly. Might as well go for it, I thought to myself, and was impressed at how composed she seemed.

Malone meanwhile, moved around Austin as if simply curious to see who her friend was talking to. That put her right in front of Kimberly. The two goons started to react and that was the cue for me and Mike.

Not having any fancy equipment like my police detective friend, I resorted to a knife-hand strike on the point where the neck and shoulder join. The guy went "uh!" and collapsed like a sack of flour.

Simultaneously, the other guy groaned, dropped to the ground, and began mildly convulsing. Considering he'd been shot from about three inches away, I imagined that was going to *really* sting.

Malone and Austin had not been idle for those few seconds. When I re-focused on them, Devon had a firm grip on Kimberly's arms and Diane had a firm grip on Kimberly's phone.

Mission fucking accomplished.

The crowd around us pulled back with a variety of screams and exclamations. I could see cops closing in from every direction. Mike had already pulled out his badge and was holding it up so they'd know we were the good guys.

He pointed at the nearest uniform. "We need the bomb squad," he yelled. "Get them here now!" He didn't have a choice. We did need the bomb squad. But it didn't exactly help with the crowd control.

CHAPTER EIGHTY

The next few minutes were chaotic. More uniforms showed up and some of them cleared out the crowd in the street while others evacuated the clinic building. Still others started going door to door to evacuate the rest of the block. They also hauled off the two goons that we'd taken down.

Meanwhile Malone had taken Kimberly's phone from Diane Austin and pulled her further away from her daughter, which I thought was good judgment. The kid was already petrified to learn that her backpack might blow all of us to hell. It was not the right time for our client to step up and say, "Hi, I'm your real mom. Let's get to know each other."

Mike and I had taken control of the girl, standing on either side of her, the three of us in the center of a very big and empty space while we waited for the Metro Bomb Squad to arrive. I kept telling myself we were perfectly safe as long as my partner didn't decide to make a call right then. I watched her pull Diane Austin to the far intersection, behind more temporary barriers that had been set up.

Kimberly had not said anything, at least anything intelligible, since her initial scream. Then it all came spilling out. "What's happening? I don't understand," she said to me. "Who are you?" she asked Mike. Back to me. "Why do you think my backpack is a bomb? I need to sit down. I want to talk to my father."

I exchanged a glance with Mike over her head. "I think she's pretty weak in the knees," he said.

I took her arm. "Okay, you can sit down. But it needs to be right here. Very slow and careful."

She started to shrug off the backpack, at which point we both got a firm grip on her arms. "No! Wait for the bomb squad. Let's get you off your feet and then we wait. They'll be here in a minute."

She acquiesced, lowering herself slowly, with our help, until she was sitting cross-legged on the pavement. "You're both crazy," she muttered as soon as she was settled. "My father gave me the backpack. It's full of literature for us to pass out when the ceremony's over. Why did you attack us? Are Marty and Sam okay?"

What could I say? "It's a long, complicated story, Kimberly. And it's not going to be easy for you to hear some of it. Now we need to just stay quiet and wait for the bomb squad. If you're right that the backpack is full of literature, I'll apologize to you and Marty and Sam. Okay?"

"I don't think that will be enough for my father," she finally said.

I didn't know what to say to that. I was very glad to see the bomb squad arriving at that moment.

Mike met them at the edge of the cleared area while I stayed with Kimberly. After a short exchange, an officer fully outfitted in protective gear joined us, carefully removed the backpack from the girl, and then sent us both down the block to join Mike. Somewhat to my surprise, Malone was with him and Diane Austin was nowhere in sight. Several men in dark suits that I didn't recognize were standing there, watching us approach.

They turned out to be Portland detectives assigned to the FBI's Joint Terrorism Task Force and they escorted Kimberly away immediately. I was worried that she'd really be in for it, but Mike assured us that the girl would be interviewed at the Justice Center in the company of someone from Child Protective Services. He'd already told the detectives that the kid was apparently an innocent victim, unaware she was carrying a bomb.

Still, I wanted to get downtown and support that story as quickly as possible. Mike said he'd meet us there, so Malone and I headed out to retrieve the Subaru.

CHAPTER EIGHTY-ONE

Having heard no explosions by the time we got to the car, I assumed the bomb squad was successfully dealing with the backpack. We settled into our seats and I noticed that Malone still had Kimberly's phone tightly in her grasp.

I gestured at it as I pulled away from the curb. "Don't be pushing any buttons on that," I said.

"Don't worry." She opened the glove compartment and tossed it in. "I never saw the damned thing."

"That works. What happened to Diane?"

"I convinced her to go back to her hotel room. As far as I could tell, Mike didn't even notice she was there."

"He was focused on his target and at that point he didn't have much idea what was going on anyway. I'm surprised Diane agreed not to follow her daughter. She's been looking for a long time."

"I described what would probably be happening downtown for the next few hours, reminded her how traumatizing all this was going to be for the kid already, and suggested that throwing in a totally new identity and family right now probably wasn't the best idea. She understood. I think she'll be a good mother when she gets the chance."

I glanced over at my partner, who was staring straight ahead looking a little flushed. I had an idea what had just crossed her mind, but I kept driving and didn't say anything about it. I wasn't bothering with the freeways. I took Glisan a few blocks as we talked and then hopped over to Burnside for the rest of the trip downtown.

While Malone was silent, I dug out my cell phone and punched in Bobby's number, putting it on speaker.

"Clint?" came his tinny voice after a couple of rings.

"How did it go at the mall?" I asked.

"We're clear. The girls woke up right after being removed from the scene and were groggy for a few minutes but they're fine. No injuries, just somewhat distraught. They weren't able to tell the detectives anything about what went on after their initial kidnapping since they were unconscious the whole time. I gathered that the dead detective is getting credit for the rescue just as you said. Certainly nobody mentioned you or Devon. They released the girls and we're bringing them to their mothers right now. Daisy is driving." I had to smile at that last. It was important to Bobby, being an attorney and the boyfriend of a police detective, that he not be breaking the law—as I currently was by being on a cell phone while driving.

We said our goodbyes and I punched off. "So far so good," I said.

"If they don't check Cluney's weapon for fingerprints— which, why should they?"

"Exactly. Have you ever heard of an officer's gun being checked for his own fingerprints after a shooting incident?"

"No. We should be okay."

We contemplated our mutual okayness for another few blocks and then Malone spoke up again. "So how did we know Kimberly was there with a bomb if Zoller didn't tell us?"

"The story I gave Mike was that we received an anonymous tip."

"He bought that?"

"I doubt that he's had a chance to think about it yet, but I suggest we stick to that story with whoever debriefs us downtown. Mike won't question it, at least not until we're all alone over a beer one of these days. And there's no way anyone can prove we're lying. We were never at the mall. We don't know what happened there. We were looking for Kimberly anyway when we got a tip. That is all."

"Did the tip include that she didn't know the C4 was in her backpack? We need to confirm her story or she could be in big trouble as a possible suicide bomber. She's already been scooped up by the joint task force."

"I didn't specify to Mike one way or the other but, yes, that was part of our anonymous tip. The phone wasn't, so it can stay in the glove compartment."

"That's good."

After another minute or two of silence, Malone suddenly said, "I'll tell you what wasn't good."

I glanced over at her again. She was still staring straight out the windshield. "What wasn't good?"

"Standing there with Diane Austin, looking at you and Mike and the girl out in the middle of that big cleared space. You looked too fucking vulnerable. It wasn't good."

"We were perfectly safe."

"Nobody standing next to a backpack full of C4 is perfectly safe. When Kimberly started going to the ground, I thought for sure...."

I reached over and put my hand on her thigh, gave it a little squeeze. "Her knees just got a little weak. You were the one holding the trigger." I tossed a grin in her direction. "I'm glad you didn't decide to make a call."

"Yeah." She finally met my next glance and offered a little smile in return.

Then I had to pay more attention to my driving because we'd hit downtown traffic beyond the Burnside Bridge. We would soon learn if it was all going to play out as we hoped.

CHAPTER EIGHTY-TWO

I've spent a lot of time in the Justice Center and of course Malone, as a former Police Bureau detective, has spent even more. But neither of us had had the experience of being interviewed by detectives with the Joint Terrorism Task Force.

Detective Farragut was the older, senior detective, bulky and a little disheveled with a full head of silver hair and craggy features. Detective Sloane was a younger and better dressed redhead, wearing glasses over somewhat squinty eyes. He seemed to be in awe of the older man.

I didn't know either one. Malone knew them both, but clearly only as acquaintances from the days when she was with the Bureau and they were not yet on the Task Force.

The city of Portland had long had a fraught relationship with the FBI around the issue of terrorism. For years the city refused to cooperate, citing human rights concerns, and only recently had agreed to add these two detectives to the task force, thus making it "joint" again in reality.

Or perhaps not. I couldn't help noticing that there were no FBI agents in the room. I wasn't going to inquire after them, however. I much preferred to deal with the locals and I'm sure Malone felt the same way.

They hadn't bothered to separate us. We'd driven in together and had plenty of time to get our stories straight—which, in fact, was exactly what we'd done. They were smart enough to know there was nothing they could do about it.

Once they had all the video and audio equipment up and had identified everyone being recorded, they asked for the story and we did an excellent job of sounding honest and sincere as we related what we'd rehearsed.

Of course they focused on the hinkiest part.

"So," drawled Detective Farragut, "you're out and about, looking for your client's long lost daughter, and you get this anonymous call that she's downtown with a bomb in her backpack? Why would someone tip you two about that?"

"We've got confidential informants just like you do, detective," Malone responded. "We had the word out on the street that we were looking for the kid. I don't know who called or how they got their information, but we're all lucky that they did."

He held Malone's gaze for a long moment, then looked at me and shrugged ever so slightly. He wasn't going to push it.

"Have you heard that the girl's father is dead?" asked Detective Sloane.

We both were suitably startled by that. "No," I said. "What happened?"

"Some of his people kidnapped the daughters of the mayor and the senator. There was a shoot-out with one of our detectives, Harmon Cluney, at Clarion Mall and Zoller was killed along with the kidnappers. Cluney died in the exchange of fire, as well."

"Wow," I said. "We both knew Harm. That's terrible. Are the kids okay?"

"They were drugged unconscious. Otherwise fine. We don't know how he got onto it yet, but Cluney did a hell of a job."

"Good for him," I said. I had a hunch they'd never figure out exactly how he knew to go to the mall or why he didn't call for backup.

"Where's the girl?" asked Malone.

"She's with a woman from Child Protective Services, waiting to be interviewed after we're done with you two. Giving her some extra time to settle down. Then CPS can contact your client and determine if she really is the biological mother."

That sounded good, like they believed the kid was a victim rather than perpetrator.

The detectives had only a few more innocuous questions and we were done. Working our way out of the building, we heard almost nothing except talk about what a hero Detective Harmon Cluney was. I poked my head in the Records Division but they said Joy had gone home for the day. No surprise.

I was feeling pretty good about it all until we hit the sidewalk and found Alison Roberts waiting for us with Murray Kravitz and his camera by her side.

We were going to have to keep all our lies straight at least one more time.

She started recording the instant they saw us.

"I'm here in front of the Justice Center with local private eyes Clint McCall and Devon Malone, the heroes of today's attempted terrorist bombing at the opening ceremonies of the Women's Hope Clinic."

She thrust the microphone at me. "What were you thinking as you confronted a terrorist carrying a backpack of C4? How did you manage to talk her down?"

"In the first place, she wasn't a terrorist," I replied. "She was the victim of a terrorist, a young girl who didn't know there was C4 in the back pack...."

CHAPTER EIGHTY-THREE

And it went from there, with Malone and I doing a good job—if I do say so myself—of sticking to the script. My partner was even civil, probably because Roberts had for once included her equally with me in the intro.

We then checked in at the office where we ignored most of the messages and all of the mail, quickly deciding to take what little remained of the afternoon off. Malone was starving by this point, anyway, as we had decided to stop a bombing rather than have lunch.

I didn't even drop by Eleanor's office to tell her we'd found the kid. She'd probably see it on TV this evening and the rest could be dealt with tomorrow.

We treated ourselves to some Thai food and I finally unlocked my front door around quarter to five. Malone was still with me; she hadn't even mentioned the possibility of going to her apartment.

Stella and Maxine were waiting in the living room, Stella near the front door and Maxine at the bedroom door, in case the second person was not Malone. Since it was Malone, she immediately moved over to the kitchen door so as to be first at the food dishes. Stella, meanwhile, just wanted some damned petting.

It was a quiet evening of getting the cats and ourselves fed, then trying to relax while watching the local news coverage and waiting for Alison Roberts' late-evening report. If anybody was going to be savvy enough to call our story into question, it would be her.

By the time I turned off the TV at ten-thirty, we knew we were clear. Harmon Cluney was a hero. Malone and Whitehall and I were heroes. Kimberly Zoller was a victim. The rest of the True Christian Brotherhood, now identified as a terrorist group, was being rounded up. We had been nowhere near Clarion Mall. Diane Austin was not mentioned by name.

"I don't want to have to do that again," Malone said as I put the remote down on the side table. She was sitting with me on the couch but with just enough space for Stella between us. We had long since changed into our casual at-home clothes, sweatpants and t-shirt for both of us. Hers were black; mine were dark blue.

"Do what?" I asked.

"Any of it. Having to wait for the bomb squad while you're out there in danger of getting your ass blown off. Getting caught up in such an elaborate lie that it was giving me a headache by the time we got through talking to your girlfriend."

"Alison Roberts is not my girlfriend. Never was. Never will be. But you're right about the lying. I don't mind a healthy fib for the greater good now and then, but this was something else. We didn't have a choice. We were leaving a scene where we'd just killed two people and witnessed a couple of other deaths. Do you think we had a choice?"

Her mouth turned down. "No."

"At least now we can get back to normal."

"Yeah," she responded thoughtfully, looking around the room as if seeing it for the first time. She ran her hand down Stella's back and got a little purr in response. "Normal."

There was only one light on in the room, a floor lamp in the far corner, and I examined her partly-shadowed face. I liked that face. A lot. "You're in a funny mood."

She turned to meet my gaze directly. "No. I'm not."

Okay. So much for sharing more feelings. There were other things we could share. I made a point of checking my watch. "Looks like bed-time to me."

Her mouth twitched into a little grin. "It always looks like bed-time to you." She glanced at her own watch. "But you're right. Let's do it."

Indeed, I thought to myself with an inner grin.

We'd been together long enough to have a routine. I brushed my teeth while she was getting undressed, then she brushed hers while I was getting undressed and appreciating the fact that she was already undressed.

She was a beautiful woman with some very prominent scars. You could see the ones on the outside, left there by a serial killer who had almost added her to his series. I didn't mind them at all. They were part of what made her Devon Malone. Watching her come back into the bedroom from the bathroom and climb into bed beside me, it occurred to me that I never wanted to be without her and her scars.

The trouble was, I still couldn't guess what she wanted.

CHAPTER EIGHTY-FOUR

We parked across from the office at precisely eight a.m. the next morning, ready for a regular Thursday of work—and hopefully some new clients. With any luck, there would be something good among the mail and messages we'd ignored the afternoon before.

But then we topped the stairs to find Diane Austin waiting in front of our door, not looking much better than the last time we'd seen her. So much for the regular day.

She spoke before we were close enough even to say hello. "I can't do it," she announced. Her voice was stressed, high-pitched, and she looked like she hadn't slept at all the night before.

"Is there a problem with your daughter?" Malone asked as we came closer.

Austin shook her head. "No, it's me,"

"Let's talk about it inside," I said as I stepped up beside her and unlocked our door. Malone put a hand on our client's shoulder, whether to comfort or to encourage her entrance I don't know.

In any event, we got her into the office. I closed the door behind us and Malone escorted her to one of the visitor chairs while I hung up my jacket and stashed the Smith and Wesson in its drawer.

Diane Austin sat, wringing her hands, until we were all three settled.

"So what's the problem?" I asked.

"The local agency, Children's Protective Services is it? They contacted me yesterday evening about meeting with Noelle today. I'm supposed to be there at ten-thirty this morning. I don't think I can do it."

"Why not?" asked Malone. "You've been looking for her all this time and now you've found her."

Austin looked at her with eyes brimming. "What do I say? She doesn't even know she's Noelle. The way she looked at me when I spoke to her yesterday.... She doesn't know who I am. She just lost her father. What do I do?"

Our client practically wailed that last question and I would swear that Malone cringed a bit. Then she glared at Diane Austin. "I don't know. I've never had a kid. I barely had a mother. Just...talk to her. Tell her the truth and let her deal with it."

Austin didn't seem to think that advice was very helpful and frankly I was a little appalled myself. There had to be some way to do more for this poor woman. Suddenly:

"I have an inspiration," I said.

Malone transferred her glare from Austin to me. "I don't think I've ever seen you have one of those," she said. "What is it?"

"The other day I met one of Kimberly's—Noelle's—teachers," I said to Diane rather than Malone, "and I think she might be a good person to go with you when you meet your daughter for the first time."

This time I got a somewhat bewildered look from Austin in return. "I was kind of thinking you two, or one of you, might come with me."

I didn't need to exchange more than a very quick glance with Malone. "No, I don't think that's the best idea. We're private investigators, not mediators or counselors. Let me give this teacher a call, see what she says."

I made the call to Summit Christian School and explained the situation to Charlotte Borden as Diane Austin listened intently on my side of the conversation. To my great relief, Borden said she'd come right over.

There followed twenty very awkward minutes of mostly silence as Malone and I checked our e-mail, repeatedly, and Austin paced the floor. Then came a firm rap on the office door.

It opened, and Charlotte Borden's head of soft white hair appeared around the edge. As soon as she saw me, she stepped into the room, nodded at Malone, and went immediately to Diane Austin. She first took her hand and then embraced her, not yet saying a word. Malone and I just watched. I was already thinking that I'd made the right call.

After a few more seconds, Borden stepped back, still holding Austin by the shoulders. "I'm so happy that you have found your daughter," she said, "I understand you are frightened and you're right that it won't be easy. But I'll do everything I can to help make it easier."

Austin actually managed a tremulous smile. "You were Noelle's teacher?"

"Yes, though I knew her as Kimberly. I think we had a good relationship and that she'll be pleased to see me. That should help. But...." Borden turned to us with a spritely grin. "I should at least say hello to Mr. McCall and...." She looked inquiringly at Malone.

My partner stood and reached out a hand to shake. "Devon Malone. I'm Clint's partner in the agency."

"Of course you are. Good to meet you." She did a quick survey of the office as she shook hands. "I'm glad you called me, Mr. McCall, and I am more than happy to do what I can, but this probably is not the place to prepare ourselves." She turned again to Diane Austin. "What time is your meeting with...Noelle this morning?"

"Ten-thirty."

Borden checked her watch. "So we have a little more than an hour before then. I know a nice coffee shop nearby. Why don't we go there and talk about this wonderful beginning to your new life?"

For a moment I thought Diane Austin wasn't going to be able to break eye contact with her new best friend. Then her smile grew. "Sounds good to me," she said. "Thank you."

She finally looked at Malone and me. "And thank you."

"No problem," I responded. "Good luck. To you and to your daughter."

"Same here," added my partner.

As they closed the office door behind them, Borden was already beginning to tell Diane Austin about the young girl she'd had as a student.

I looked across the partners desk to find Malone giving me an appraising look. "What?" I asked.

"Just good to know that you can have inspirations," she said.

CHAPTER EIGHTY-FIVE

Two hours later we were still at our desks, all e-mail and regular mail read, some bills paid, a couple of telephone inquiries fielded, and no new clients. We had ignored any calls with blocked Caller ID on the assumption that they were probably reporters—and with the hope that, if they were clients, they'd call back after the media storm died down.

We did have a couple of minor jobs left over from before Diane Austin showed up, but one had gone cold and the other just needed the final report written.

Since the latter was mine, I was thinking that maybe I should start on the report when Malone stood up and reached in her top drawer to retrieve her Glock.

"Where are you going?" I asked.

"Thought I'd hit the Home Run before the lunch crowd."

I checked my watch. Just past eleven-thirty. "I'll come with," I said. Better than writing the damned report. And we could speculate over burgers about how Diane Austin's meeting with her daughter was going.

I was pushing to my feet when my line rang. "Hold on," I said to Malone, then glanced down at the Caller ID. "Speaking of lunch places, this is the Pen and Pastry. Gotta be either Veronica or Colleen."

It was my daughter, who—it suddenly struck me—I hadn't heard from for several days. Usually she would have been on the horn right away after I made news, wanting to be sure I was all right.

She didn't seem interested in inquiring now, either. After a quick hello: "Dad, are you free for lunch? I'd like you to meet me here at the Pen and Pastry if you're free. It's kind of important."

"Oh? What's up?"

"I don't want to talk about it over the phone. Can you come down here for lunch?"

"Well," I said, "we were just heading out to eat. I suppose we could go to the Pen and Pastry rather than the Home Run." I caught Malone's eye as I said it and she shrugged an okay.

"Good," said my daughter. "That's good."

She sounded like she was about to hang up, but I had to check: "I'm surprised you didn't call sooner after all the news coverage."

Long moment of silence. "What news coverage? Are you okay?"

That explained the lack of a phone call, but it was still highly unusual. "I'm fine, but you mean you haven't seen any news in the last day or so?"

"I've been kind of...busy. You can tell me all about it when you get here." With that, she did hang up.

"What was that about?" Malone asked as I got to my feet.

"Beats me," I said and retrieved my own weapon from the drawer. "It's important to meet her for lunch and she's been 'busy.' Why and with what, she didn't say."

"Huh," offered my partner, and we headed for my car.

I wasn't much of a conversationalist on the fifteen-minute drive. I was thinking about how Colleen and I had been out of touch the last couple of days even though we'd both just been in life-threatening danger. The older she got, it seemed, the more we were growing apart. And I wasn't sure what I felt about that.

As usual, I parked in my own driveway since the café was just around the corner. I had just beeped the car locked and Malone was coming around to join me when my cellphone trilled. The number was unfamiliar. I punched it on and put it to my ear.

"McCall."

"This is Charlotte Borden, Mr. McCall. I thought you'd want to know how things are going."

"Miss Borden, yes, I would."

"Diane, Kimberly, and I have finished our meeting with the social worker and we're now at lunch together. I just stepped away for a moment to make this call, but I can see that they are talking. It's going quite well."

"Kimberly? Not Noelle?"

"Not yet. A daughter by any name is still a daughter, Mr. McCall. The girl has had a peculiar upbringing, to say the least, and a lot of trauma lately. I'm not saying it will be easy or quick, but the bonding has begun and I believe it will endure."

"That's good to hear."

"Well, I need to get back now. I'll stay with them as long as they need me. Thank you for calling on me, Mr. McCall."

"My pleasure, Miss Borden. Have a good lunch."

She disconnected and I stuffed the phone back in my pocket.

"So it's going well?" asked Malone as we started walking toward the café.

"So far so good," I said.

"The teacher was a good call."

"Thanks."

I said nothing more, focusing on the entrance to the Pen and Pastry as we approached. Inside, the place was packed but it didn't take long to pick out Colleen sitting at a back table. With Hoke Moseley. Holding hands with Hoke Moseley. Exchanging a fond look with Hoke Moseley.

Crap.

CHAPTER EIGHTY-SIX

Malone nudged me as we worked our way through the room to Colleen's table. "Remain calm," she muttered.

I said nothing, but I knew it wasn't going to be easy to take her advice. I wasn't even sure I wanted to. The last time I'd talked to Hoke Moseley, it was to tell him his mother—who had tried to kill me—was at the Justice Center.

Before that, of course, *he* was threatening to kill me.

Yes, he'd pointed out the bomb under my car, and helped rescue Colleen, and supposedly forgiven me for killing his brother...but that didn't make us buddies, certainly didn't give him the right to be sitting there *holding hands* with my kid....

Talk about complicated.

Meanwhile, his expression as he watched us approach reminded me of someone who'd just realized a rattlesnake was within striking distance. Apparently he also understood that it was complicated. And that our original roles might soon be reversed.

He was wearing a blue checkered flannel shirt, long-sleeved, and I noticed that he'd begun to grow his blond hair out again. My daughter, sitting close beside him, still looked older, her granny glasses glinting in the café's fluorescent lights. I found myself wondering if his hair, once grown out, would be the same color as hers.

"Hi, how are you guys?" my partner inquired cheerily as we arrived at the table. It didn't help that she was having such a good time with this.

"We're fine," Colleen said. "Hi, Dad."

I jerked a chair away from the table and sat down. "Colleen," I replied. Malone gracefully joined me. I transferred my gaze to Moseley. "Hoke." Then I looked at their joined hands—which were getting a little white-knuckled on Moseley's part, I noticed. Somehow that made me feel a little better.

"Dad, I...."

My daughter broke off whatever she was going to say as café-owner Veronica Fortune swept up to the table, waitressing during the lunch rush as she often did. Today she was wearing some sort of magenta caftan, spectacular as always. "What can I get you guys? On the house for Clint and Devon, here, since they're the heroes of the hour."

Colleen gave me a wide-eyed look. "Heroes? What...?"

I held up a hand to interrupt her again. "I'll tell you about it. How about a ham and cheese croissant, with coffee," I said to Veronica.

"Make that two," Malone chimed in, then added, "I mean two for me. And coffee."

"Veggie wraps for us," said Colleen. "And tea."

"Good enough," said our hostess and swept away again.

As soon as she was out of earshot, I looked again at those hands still holding on, then up at my daughter. "So you two...?"

"Yes," she said firmly. "We two. Hoke saved my life and he's a good guy. You know he is. I went with him to get his mother and get her settled and then we went to dinner and then we talked for a long time and then.... Well, that's why I haven't seen any news lately."

"Colleen," I said through gritted teeth and then grunted as Malone kicked me hard under table.

"How old are you, Colleen?" she asked sweetly.

My daughter grinned at her real big. "I'm twenty-four," she said. "Now, tell me why you two are heroes this week."

CHAPTER EIGHTY-SEVEN

Somehow I managed to eat my lunch while we brought Colleen and her new boyfriend (shudder) up to speed on why we were currently in the news. The soreness in my lower left leg, where Malone had kicked me, was a constant reminder that my daughter is a grown woman and there is little I can do about her taste in men.

Malone and I remained at the table, nursing our coffees, when Colleen and Hoke excused themselves to go do whatever it was that kept her from watching the news. I couldn't help glaring at their backs as they left the now half-full café.

I finally sat back with a sigh and looked over at my partner. She was giving me a wide-eyed innocent look over her cup as she took a sip. Then she grinned as she set it down. "Aren't they just the cutest couple?"

I'm afraid I snorted. "Give me a fucking break. He's not the right guy for her."

She lost the grin and leaned forward. "It's not your decision. He's a young guy who cares about her—hell, who's willing to put his life on the line for her. A young guy with enough heart and brains to understand what happened with his brother.... Sounds pretty good to me."

I took a good swallow of my own coffee, finishing it off, and set down the cup next to her. "Well, I'm going to keep an eye on it. I hear what you're saying and, yes, she's a grown woman, but I don't entirely trust him yet."

She sat back. "So? I don't entirely trust anybody."

"Not even me?"

She held my gaze for what seemed like a full thirty seconds. "Maybe you."

And I realized I'd come to a decision in that half-minute. A feeling ran down my back that could only be described as terror, the kind you would feel if your world turned upside down —which mine might, at any moment because it was time.

"We need to talk," I said.

"Oh, yeah?"

"You know I love you, right?"

"Yeaaah."

"And I know you love me, right?"

"Okay."

Okay? Just okay? Oh man, this could be a major clusterfuck. I took a deep breath. "So what would you think about...."

"Moving in together? We just did that. Now that Sherry has left...."

I shook my head, resolved to soldier on no matter how miserable my failure might be.

"No, not that. More than that."

She put a hand firmly on my arm that was resting on the table. "Really? You're really going to do this?"

"Yes, I am."

She kind of winced. "Well don't go down on your knees, for fuck's sake."

"Don't worry. And I don't have a ring, either." Even if I had known I was going to do this, a ring would probably be too traditional for a marriage proposal to Devon Malone.

We sat there looking at each other for a moment. I would have sworn the entire café had gone quiet even though I was sure no one had overheard our quiet exchange. I was desperately trying to read her expression, her body language, *something*, and failing completely. It was like my brain wouldn't even work.

"You know that I probably can't have kids," she said.

"Been there. Done that. No problem."

Then: "And you do realize you haven't actually asked me yet."

"Oh, shit. You're right. Will you marry me?"

"You really think it could work? Why get married? Aren't we doing fine as it is? There are a lot of things we haven't talked about, things we don't know...."

"Has the team of McCall and Malone ever encountered a problem they couldn't deal with, a case they couldn't solve? There will always be things we don't know. And we should get married because we love each other. Call me old-fashioned, but that's what people who love each other do. It's a public declaration that we have each other's backs."

"You're old-fashioned. But I do like that idea of what it means." She paused. I held my breath.

"I want to keep my apartment for now."

No surprise that this was going to be a little different, but I assumed I had a reason to breathe again. "Okay."

She pursed her lips, gave me the gimlet eye, and...

"I'll marry you. Probably. One of these days. If you haven't pissed me off too much by then. Now let's get back to work."

With that, the world stayed right side up.

Pretty much.

THE END

ABOUT THE AUTHOR

Glenn Harris lives and writes in the middle of the Columbia Gorge National Scenic Area (Hood River, Oregon). Besides creating detective novels and short stories, he serves as staff to the same two cats that live with Clint McCall. His former lives include college English teacher, private K-12 school director, graphic design business owner, weekly newspaper managing editor, corporate manager, and taekwondo instructor.

Keep reading the McCall and Malone mysteries! Stay tuned for *Death Comes Around* and be sure to visit Glenn Harris' website www.glennharris.us where you can subscribe to his free e-mail newsletter to get updates and background of the series!